SIX WEEKS

(A C. J. Cavanaugh Mystery)

Also by Michael R. Lane

<u>Poetry</u>
A Leap Year of Haiku
Love & Sensuality
Mortal Thoughts
Sandbox
A Drop of Midnight

<u>Fiction</u>
Exchange Student
Long Journey Home
The Butcher
The Family Stone
Blue Sun
UFOs and God
The Gem Connection
Emancipation

SIX WEEKS

Michael R. Lane

BARE BONES PRESS
P.O. Box 9653, Seattle, WA 98109

ISBN: 979-8-9891948-0-3

Published by Bare Bones Press, LLC

Printed on acid-free paper.

Design: Bare Bones Press, LLC
Production: BookLocker.com
Cover Art: Michael R. Lane

Bare Bones Press, LLC
P.O. Box 9653
Seattle, WA 98109

www.michaelrlane.com
www.barebonespress.com

First Edition: November 2023

CHAPTER ONE

Driving along Oregon I-5 South, midway between the Rose City and the state capital, you will bear witness to a stretch of modern development that is as pleasing to the eye as any scenic view from the air. Monroe Industrial Park is both an ascetic and functional landlocked island. You can see stretches of bright green lawns, boundaries of vibrant clipped hedges, interspersed plots of colorful native shrubs and wildflowers from the freeway. Oregon crabapple trees picket road medians with white and pink flowers in full bloom. Fashioned forest touches frame concrete roads, driveways, and parking areas. Fully occupied by over one hundred diverse businesses ranging from an auto parts distributor to Chinese fast food make their home on this triennium island. The commercial office buildings range from ultra-modern with plenty of glass and artistic facades to conservative brick, stone, or steel structures. A conventional, tan brick office building named Globe looms three stories high and is easily identifiable above its one and two-story mates.

On the first floor of the Globe Building are a real estate agency, insurance agent, clinical psychologist, attorney, periodontist, and dentist. On the second, a research and consulting firm devoted to clean technology occupies the entire floor. On the third are a digital marketer, software and video game developer, eBook and audio book retail and distributor, accountant, and brokerage. DEA had done a thorough background check on each of the businesses in Globe, building management, and the building owners. Standard procedures to vet out any illegal activity before you make your nest. All shook out as legitimate.

The eBook and audio book retail/distributor is sandwiched between the digital marketer and software developer on the southwest side of the building. It also serves as a front for a DEA surveillance team.

From the west windows of our cover office across the grass medium and over the tops of the crabapple trees is a perfect view of Epitome Self Storage, a modern self-storage facility that offers station locker rentals as well as climate controlled storage units. The 24-7 accessed facility is well lit and foot patrolled by armed security. High-tech security cameras cover every public square inch. Anyone wanting to rent a locker or unit would feel safe knowing their possessions are so well guarded. Narcotics distributors felt the same way.

Portland DEA Deputy Director Patrick O'Malley had received intel from a couple of his most reliable undercover agents that there was a lot more going on at Epitome Self Storage than people stowing their out of the way items. Having an agent go in and rent a unit confirmed their suspicions. "How many self-storage facilities do you know that have armed patrols?" Patrick asked me, echoing a portion of his agent's report. None was my answer.

A routine background check on Epitome Self Storage unveiled some very interesting facts. The Chattaway Company owned the facility. The Chattaway Company is a sole proprietorship. Louise Stipes is the owner. Louise Stipes happens to be the maiden name of Louise Westmore. The same Louise Westmore, who is the wife of Kellen Westmore. The same Kellen Westmore, who happens to be the biggest illegal narcotics distributor in Oregon.

I remember my first meeting with Kellen Westmore. It seemed as though it happened in another lifetime. I was a green licensed PI still figuring out the lay of the land. Destini and I were unacquainted. Renita had not entered my life. A time before, I met Carl Wheaton and became a contracted Lunsford Insurance fraud investigator. Most of my cases involved background checks, civil investigations, infidelity, and surveillance. It was early August. Late summer in Portland, Oregon, is typically clear skies, sunny and warm if you considered in the eighties warm as I do. I had nothing pressing for the week and decided to take a late lunch on hump day.

Some delicious and varied fare can be found in downtown Portland, where my office is located. For some reason—one I cannot explain until this day—I wanted to venture out a bit. Fullman's Restaurant had some of the best service and food in the area. The upstairs, commonly referred to as The Lair by regulars, had a reputation for being frequented by criminals and thugs and reported to be owned by the same. The criminals and thugs patronage turned out to be true. The ownership rumor was false.

I was reading at a downstairs table for two enjoying some delicious stuffed portabella mushrooms. It was a little after three, but the restaurant was still half-full. Soft instrumental Jazz adding to the ambiance.

"What are you reading?"

I looked up from *Things Fall Apart* by Chinua Achebe. A fit, sun-brown man of about six-four, with classic tapered brown hair, cool brown eyes, and chiseled features, stood by and calmly awaited my response. He was wearing a light gray fresco suit of European design that must have set him back at least four grand. His expensive light blue dress shirt, navy suede belt, and navy leather boat shoes hinted at his financial status. The platinum Rolex and diamond-studded wedding band brought it home. He could have stepped right onto the cover of *GQ* magazine. Nothing like my off the rack duds and Fossil watch. Good thing I didn't adhere to the philosophies that clothes or accessories make the man. When purchased with corrupt money, they do not alter the quality of the man. I showed him the book cover.

"Interesting," he said with a slight nod.

"It is," I said. "May I help you?"

"I'm Kellen Westmore," he stated as if expecting some expression of recognition from me. Westmore extended his large manicured hand for a shake. I placed my book aside, stood, and shook his hand. His grip was like a vice. We had that in common.

"C. J. Cavanaugh," I said.

"I hear you're a private dick, Mr. Cavanaugh."

"Private Investigator, Mr. Westmore."

"There's a difference?"

"When it comes to investigative work, 'dick' is a moniker commonly used in reference to a detective. A detective works for a public law enforcement agency. An investigator works for either the public or private sectors. In my case, I'm private, thereby an investigator, not a detective. That's my take on it anyway."

"Isn't a detective anyone who detects?"

"Not officially. Anyone can detect, but most are not given legal authority to do so."

He blew off my explanation with an amused chuckle. "What's your going rate, Mr. Cavanaugh?"

I fished out a business card from my inside breast pocket and handed it to Westmore, giving him my usual pitch about it dependent upon the case. He looked at my business card, nodded his approval, and slipped it into his flap pocket.

"I also heard you're DEA."

"Ex-DEA," I said.

"Once an agent, always an agent," Westmore said. "It remains in your blood like military training. Am I right?" He winked at me. I stared at him. Not changing my poker face expression.

"I had a complete transfusion into civilian life when I left the DEA." I was lying. The military and DEA would always be a part of me. If he knew I wasn't telling the truth, he didn't let on. We eyed each other for a long silent moment, neither of us giving a centimeter.

"Were you ever in the military, Mr. Westmore?"

"Never had the pleasure."

"I doubt you'll hear many ex-military personnel describing their time in the service as pleasurable."

He gave me what would best be described as a wry grin. "Suppose not. Business good?"

"Making enough to pay the bills."

"Step down from DEA money, I'd expect."

"Yes, also a lot less dangerous."

Again with the wry grin.

"And why does what I do and what I was concern you, Mr. Westmore?"

"I'm considering hiring a private *investigator* to do routine detective work for my business."

"This is a job interview," I said.

"You could say that."

"Would you like to join me?" I asked.

My smiling invitation was extended under the guise of prospective business. The truth is I knew Kellen "Missile" Westmore without ever being introduced. I had seen him and his wife, Louise, a few times at The Lair. I learned about him the same way he learned about me by asking around. I knew who had told me about him. I wondered what sources told him about me?

He acquired the nickname "Missile" from his days as a high school quarterback. Westmore had a reputation for firing the football with force and accuracy to his receivers. "It was as if he were launching a heat-seeking missile from his right hand," one sports writer wrote about him as a high school junior. Hence the nickname "Missile" was born before his senior year when a broken right arm injury ended his college and professional prospects. It explained the only item on his person that appeared out of place on his *GQ* image. The high school graduation ring on the ring finger of his right hand.

"Thanks, but I'm here with my wife," Westmore said in answer to my invitation.

Westmore wanted something. What was it? Something specific from me, or was he trolling in an attempt to discover if I was still DEA connected? I continued my performance.

"Mr. Cavanaugh, I've heard good things about you."

"Whatever you've heard, divide it by half. You'll be closer to the truth."

I looked past the smile and focused on his steady eyes. He was reading me. My act wasn't deceiving him at all. Westmore was no fool.

"I'm getting together my shortlist of potential *investigators*, and I wanted to take this opportunity to touch base."

"What kind of work do you do, Mr. Westmore?"

"Pharmaceutical supply and distribution."

Illegal narcotics were more like it. In a big way, from what I'd heard.

"That seems…interesting," I said, deliberately sounding as if it were not.

He chuckled. If nothing else, he was being entertained. "It is to me, but most people find it boring."

"It's profitable." I gestured toward him with my palms up and arms open.

"I do alright."

"What kind of investigative work would you need me to do?"

"We'll cross that bridge if and when we come to it. Nice meeting you, Mr. Cavanaugh."

"The pleasure was all mine, Mr. Westmore."

We shook hands again. Upon release, we both appeared pleased with the outcome. Westmore joined his wife, Louise, who had not taken her eyes off us. He kissed her cheek before sitting down. His broad back blocked her from view, leaving my ability to read lips useless. I ate my lunch and returned to reading *Things Fall Apart*. Soft jazz returned. For an instant, I noticed the music had somehow gone silent to my ears during my brief conversation with Kellen Westmore. He never hired me to do any investigative work.

As owner of the facility, Mrs. Westmore—as a proxy for her husband no doubt since money for establishing Epitome Self Storage had to come from him, seeing as Louise Westmore had no visible means of income—controlled all aspects of its operations from employees, security, and renters. What better way than a public storage facility that can also cater to your drug trafficking ventures and colleagues? On the other hand, Epitome Self Storage could be legit. Narcotics dealers are always searching for ways to launder their money. The DEA believed it was a combination of legitimate and nefarious. That was my guess as well.

Our cover is as follows. When you walk into Blue Wonder Digital during business hours, you will see four people hard at work. Their open office computer workstations are each accessorized with personal touches. The office is neat and orderly with a copy room, a fully stocked functional kitchenette, and a unisex bathroom. Left of the kitchenette at the back wall is a digitally locked door with the attached sign STORAGE ROOM. Through the storage room door is an area large enough to comfortably accommodate the two agents who oversee the surveillance operation.

The surveillance teams work eight-hour shifts. Dayshift consisted of six agents, four in the front offices, while two staffed the surveillance station. Swing and graveyard shifts posted four agents—two in the surveillance room, two in the front offices. The front office agents act as sentries during business hours. If anyone enters the office for whatever reason, the front office agents intercept and appease the intruders. They make it clear we are merely a digital distribution and retail center, giving the curious business cards that will usher them to a professional website that will fool everyone but is as phony as the person's identity on the business card. After and before business hours, office agents act as security when the front door is locked.

The surveillance room consists of gray mesh ergonomic office chairs and a granite white-topped banquet-folding table. Two 43" HD Color monitors. A high performance desktop computer. A high performance laptop with a seventeen-inch touch screen that primarily serves as an emergency backup. A couple of pro electronic tablets, used mostly for operation diaries and entertainment, could be found abandoned at the opposite end of the table when not in use. The usual wire and cord accouterments accompanying such electronic devices snaked their way from inlet to outlet. Blackout curtains had been hung behind closed white miniblinds, depriving us of natural light while masking the world of our covert existence.

A customized wireless video interceptor capable of capturing video signals as far away as a mile is connected to the desktop computer. More than enough range to tap into the wireless security camera video feeds of Epitome Self Storage. The tap allows us to see and record everything their security cameras witnessed. Some of the close-ups on drug dealers and their contraband coming out of their security station made us wonder if their security people had been instructed to record footage of illegal transactions for possible use as leverage for future blackmail or extortion schemes. Common business practices would disdain such thinking. Such conduct could only serve to taint your reputation and breed distrust, souring future enterprises when wealth and power are your primary motivations with no regard for the law. I have found few restrictions one would self-impose to satisfy the gluttonous appetites of those ravenous twin wolves.

How did a retired DEA agent become involved in an active DEA surveillance operation? Necessity, convenience, and familiarity would be the most accurate words to describe why I was invited back into the fold.

Of the fourteen regular agents assigned this rotating surveillance operation, four had been pulled away due to personal matters ranging from sudden death in the family to a sick child from food poisoning. Not to mention that a flu epidemic had raged through the Portland DEA office like a wildfire leaving them shorthanded of field operatives. Patrick asked if I would step in for a minute until their field staffing could return to normal. I was happy to help as long as it didn't involve deep cover. I was through with that.

While I didn't expect to be recognized by anyone at Monroe Industrial Park, being 6'-4" and 225lbs can make one stand out. The simpler the disguise, the less memorable the person. I wore a winter beanie, waterproof multi-sports shoes, straight fit jeans, a sports shirt, and a lined hooded rain jacket. Northwest casual. I topped it off with plain black-rimmed glasses and a plain gold wedding band. I had been experimenting with a petite goatee that I decided to continue to grow into what is known as a circle beard, where the goatee is connected to the mustache. The new look hid my chin scar. Cheek stubble gave bystanders the impression I was a family man that did not always have time for facial grooming, or I was making a style statement. Patrick thought it was overkill. It's a small world is my motto when going undercover. In this small world, anyone at any time can make you at the worst possible moment.

Surveillance by nature is flat out boring. Most criminals are not criminals 24-7. You need to catch them when they are — in the act, so to speak, no easy task for the smart ones. The ultimate objective can keep you focused. Maintaining that focus is easier done in teams. A minimum of two, depending on the size and scope. The other person serves not only as a backup but will also keep you from prolonged distractions or even dozing off.

We were recording the comings and goings of all renters. Our job is to make certain our wireless taps on their security cameras held and recorded footage made it from our desktop to the DEA Cloud, where it would be downloaded onto Portland's secure storage system. More like a reconnaissance mission than surveillance when you thought about it, gaining information on enemy activities to report to command.

Our teams had confirmed twelve units and seven lockers as drug drop-off and pickup stations. We had already tied ten known narcotics dealers with six of the units and four of the lockers. The others introduced us to fresh players in the mix. Undercovers had looked into the involvement of the new faces. All were assessed as middle management. The DEA could convict the middle management people and work their way down the line with what they had. A ladder to climb was not yet in place.

Louise Stipes would walk, claiming ignorance of what was stored in her rented lockers and units. Unless drug enforcement could uncover a paper or money trail leading back to her, which was highly unlikely. In the absence of concrete evidence, getting someone to roll over was the agency's only hope. Warrants for searches and seizures were on the table, awaiting Patrick's approval to proceed. Patrick wanted to hold out a little longer to see if they could net any big fish.

Luca Olsson and I were on our fifth swing shift together. Five-eight, fit with medium brown hair and crisp blue eyes looking out of a thirty-two-year-old baby face. Luca was a high-tech guy who loved sci-fi, video games, spelunking, photography, videography, camping, hang gliding, catching bad guys, and his wife, Caja. Luca talked incessantly about Caja when we weren't discussing the operation. The topics of her pregnancy and their plans for the baby seemed to be on an endless loop.

Luca walked me through the technical aspects of the operation. Showed me how to execute uploads and check the video interceptor equipment and signals. Easy stuff. I didn't tell Luca I already knew how to do those things. My professional partner and techie extraordinaire, Renita Harris, had educated me on such matters. Still, I followed Luca as he directed me as if I were a novice. It doesn't hurt to listen. You never know what else you can learn.

Luca was late. I received a call from him at 5:47 p.m. from the hospital. He sounded panicked. Caja had gone into labor. When I asked him how Caja was doing, he said, *"Who?"*

"Caja, your wife."

"Oh yeah! *She's gone into labor. We're at the hospital.*"

I couldn't help thinking it might be best if Luca were not allowed in the delivery room. At least make certain an empty gurney was available to cart him away when he passed out.

"I'll take care of things here, Luca," I told the freaked out father to be, wishing him and Caja well.

"Thanks, C. J., I appreciate it," he managed to say. Luca forgot to hang up. I could hear Caja between fitful bouts of abdominal breathing ordering her husband to calm down. I ended the call and phoned Patrick.

As I suspected, Luca, in his rattled state, had forgotten to inform his boss of the situation. Patrick was going to have one of the dayshift people circle back and join me. I told him not to bother. I could operate the fort solo. That was not false bravado. I'd done lone surveillance before for the DEA, military intelligence, and my investigation practice. Patrick was familiar with some of the DEA portion of that history. Fortunately, I had purchased a few books from Powell's Book Store that I didn't have time to drop off at home. Hardback first editions, my favorites. They could keep me company.

I typically purchase two copies of a book these days. A physical copy and a digital one if available. The digital copy is for my digital library and to read when I travel or in situations like the current one. The physical copies are what I mostly read and for my home library. You could also say the digital copies are my backups. They would come in handy in case of a house fire or other unforeseen catastrophe. Since I keep offsite copies of almost everything on my home computer, music, books, photos, personal finances, etcetera, I can reproduce my losses should I incur such misfortune.

A couple of hours into my shift, I had finished Chapter 5 of Horizon, the voluminous, graceful, and vibrant recollections of the brilliant nature writer Barry Lopez, when I glanced up to check the camera signals. All sixteen channels had crisp, clear video feeds. A person walking down a corridor of climate-controlled units came into view on Camera 7. His stride was cool and confident. He was wearing an off the rack inexpensive dark blue suit, black fedora, and black athletic shoes. Something about him was familiar. I saved my place with my Ernest J. Gaines bookmark and set *Horizon* aside. He stopped in front of Locker No. 137. A locker we had identified as a narcotics transfer station. Someone in the storage security office enlarged the shot of his profile before I could. The man was wearing dark sunglasses and a fake beard that looked as though he had picked it from the bargain bin of a costume store.

He looked left then right, checking to see if he were alone. He punched in a code, stepped inside, and was out in less than a minute. The man in question placed a slate blue business case covered in travel stickers on the concrete floor next to him. He closed the unit door, tugged on the door handle to verify it was locked, extended the telescopic handle from the business case, and wheeled back toward Camera 7. I observed him closely as his image passed from Camera 7 to Camera 5, then 3, emerging on Camera 1 in the parking lot. He loaded the shipment into the back of a gray Ford Focus hatchback. The vehicle I didn't recognize. It was a rental. I could tell by the barcode stickers on the windows and the Thrifty Car Rental rear license plate frame. I made a mental note of the license plate number rather than post it in my electronic DEA journal. I watched the car exit the facility until it was out of view as if looking after someone I was not ready to say goodbye.

I rolled back the captured footage of the man in question on the computer. I zoomed in on the business case. Bombay, Australia, California, New York, London, Paris, Canada, Holland, Brazil, and Japan. I suspected those specific decal combinations were a buoy, a signal to someone what was inside. That person had retrieved the case from wherever and deposited it into the locker. Finding out who they were would simply be a matter of checking previous footage on Locker No. 137.

I zoomed in on the man's profile, focusing on what I could see of his face. Peeling away the facade in my mind. His face was unveiled. My jaw dropped in disbelief when his identity registered. If my revelation was correct, then what in the *hell* was he doing there? I needed to talk to this man before the DEA figured out who he was.

CHAPTER TWO

2:26 a.m.

The last of the Vista Cleaning crew cleared out of the four-story colonial brick building situated on a lot in the southeast corner of Multnomah County, Oregon. The only commercial office building in an affluent, predominately residential area. The building was now empty. What remained of security was an electronic alarm system triggered by forced entry and wireless digital cameras recording and storing video, but not monitored in any way. Lawful entry outside of normal business hours required electronic photo ID recognition coupled with a keypad passcode that changed every three months.

He had been casing the Cronus Building for two weeks from several locations using varied disguises. Since midnight, the man now impersonating a Vista Cleaning employee had been watching from the paid parking lot across the street. Perched inside his cargo van disguised as a Vista Cleaning vehicle complete with advertising decals, a lit cigarillo dangled from his bearded lips. The raw, earthy smoke formed a diaphanous gray spiral about his black curly head. Unlike a genuine Vista work van, his was equipped with surveillance equipment and computer hardware rather than cleaning supplies and materials. The parking lot made for great cover. Local apartment residents had prepaid assigned spots grouped within the lot. He paid for his online. His parking space situated his van between two residential SUVs to avoid local police patrols. Vista cleaning vehicles were regular sights in this neighborhood. Police patrols did not even look twice at his vehicle.

2:53 a.m.

Lucas Perez was the area manager for Vista Cleaning. Perez was away on vacation with his family. The bearded man had broken into his home. He stole the area manager's encoded Photo ID badge and security clearance code that Perez had conveniently written on a yellow post-it and stuck to the back of his badge.

It was time.

He ground out his cigarillo in the "COFFEE COMPLETES ME" mug empty of the dark roast coffee he had enjoyed earlier. Pouring a little water in the cup to assure the cigarillo flame was doused. In his first week, he tapped into Cronus' central security Wi-Fi connection, easily tearing through their off-the-shelf firewalls, establishing a backdoor into their network. He also recorded three hours of video footage from the surveillance feeds from a previous night. He combined the video footage with specific software instructions then downloaded it as a sleeper file into the security system awaiting his command. Once the sleeper file released the pre-recorded footage, it would appropriate any camera fed monitor footage and block real time surveillance video from ever being recorded. He opened the system backdoor, located his sleeper file, and released it.

Cigarillo man slipped from the back of the cargo van into the driver's seat without leaving the van. He pulled the van around to the back of the Cronus Building and parked. It was a blind spot from the street but well in view of a security camera.

Killing the lights and the engine, he returned to the back. He checked the tap he had on the building's wireless security cameras. The prerecorded video was working. Complete with reset timestamp. He could tell. On the day he planned to record the footage, he had entered the Cronus Building disguised as a delivery person. It was 4:58 p.m. The concierge was set to leave at five. A deliberate ploy on his part.

"Who's the package for?" the stout middle-aged concierge irritably asked. Walt, his nametag read. A fact the man already knew from his quick background check on the Cronus concierge.

"Mr. Paul Adams."

"Adams Industries?"

The fraud checked the package label. "Yeah, that's right."

"They're gone for the day."

Cigarillo man was well aware of that fact. The company was celebrating its fifth anniversary and had closed shop early to party.

"They told dispatch they needed it no later than first thing tomorrow morning." He feigned apprehension.

Walt checked the time on his cell. The fraud could read it upside down: 5:01. Cigarillo man knew from his daily surveillance of the Cronus Building Walt punched out at five sharp Monday through Friday. The concierge was anxious to place the building on lockdown and go. "Can I leave it with you?" Cigarillo man asked, continuing his act.

Walt sighed. "Sure. I'll see Mr. Adams gets it first thing in the morning."

The fraud expressed relief. "Sign right here." Walt gave Cigarillo man his electronic signature.

"Thanks," the fake delivery person said and hurried off. The concierge not far behind.

That night he saw the package on his monitor, sitting on the small table behind the concierge desk within direct sight of one of the security cameras. It was his marker. In real-time, the package containing a vegan snack box packed in crumpled newspaper was long gone. It was in plain view on the footage he was viewing. One final check was the camera panel where he was parked. There was no sign of his van.

He stripped out of his disguise and put on flame-resistant coveralls, balaclava, and safety toe boots. After putting on his flame-resistant gloves, he grabbed a black duffle bag that contained everything he needed for the job and exited the van through the sliding side door that faced the building. You couldn't be too careful, he believed. Even with prerecorded video circumventing actual footage, getting dressed before he exited the van provided him with cover that would protect him in case he missed some security measure. Cigarillo man was a stickler for detail and caution. Two qualities both he and his employers embraced.

Aren Jakande would be first to arrive at approximately 6:30 a.m. An investment counselor who leased a fourth-floor office and could not wait to start his day. Jakande would be followed ten minutes later by Walt, who would organize his lobby station and by 7:00 a.m. sharp officially open Cronus for business. Cigarillo man had at least three hours to execute his plan. More than enough time for what he had in mind.

3:11 a.m.

Cigarillo man flashed Perez's encoded photo ID badge in front of the reader. A small green light blinked top left of the reader. He punched the passcode into the keypad. The door unlocked. He slipped inside and went to work.

CHAPTER THREE

The soothing yet treacherous patter of hard rain pounded the gray Ford Focus. The rhythmic thump of wiper blades cleared the water-blurred windshield. High winds added their voices to the song. A heavy shroud of darkness gobbled up light like a ravenous black bear. The man in disguise had taken off his dark sunglasses to see. He had settled into the right lane of Oregon I-5. The slow lane. Traffic flowed smoothly despite the stormy weather. He had set the car's cruise control at fifty-five. Ten miles under the 65 MPH speed limit. Resisting the urge to lock in the electronic device at forty-five. Believing forty-five to be a safer speed under current conditions.

He wasn't certain, but he believed driving a passenger vehicle too slow on a freeway was against the law. In any case, poking along on I-5 could attract unwarranted attention from Oregon State Highway Patrol. He could be pulled over if a State Trooper regarded his snail's pace as a safety hazard to other drivers. An attentive Trooper might regard his disguise as suspicious, which could result in a search of his rental car. That would be a disaster. Fifty-five in the right lane during a rainstorm in a lightweight vehicle should keep him safe from law enforcement scrutiny.

An SUV, sedan, and a couple of pickups tailgated him, flashing their high beams in aggressive efforts to force him to accelerate or pull over. He refused. One of the pickup drivers became so angry that he flipped him off as he zipped by in the left passing lane. Vehicles sped by him as if hydroplaning were a myth. He was normally one of them. While he was in a hurry to get to where he needed to be, he would not be joining their ranks tonight.

The man in disguise was sweating, partly because of the hot air from the car defroster being on full blast. In part, because of the fake beard and wig he was still wearing. Largely because he was nervous and scared. Two abnormal conditions for him.

His emotions kept fluctuating between anger, fear, and self-loathing. Neither having enough fight to dominate the other. He had done as instructed. The luggage pickup from Epitome Self Storage Locker No. 137 had gone without a hitch. He had asked about the case contents before making the pickup. He was told it was none of his business. Knowing would have mattered. He was an advocate of the complete legalization of marijuana. Believing cannabis should be regulated in the same manner as alcohol. He was warned what would happen if he tried to open the case. They didn't have to spell it out for him. He knew with whom he was dealing. Marijuana was not his cargo but a more lethal narcotic. Cocaine or heroin was his guess. The case contents did not matter. He had no choice. He had become something he despised. A drug trafficker.

Making a clean getaway did not make what he was doing any easier. Knowing he had become a part of a narcotics distribution network made him sick to his stomach. If there was a way out, he did not see it. It was the only way. The person holding all of the cards made that crystal clear. If he did not do as told, people he cared about would go to prison or worse. He could not allow that to happen.

He drove the gray Ford Focus hatchback with caution, not due to lack of familiarity with the vehicle or the road but in a concerted effort not to attract attention. Obeying traffic laws like a newly minted driver seeking to prove they belonged behind the wheel. Keeping a wary eye out for cops. The drive felt as though it was taking an eternity. He let out a prolonged audible exhale when he finally arrived about a half-hour later. Parking in the same area of the Tigard, Walmart Supercenter parking lot where he had picked up the car. A good distance from the store entrances.

He took a moment to try to compose himself. He released his death grip on the steering wheel. He had not realized how intense his shoulders had been until he felt them relax. He wondered if rookie drug mules felt as he did. Experienced the same cavalcade of emotions. Wanting nothing more than to get the whole terrifying event over. Tossing the keys into the glove compartment as instructed, he put on his dark sunglasses and exited the rental leaving the driver's door unlocked. The cold rain felt refreshing on his sweaty face. Blurred his sunglasses but not enough that he could not see where he was going. He had parked his car a few rows over. He dared not strip off his disguise out of concern he might be recognized. He jumped into his car, removed his sunglasses to clear his vision, and drove the hell out of there as fast as he could.

Two men watched him pull away from a charcoal sedan with tinted glass. They had been waiting for him unbeknownst to the driver. They had seen him park the gray Ford Focus. They recognized the Thrifty Rental Car. It was the same one they had rented earlier and left near the same parking spot for the man in disguise to pick up. When they saw the driver leave in his own car, the man in the passenger seat wasted no time rushing to the Focus. He got in on the driver's side and retrieved the keys from the glove compartment. He popped the trunk and looked inside. The slate blue business case covered in travel stickers was in there. He gave his partner a thumbs up, closed the trunk, got in, and drove away. His partner followed in the charcoal sedan.

CHAPTER FOUR

I rang the doorbell. The distinctive first few measures of Beethoven's *Fifth Symphony in C Minor* came from inside. A surprising elegance for a paint-chipped, green vinyl-sided, single-story, blistering asphalt roof home in a small community of similar houses whose name I did not catch. I had followed Gerek Choinski from his three-story northeast Portland home seventy-three miles southeast to land on this front stoop. I already had the answer for why I was hired. Gaining this knowledge might add enlightenment to his motivation.

I learned from his insurance file that Gerek Choinski had just turned forty-two. Married with two children. He had worked for Heritage Supplies for twenty years. He began his career with them as a stock and delivery person. A decade ago, he wrenched his back. The injury left Choinski bedridden for four weeks. Bedrest averted any need for surgery. Heritage had all of their employees on Lunsford Insurance top of the line policy. Choinski received 80% of his salary during his recovery and had all of his medical expenses paid. It took another three months of physical therapy for him to be back on the job with the stipulation of only light lifting. He was a Grade A employee, and the company wanted to help him as much as they could. They offered him a supervisor position that required little physical labor. He took it.

Months of additional physical therapy returned Choinski to full strength. Granted a choice to return to his old job or remain at his current position, he opted to stay put. All had been well with his career of late. Choinski had been taking sick leave for what he claimed were recurring back problems, forty-eight days over the past year. Doctors could not find anything physically wrong with him. Diagnosing on the side of caution, they prescribed a couple of days of bed rest in hopes his condition improved. It always did.

Choinski had exhausted all of his company sick leave. Lunsford was again obligated to reimburse Mr. Choinski to the tune of 80% of his lost income. His suspicious sick leave pattern had caught the attention of Lunsford's claims department, who passed it upstairs to their investigation division. Lunsford's investigative team had more on their plate than they could handle for the moment. Struck by the flu bug that was going around. Carl Wheaton, head of the division, asked if I'd look into the Choinski case. Cavanaugh Investigation Agency is on retainer with Lunsford Insurance. They call, and we typically answer. I was happy to investigate on their behalf.

I rang the doorbell again.

A downpour had backed off to a steady rain. Winter in Portland, Oregon, what would you expect. I sat in a leased gray car with dark tinted windows. I had a Lunsford expense budget I decided to put to use. Leasing a car for stakeouts is a good idea whenever possible. Better than using your personal vehicle for obvious reasons. I parked in front of a house where I knew no one was home. No one could see me, but I could see everyone. Three houses up and across the street lived my person of interest.

Today was my first day on the Gerek Choinski investigation. Using my telephoto lens and digital camera from my car, I got good photos and video footage of Mr. Choinski taking out the trash and recyclables, replacing his old wall-mounted personalized mailbox with a new one even going for a run with his dog. There was no indication at any time that he suffered any discomfort. I was packing it in when I noticed Choinski drive away. Curiosity got the better of me. I followed him.

"Can I help you?" A voice asked from the other side of the weathered wood panel door. It sounded like a woman.

"My name's Cavanaugh. I'm a private investigator." I held up my PI photo ID to the peephole centered in the upper cross of the door for the faceless voice to see.

"And?"

"I'd like to speak to Gerek Choinski."

"Nobody here by that name."

"Then I suppose that wasn't his blue SUV that pulled into your garage just a few minutes ago."

"I don't know what you're talking about. There's no one here by that name."

"Suit yourself. If by chance you encounter Mr. Choinski, please mention to him that the person hired by Lunsford Insurance to investigate his rash of work absentees was here."

The door opened a few moments later. I walked in. She had dark shoulder-length hair, blue eyes, and skin the color of iceberg rose petals. Her relaxed-fit jeans and elbow sleeve teaberry blouse were a comfortable fit on her five-six athletic frame. She immediately closed and locked the door behind me.

"Your name?" I asked.

"You can call me none-of-your-business," she said with attitude.

She walked. I followed. She led me to a fully furnished, carpeted, functional living room with a slate and copper theme. The same man I photographed earlier stood in the middle of the room, five-ten, about one-ninety, broad shoulders, short dark ash-blond hair, and a full matching beard. He was brawny despite a middle-aged paunch that was beginning to sprout. He wore steel-toed work boots, and a tan polyester Heritage Supplies work uniform.

"Why is someone playing hooky from work dressed for work?" I asked Choinski.

His light gray eyes glared at me. His jaw tightened. His arms hung loosely by his sides like a boxer awaiting the bell to come out swinging. The woman went over and stood beside him, crossing her arms over her chest.

"Lunsford hired you to spy on me?" he asked, sounding more like a demand than a question.

"They hired me to find out if your back injury was real. From what I've witnessed, it's not."

I noticed a shared hint of relief between them. The woman dropped her arms to her side. Their shoulders relaxed, as did their expressions.

"You got proof," Choinski said.

"Video and photos of you doing everything but break dancing."

"How much will it take to make them disappear?" Choinski asked.

"Are you offering me a bribe?"

"Are you taking?"

I shook my head.

"Then I'm not offering." Choinski tilted his head slightly to one side as if he had just witnessed an odd curiosity. "Why are you showing your hand, PI?"

"Meaning?"

"Investigators under surveillance operate in the shadows. There's no reason for you to step into the light."

Choinski was sharp. It made me wonder why he was being so stupid with this back injury scam.

"Here's the deal," I said. "I'll file my Lunsford report with a caveat. I'm going to request the person I report to for leniency on your behalf. On two conditions."

"They being? Choinski said.

"You show up for work tomorrow, miraculously healed, and you don't pull another stunt like this one again on Lunsford's dime."

"What's in it for you?"

"Warm and cozy butterflies in my tummy for having done a good deed."

"I don't follow."

"Family."

Gerek and the woman looked quizzically at each other.

"You've invested fifteen years with Lena, your wife, remember her? The mother of your two children, Monika and Oscar. You will lose your job without my appeal for clemency. Lunsford will prosecute you to the fullest extent of the law to make an example of you. Now you might catch a break and get probation, but I wouldn't count on it. In all likelihood, you'll be sentenced to the max and wind up another member of the American industrial prison complex."

The two of them stared at me. Their expressions were equally blank. The kind of poker faces common amongst people accustomed to the give and take of deceit.

"Thanks," Choinski said flatly.

"I'm not doing this for you, *idiot*."

Anger darted through Choinski's eyes. His jaw flexed.

"I'm cutting you a break for *your family*. They deserve better."

"You don't even know my wife and children."

"I know family means more to most people than skipping work to have an affair."

"We're not —" the woman coughed before Choinski could finish. Choinski looked at the woman in time to catch her quick glare. She looked down at the carpet then back up at me with defiance.

"What's going on here?" I asked them. Choinski and the woman looked at each other, then at me.

"That's none of your business," Choinski said. The woman nodded her agreement.

"Isn't that your name?" I quipped to the woman. She smirked. Choinski, oblivious to the inside joke, dismissed my question as irrelevant.

"You've made your conditions clear," Choinski said. "I'll be at work bright and early tomorrow."

"Then we understand each other," I said. "No more mysterious back injuries causing you to bail on your job."

"Not a one."

"I'm going to hold you to it. If you try double-crossing me, I'll make sure Lunsford fries your ass and your wife gets everything you own if she decides to divorce you."

"Tough guy, huh."

"A little," I said. "Mostly honest. I keep my word."

There was a moment of quiet tension. Choinski and I were sizing each other up. It felt as though the bell was about to ring.

"You've made your point," the woman said. "Now leave."

I left with the most peculiar feeling. My initial assumption was I had uncovered Choinski's marital unfaithfulness. Most people caught at infidelity become remorseful or defensive. They may cling to each other for emotional support or repel the object of their guilt. That is, people with a conscience tend to respond in that manner. While the mystery woman and Gerek Choinski stood next to each other, they had no physical contact or seemed to desire any. Neither appeared humiliated or even embarrassed by the situation. If anything, they seemed cool and detached. As if they had been in the middle of a business meeting before my untimely interruption.

Maybe she was a prostitute, and it was merely a business transaction, I thought. Nothing about the mystery woman confirmed that suspicion. My job was done whatever the issues, and so was my good deed for the day. Unable to shake the oddity of what had just transpired, I hopped in my car and headed back to the office.

CHAPTER FIVE

I didn't have time to go to the office when I returned to Portland. The DEA surveillance team was expecting me at five. I uploaded the photos and video of Gerek Choinski to my agency Cloud storage from my laptop. I could download them later at the office when I wrote my report to Carl Wheaton.

I made a quick call to my Homicide Detective woman friend to see how she was doing. Communication with non-DEA personnel was prohibited during stakeouts. Homicide was busier than ever. Destini and I agreed that was not a good thing. We had plans to get together on Saturday. An opportunity to squeeze in any quality time before then was not in the cards.

I spent a few moments with my tropical fish, my singing finches: Toussaint, Coretta, Claude, Truth, and my twin Scottish terriers, Andrew and Booker. Assured they had all they needed for the night, I darted over to the Globe Building for my DEA stakeout shift.

Felissa Maddison Olsson was born at 9:47 a.m., 19.5 inches, seven pounds two ounces, according to the text message we received from the proud father. He had included a pic of the beautiful mother and daughter. Caja is exhausted but happy after fifteen hours of labor. Felissa is sound asleep on her mother's chest.

Patrick informed our team that Luca Olsson was taking time off to be with his new family. Special Agent Lamar Parker, one of the front office sentries, filled in for him. A clean-shaven ex-naval lieutenant. Six-three, lean and muscular, with skin the color of desert sand. With his designer eyewear, business casual clothing, and sponge twists hairstyle, he looked the part of a trendy professional. We sat parallel about an arm's length away from each other, facing the two color monitors.

Lamar was married. He showed me pictures of his bride on his phone. Belinha had mocha skin, flowing lioness curls, a graceful neck, large amber eyes, and a 1000-watt smile. Her head topped right at his shoulders. Happiness beamed from their eyes and face during every comfortable embrace. Some couples belong together as if cast as one. Belinha and Lamar appeared that way to me. In the adoring way he spoke of her, It was more than conjecture on my part. It also made me wonder if Destini and I were cast the same.

Our conversation made its way from personal to shoptalk. Most of his fieldwork had been surveillance. Lamar had been involved in a few drug raids. One resulted in a brief skirmish. Shots were fired. No DEA agents were injured. Two perps suffered minor gunshot wounds.

He enjoyed the work he was doing but admitted there were times he craved more excitement. Lamar had done some undercover work and enjoyed it. He was seriously considering doing deep cover. I cautioned him that regular undercover work might last a few weeks to a few months. Deep cover can go on for years. He said he understood. I didn't believe him.

"Have you spoken to Director O'Malley about your desire to do deep cover?" I asked Lamar.

"Not yet."

"How many undercover ops have you done?"

"A few. I'm doing one now in the front office."

"What's the closest you've come to direct undercover work with drug dealers?"

"A year-and-a-half ago. Went under as a drug dealer in Houston."

"For how long?"

"Six weeks."

"How'd you feel?"

"What do you mean?"

"I mean, how did you feel being a drug dealer, Lamar?"

"Disgusted. I did what was required to bust the real dealers."

"You got a taste of how they lived. Who they were. Experienced the world through their eyes."

"Yeah."

"Did you see them sell drugs?" I asked.

"Of course."

"Who'd they sell to?"

"All sorts of people."

"Students, professionals, laborers, kids, moms, dads, pregnant women."

"Yeah. You name it. I saw it, C. J. If 'a sucker'— as the dealers referred to their clientele — had the money, they'd sell them drugs."

"Did you ever sell to anyone?"

"I made my policy clear. I was strictly a distributor. I didn't do direct sales."

"You sold them product to sell to the suckers."

"Again, part of the job. Bait to catch the bigger fish."

"Did you see them hurt anybody?" I asked.

"Yes."

"Did you see them kill anyone, Lamar?"

"No."

"Did you hurt anyone on their behalf?"

"No. I told them to handle their own problems and not involve me in that shit."

"Good line."

"What's with the interrogation?"

I ignored Lamar's questions and pressed on. "How long do you think they would have let you get away with being on the outside looking in?"

"As I said, I was gone in six weeks."

"I give it three months tops before they started making you prove you were one of them, Lamar."

"Prove how?"

"By street selling, physically hurting some people, and if you're in the gutter long enough, forcing you to take a life."

"I wouldn't do it." Lamar sounded certain. Famous last words of a naïve deep cover op.

"I believe you have the integrity and grit to say no under normal circumstances," I said. "The real test would come when your life is threatened. A dealer places a gun to your head and tells you to smoke someone, or they will drop you where you stand. This threat coming from someone you have heard about, maybe even witnessed, take life and laugh about it."

"Did that happen to you?" Lamar asked.

I was on vacation in Hilton Head, South Carolina. Addison Dunn— who everyone except myself and her mother called Addie—and I happened upon an automotive exhibition that we decided to check out. Addison was a DEA financial manager. We were both stationed at the DC office. Addison was my girlfriend at the time. Addison was into building and restoring vintage cars. The owner of a 1936 Mercedes-Benz 500 K Special was giving Addison and me some history on the hickory brown beauty when an apple red 1964 Chevrolet Corvette Coupe caught my eye. I'm partial to Chevy Corvettes. My uncle taught me how to drive in his. Addison was taking it all in when the owner popped the hood on the Benz. I excused myself to stray over to the Chevy.

The Corvette was in immaculate condition. Jeremiah Gillis, the owner, was equally proud of his creation. He said he happened upon the 'Vette in a junkyard. Rusted out body, broken windows, and water-soaked, rancid upholstery. When he towed it back to his garage, cleaned it up, and stripped it down, he discovered the engine, transmission, and frame were in good shape. Jeremiah rebuilt it all himself with occasional help from his friends. Jeremiah—or Jerry if you preferred—was a clinical psychologist. I told him I was a short-order cook between jobs at the moment. No one who works for the DEA tells a stranger they work for the DEA. Especially a field operative. That information is treated as classified and doled out only to a very few. Jerry—or Jeremiah as I preferred—said he might have some work for me if I were interested. I found that strange. What use would a clinical psychologist have for a short-order cook? Jeremiah wouldn't be specific but asked me to meet him the next day at a diner on Dunnagan's Alley. I knew the place and agreed. My instincts were telling me that Jeremiah was up to something. I needed to know what.

Addison was still asleep when I stepped out to meet Jeremiah. We had been up late partying with the vintage car crowd. Addison had a lot more to drink than I had. She wouldn't be awake before the afternoon. Midway through our sausage, eggs, and toast breakfast Jeremiah made me a job offer. Complete with a salary and commission on all of my sales. The only catch was the product, marijuana. I took the job.

I reported to the local DEA office about what I had come across. Jeremiah Gillis was not on their radar. After clearing it with the DC office, I was granted permission to go undercover. Addison was none too happy about the development. Cut both our vacation and relationship short.

Jeremiah exclusively dealt marijuana. His operation was run out of a small apartment building that he owned. Jeremiah lived there. The rest of the apartments were occupied by his managers. As a seller, you had the option of pick up or delivery. Payment was made in the same way.

Jeremiah and his managers were true believers that cannabis should be legalized and recreational marijuana usage treated no differently than alcohol. I suppose you could say he imagined himself a visionary. Jeremiah even handed out a self-made booklet on marijuana published on hemp paper. The booklet touted the industrial and medicinal uses of cannabis. They even had a name for themselves, The Kali-Ma Alliance. I was impressed. Secretly, I was a proponent of legalizing marijuana. Federal laws had not progressed to agree with them. My job was to enforce the law.

I received intel from the local DEA office that Jeremiah's operation had come to the attention of some hardcore dealers. In general, those who sold Heroin, Cocaine, Crack, PCP, the more physically and mentally addictive narcotics. They had gotten wind that Jeremiah was making a sizable profit. A plump hog ready for the slaughter. Rather than moving into his market, they were looking to take over. Jeremiah employed muscle for protection and collection. The collection would sometimes be necessary from an occasional seller who would try to stiff them. Customers always paid upfront and were never strung out like junkies. I never knew or heard of a case where anyone was killed or seriously injured under Jeremiah's watch.

I busted the Kali-Ma Alliance. Rather the DEA did. I made the call. In part because I was doing my job. Mostly it was to save their lives. The hardcore dealers had plans to hit the apartment building, killing them and making off with their cash and product. Ours was a preemptive strike to prevent those things from happening.

Needless to say, Jeremiah and the rest of the Kali-Ma Alliance were furious with me when they discovered I was DEA. I didn't talk to or see any of them after the trial. They agreed to be tried together. They had great legal counsel. The best money could buy. It helped that I curbed my testimony to show that the Kali-Ma Alliance were not vicious, sadistic, greedy drug dealers. It made them appear as believers in an illegal product to sell for money to further their cause while having a good time in the process. They got off with a large fine and a few years in prison. They were out in no time for good behavior.

I did check on Jeremiah through my law enforcement connections. He changed course on the same river, you might say. It turned out Jeremiah had earned a Master's Degree in Psychology. He started dealing marijuana in college to help pay for his education. Upon graduation, Jeremiah discovered dealing to be far more lucrative than any job he was offered. He decided to stick with it. Jeremiah put his degree in psychology to good use, starting in prison. Counseling drug-addicted inmates per the warden's request. Jeremiah Gillis became a licensed clinical psychologist specializing in drug addiction. I didn't bother to ask how an ex-felon could obtain such a license. His methods have become so successful that he has opened treatment centers throughout the U.S. and Canada. The Kali-Ma Addiction Treatment Centers, to be exact. Jeremiah Gillis embraced his true calling.

I don't know why I thought of Jeremiah Gillis now. An experience so far afield of our current conversation. Somehow, someway, on a deeper level, I must have seen some parallelism between Jeremiah's life choices and Special Agent Lamar Parker. A Hopi proverb came to mind. *What should it matter that one bowl is dark and the other pale if each is of good design and serves the other well?*

"More than once," I said, back in the present.

"Did you do it?"

"I knew what I signed up for. I also knew how far I would go to nail those bastards. The short answer is no. I didn't do it."

"You're still here," Lamar said with a satisfied smile.

"I was lucky. I was able to either talk my way out of it or catch a killer on a good day." There was a lull in our conversation. I let what I said sink in. "How long have you been married, Lamar?"

"Coming up on a year."

"Newlyweds, cool." That comment caused his smile to widen. "Plan on having children?" I asked.

"Yep."

"Sounds like you want a normal life."

"Pretty much."

"How long have you been in love with Belinha?"

His smile disappeared. "That's a strange question."

"I'm a strange guy," I said. "Humor me."

Lamar looked at me quizzically. "Since we met about three years before we were married. What's that have to do with anything?"

"The longer the love, the stronger the bond," I said. Lamar nodded. "Does the DEA still shy away from placing married people and parents under deep cover?"

"Yes."

"Why do you think that is?"

"It's stressful."

"It's also extremely dangerous," I added. "Deep cover is typically done for high profile targets. Your chances of winding up dead before achieving your goal are high. The mark doesn't even have to know you are DEA. If they suspect you're not legitimate, you are mulch."

"You did it."

I wasn't surprised Lamar knew I had gone deep. Everyone at the Portland office knew of my DEA background. Deep cover ops had become my specialty during much of my DEA tenure. My storied DEA career was legend to some, overblown to others. The reality lay somewhere in between. Lamar prodded me for details on my experiences. None was forthcoming. Undercover operations are classified as he well knew. It didn't prevent him from probing.

"To circle back to your original statement," I said. "I don't have children and was not married when I did it," I stated the facts in that order since having children and marriage often do not go hand-in-hand. "Did you see combat while you were in the navy?" I asked Lamar.

"Yes."

"Any hand-to-hand, in the trenches."

"None," Lamar said. "I was stationed on a first-class battle cruiser. I got in more scrapes on shore leave or in stateside bars than in naval combat." He chuckled. I chuckled too.

"You didn't miss anything," I said. "Deep cover is like constantly being on the edge of a firefight except you don't know when or where it's going to set off. You're always on guard. You are left to your own devices, armed mostly with your wits and training. You have to watch and maybe even participate in things that will turn your stomach, even make you hate yourself. If you're in long enough, you could devolve into the same type of person you're trying to bring down."

"Did that happen to you?"

"No. I was fortunate. A couple of special agents I knew bottomed out during deep-cover ops. Once they were pulled and realized what had happened, they quit the DEA."

"You're saying that could happen to me, C. J.? Bottoming out, or winding up dead?"

"Maybe. There's no such thing as a superman, Lamar."

There was a quiet lull in our conversation. I could tell Lamar was mulling over what I had said. I knew I was overstepping my bounds, but there was something I needed to spell out for Lamar that was as clear as the video feeds we were receiving from the wireless tap. I was trying to scare him. From the wary look in his eyes and nervous jerk of his head, I would say it was working. Good. What he was proposing was parachuting into the belly of the beast. Not a video game, not a TV show or film, real-life and death scenarios with no stop, pause or reset buttons, the kind of brutal toughness, unwavering constitution, and razor focus required of an individual to be a successful deep cover agent I did not see in this young man. Without stating it, I was hoping to get him to catch a glimpse of that reality.

"What would you do for your wife?" I asked. "Your family?"

"Anything," he said.

"Would you give your life for them?"

"Of course. That's why I joined the DEA. I want to make a positive difference for them and future generations."

He wanted to make a positive difference, common sentiments for most law enforcement personnel. I didn't press him on the typical follow-up question because I already knew the answer. Most of us discovered we were like the Dutch boy who put his finger in a dike. The holes were becoming more bountiful with too few fingers to plug the leaks.

"Why not live for them?" I asked.

Lamar glared at me. "I didn't join the DEA to play it safe."

"It's not just about you anymore. You made a commitment to Belinha. Part of that commitment is to consider her with every decision. Your wife has to become your top priority."

"I know that! Belinha is my top priority!" Lamar sounded offended. I took his tone as a sign I was breaking through.

"I can promise you if you become a deep cover op, you can kiss any hope of having a normal life with Belinha goodbye. It's simply too much to ask from your significant other. There's no future for love when you're in that line of work."

I thought of the issues I had with Destini being a homicide detective. It was the blockade in our relationship. Wondering how much of my baggage I was placing on Lamar. The ex-Naval lieutenant didn't say anything. He stared at me for a long moment. I could see in his eyes that I had hit pay dirt.

"The level of commitment required to go deep cover is like nothing you have ever experienced, Lamar. It's not like a sports challenge or field combat. You will be rubbing shoulders with some of the most dangerous and often sociopathic, psychopathic, and paranoid people you will ever encounter in your life. Your job is to infiltrate and gather as much intelligence as possible to convict them. You can only achieve that goal by convincing them you are one of them."

"You're not married, C. J. Would you go deep cover again?"

"*No*," I answered without hesitation. I questioned why I felt so strongly about it.

"Why not?" Lamar seemed incredulous at my answer as if he were expecting some glory days' bravado stories to ensue.

"Seen too much insanity. Experienced too much horrible shit."

"Was it worth it?" Lamar asked.

I had to think. Surprisingly, I had never asked myself that question. "It seemed so at the time," was my honest answer.

"And now."

I shrugged. "I'm not so sure." We both watched the monitor in silence.

"Would you?" Lamar asked after a few quiet measures.

"Would I what?"

"If you were married, had children, or both when you were deep cover? Would you have killed someone when they threatened your life to prove yourself?"

"That's speculation."

"That's avoidance."

The question made me uneasy. I thought about Destini, Renita, and others who had planted seeds in my life since I retired from the DEA. What would I have done to return to them? How far would I have gone if my current circumstances existed then?

"I don't know," I answered.

Lamar nodded. As we continued to watch the monitors, we did our due diligence, documenting more recorded drug transactions by uploading our footage to DEA cloud storage. Most were repeat offenders. A few faces were new. We drifted off, discussing his DEA career options aside from deep cover, and shared our views of critical modern world strife. Our conversation fizzled. Lamar took that as his queue to remove a sketchpad and set of sharpened charcoal pencils from his vintage leather shoulder bag.

I checked the monitors then glanced over at Lamar. "You're an artist," I said.

"Some might say that," Lamar mused.

He shared with me some of his artwork by both hand and digital. They were excellent, as far as I could tell. He was very interested in animation, manga, and anime and was considering a career change if the right opportunity came along.

Lamar settled into his sketching. I pulled out *The Oregonian* that I didn't have a chance to read that morning. There was an article about the Cronus Building fire. The building was destroyed. It turned out it was the fourth such fire in the last three months in Multnomah County. The other three had been confirmed arsons. The Cronus Building fire was still under investigation. My focus was elsewhere. I kept a sharp eye on the monitor. I was looking for the person I'd seen the night before. He never showed.

CHAPTER SIX

Janet Proctor could not stop thinking about C. J. Cavanaugh after the conclusion of her business with Gerek Choinski. The PI had followed Choinski on another matter and stumbled upon their secret meeting place. Janet couldn't blame Gerek. There was no one way for him to anticipate that anyone would be spying on him. Cavanaugh had assumed they were lovers. Janet knew Choinski destroyed any credibility in his theory when he started offering up a denial that she tried in vain to intercept. If Gerek had gone along with Cavanaugh's presumption, then maybe the whole matter would be behind them. Janet could tell Cavanaugh became suspicious of their motives afterward. She imagined even the prostitution angle he was probably considering disintegrated. The bent of his comments and questions made that clear. Until Cavanaugh showed up, everything had been going well for her and Choinski. This was the first serious bump in their arrangement since the beginning of their partnership.

Janet did not like anyone sticking their nose into her business, personal or professional. She especially did not care that said nose belonged to a PI in this particular instance. Cavanaugh could present a problem. His involvement should be concluded with Gerek. If Cavanaugh was as good as his word and Gerek was the same on the Lunsford Insurance issue. If Cavanaugh proved to be the curious type or an opportunist, as some unscrupulous PIs were known to be when it came to money, then he could present a serious problem.

A quick internet search on her laptop on the day of Cavanaugh's intrusion revealed some information about the man. Janet learned his office was located in the Stevens Building in downtown Portland from his business website. Uncomfortably close to her residence in Portland Heights. He had a junior partner, Renita Harris. The Cavanaugh Investigation

Agency handled insurance, civil, criminal, and domestic investigations at reasonable rates. Although none of their reasonable rates were posted.

Cavanaugh had no social network or social media accounts under his name that she could find. Not even a professional LinkedIn profile. Janet found that odd. Upon closer examination of his website, it contained no background information on Mr. Cavanaugh. Was he from the northwest? Had he been in the military? Had he served in law enforcement in any capacity? Did he have any law enforcement or criminal justice degrees? It was as if this Cavanaugh person simply dropped out of the sky and became a licensed private investigator. Janet knew a few scam artists. Setting up a PI swindle would be easier than ever in this day and age. If she were running such a scam, Janet imagined she would want to entice her marks with more phony contextual information. It was piss poor marketing as far as Janet was concerned.

Cavanaugh appeared to have no shortage of satisfied customers if his website testimonials were to be believed. Most of the agency's reviews were glowing. The few that were not Janet could easily dismiss after having met Cavanaugh. If his positive reviews were legitimate, then Mr. C. J. Cavanaugh was someone to be wary of. A big shot like Lunsford Insurance showed confidence in him by hiring him to investigate the legitimacy of Gerek Choinski's suspicious series of insurance claims. Cavanaugh delivered and then some cutting Gerek a break if he straightened up for the sake of his family. That was something a good cop might do after busting a first-timer. Lunsford could have their pick of any PI in the state—in the country, for that matter. They chose Cavanaugh. There was a lot more to this PI than met the eye.

Janet had her ritual morning five-mile run. Showered, groomed, and dressed in a pair of faded jeans and an ivory turtleneck pullover sweater. Rain was steady with intermittent gusts of wind. Inside was warm and cozy. Classical piano played on her stereo, drowning out the sound of forced warm air flowing from the baseboard registers. Janet had made herself a Greek omelet for breakfast. She meditatively chewed a forkful of omelet. Her strawberry-scented shampoo reminded Janet to add the fruit to her grocery list. It was the first she'd had time to reflect on the scene of Cavanaugh crashing their meeting. Perhaps she should pay him a visit. Crash his turf as he had done hers.

It had taken Janet almost half an hour to calm Gerek down after Cavanaugh's intrusion. Contrast that to Janet's initial take on Cavanaugh, who appeared cool, confident, and persistent. Professional qualities in a person who is accustomed to getting a job done. The positive reviews on his website bore out her first impressions. The fact that he had tracked Gerek to their secret rendezvous on what was a gut whim lent credence to her tenacity notion as far as Janet was concerned. *I wouldn't mind having this guy on my payroll,* she thought. Although she did not know how upper management would feel about hiring a PI, particularly one who may prove to be enterprising in a self-serving sort of way.

His resolve also made Janet believe Cavanaugh had a hunger for the bottom line truth, making him especially dangerous to their operation. This guy could bring the drama. Cavanaugh could become a serious problem if he became curious about her and Mr. Choinski. That sort of attention was bad for business. Janet did not like problems. They often led to complications. Enough of them could turn a currently successful operation into a bust. There was no way to tell from the information she had mined on Cavanaugh whether he was an opportunist. Their first meeting had not made it clear to Janet whether he might cultivate exploitive intentions. Janet decided that if Mr. Cavanaugh proved a nuisance, she would need to neutralize him. An obstacle to be removed. It all hinged on whether Mr. C. J. Cavanaugh was willing to have a case of amnesia regarding her meeting with Gerek Choinski without compensation.

CHAPTER SEVEN

Renita had accrued eight weeks of vacation time. I convinced her to take six. Renita was not due back in the office until the second Monday of February. Ernest Fullman, Renita's muscular, seven-three gingerbread man-friend, had whisked my junior partner away. The bouncer and half-owner of Fullman's Restaurant met my five-six, athletic, latté skinned partner while we were working a dangerous case some time ago. Ernest was charming and sophisticated and fell in love with Renita at first sight. Renita had not yet developed the same clear vision of their relationship.

They left Portland International Airport on a gray, cold, wet Saturday morning for the initial leg of their journey to a first-class sunny resort on the southern Pacific coast. A well-earned escape for my partner. We had been at it nonstop for almost the entire year. Working a variety of Lunsford Insurance and private client cases independently and as a team, business was great. It hit us like a sledgehammer strength tester ringing our bells to tap out from mental fatigue when the lull happened. We worked around Thanksgiving. We closed shop between Christmas Eve through the New Year. I went home to Pittsburgh. Destini and Renita stayed put. Renita being a child of the northwest, family surrounded her. Work did not allow Destini to break away. Ernest surprised Renita on Christmas with an invitation to join him on a winter escape to Ixtapa, Mexico. She accepted. I asked Renita if accepting Ernest's invite officially made them a couple. She gave me a mischievous grin before answering, "We're getting there."

The Cavanaugh Investigation Agency is located on the ninth floor of the Stevens Building in downtown Portland. When you enter my office is to your immediate right. Renita's office is directly ahead. On Renita's side are the workout area, shower, and bathroom. The kitchenette, copy, storage, and server rooms are on my side. I made a beeline to my office, carrying the company camera equipment. The office was quiet. When I began my agency, this was the way it was. I operated solo and was comfortable with that arrangement. Then this hardheaded, outspoken, brilliant young woman entered my practice, and my professional and personal life has not been the same.

I missed Renita telling me about her personal life. Expounding on her methods of solving her cases and sharing with her mine. I missed teaching Renita about prudent investigative practices and her teaching me about the modern technological world. I missed her enthusiasm and unbridled passion for life and justice. I missed our banter. Mostly, I missed her because she is my friend.

Renita sent me an internal email. My partner had overhauled my dinosaur office into a modern work environment. At least as much as I would allow. We now had remote access to our network, PCs, and laptops by two methods, WAN (wide area network) or the Cloud.

I activated the link Renita had included in the email. It took me directly to a "MexVacpics" folder she had created under her directory on our network. Breathtaking photos of turquoise water, azure skies, and stunning beaches suitable for postcards. Her luxury suite wasn't bad either. A little sampling of what I was missing, as she phrased it in her email. She went on to rave about how amazing everything was. The delightful people and the delicious food. Although her donor was featured in a number of the pics, both solo and coupled with Renita. My partner did not mention Ernest. Deliberate omission or not, I could not say.

Judging by the time/date stamp on the folder, Renita must have created the "MexVacpics" folder before downloading the Choinski files from our Cloud storage. Had my partner seen the Choinski files, she would have wanted to know all about the case. Any attempt to thwart her curiosity would end in vain. I would feel obligated to fill her in. From there, my partner would hound me to keep her posted. The last thing I wanted was to interfere with Renita's getaway. Luck was on my side in that regard.

I entered Renita's office to ask her to proof my Gerek Choinski report before sending it off to Carl at Lunsford Insurance. The instant I saw her empty chair, I realized my mistake. The moment saddened me. There would come a day when Renita would strike out on her own. Funny how attached we become to certain people. They become permanent fixtures we assume will always be present. Not until their absence do we fully appreciate them. While I have no doubt Renita and I will remain close friends, it will not be the same as working with her. Renita's empty office chair spelled that out for me. I shook off my mistake and sentimentality, returned to my office, and emailed my findings to Carl.

I prioritized my current caseload. Enough to keep me busy but not overwhelmed. Patrick had informed me that after this week, the DEA would no longer require my services. Maybe in the coming weeks, I could squeeze in a little retreat to some sunny part of the world? Maybe I could coax Destini into joining me?

First up was a background investigation. I contacted my honed inside connections to compile financial, criminal, and commercial data on the individual in question. I checked him out on Facebook, Twitter, Instagram, Pinterest, and LinkedIn using our agency's fake social media accounts. I followed that up with phone calls to his personal and professional references, identifying myself as an agent of a potential employer verifying their validity.

Professional references were eager to help. The personal ones could be a little tricky. Can you blame them? A stranger contacts you to ask questions about a close friend. It would give me reason to pause. Maybe even hang up. That is why I pre-empt my personal reference calls with a certain message and tone. I strongly hint refusing to talk to me could result in their friend not getting the job. Any decent friend would take the chance. Once the interview was over, and they discovered the questions weren't that bad—as was often said in such cases—they were not only relieved but also glad they could help. I had also gotten the information I needed.

I had a rough draft of the report written before lunch. The person in question had a couple of outstanding parking tickets and a drunk and disorderly conduct arrest a few years back that had been dismissed. His personal and professional references were glowing. His financial situation was what was likely to sink him. He had maxed out three credit cards. He was also frequently delinquent on his child support and alimony payments. He had no savings and regularly withdrew money from his suffocating 401K in order to stay afloat. I telephoned the client to give her an overview of my findings. I mentioned I would have a formal written report to her by tomorrow afternoon. She told me not to rush. She sounded disappointed. My guess was she liked the person. There was no way she could hire him as an accounting manager based on the information I had given her.

When I hung up, I realized something. My normal background procedure was to meet my contacts and the potential employee references in person. I always like to get a feel for people. The only real way to do that is to be in close proximity to them. I had foregone my usual investigative process for time and convenience. The digital age had affected me more than I realized. I was becoming Renita when it came to background investigations. This, my partner, could never know.

I contacted Destini to see if she was free for lunch. She begged off. She had just landed two more homicides. On top of the stack, she was already working. Destini simply did not have time. I offered to pick her up something to eat. Destini informed me she was out in the field and did not know when she would return. I opted for Lunch Plan B.

I picked up a veggie burrito, grabbed a pomegranate juice from the fridge, and settled in. The paperwork I had been procrastinating on was piling up in my inbox. Business-related stuff. I still required anything in need of my signature or had a direct effect on our agency to be on paper. Renita was the one who prodded me. "Take care of those papers before I burn them," she would say. An empty threat, we both knew she would never follow through. It still served as a motivator. I took a deep breath and plunged.

My snail's pace picked up momentum. Whenever I found myself slowing down or wanting to quit, I would repeat my partner's fire mantra. Three hours later and I was done. I took the organized stack of paperwork and deposited it onto Renita's desk for filing. A welcome back from vacation gift if there ever was one. Being senior partner still had its benefits. I had time to check in on my family of pets before heading over to Globe. I grabbed my winter coat, wool fedora, and canvas shoulder bag, locked up the office, and headed home.

*   *   *

The remainder of my DEA surveillance experience of Epitome Self Storage was uneventful. Lamar mentioned he'd discussed his DEA career goals with Belinha. Together they decided it would be best for him to drop his pursuit of deep cover ops. That was good news to me. With his artistic talent, it wouldn't surprise me if a career change were not in his future.

Another routine night. We did our due diligence. Uploading saved video files every two hours from our PC to DEA cloud storage. Lamar sketched. I read. Both of us checking the monitor enough not to miss anything. The individual I was keeping an eye out for never reappeared.

CHAPTER EIGHT

I had stepped out for lunch on a drizzly autumn afternoon at Pioneer Courthouse Square, months before Renita's winter vacation, when I encountered a mocha-skinned man with a trimmed white beard wearing a baseball cap and stylish trench coat. With him was a man with a deadpan expression and fervid eyes dressed in crisp jeans, a hooded rain jacket, and a black safari hat. Smoky and Winston had been writing music all morning and had decided to take a break to grab a bite to eat.

"Mind if I join you?" I asked.

"You buying?" Winston said. I had never seen Winston buy a drink or a meal when it was the two or three of us.

"Of course," I said.

"Glad you could join us, C. J.," the decorated Korean War veteran said with a grin. I enjoyed the company of these gifted jazz luminaries. They were as brilliant conversationalists as they were musicians.

"I'm a proponent of socialism," Winston said as we strolled down Yamhill toward the Pearl District. "The fair distribution of wealth."

We had segued from a discussion of their latest musical renderings into a debate on socialism versus capitalism. Not unusual. The three of us were comfortable shifting topics without a hitch.

"So if you were a millionaire or billionaire," Smoky said, "you would have no problem with the government stepping in and telling you what to do with your hard-earned money?"

"As long as my contribution serves the greater good, I have no problem with it," Winston said.

"Says someone without a lot to lose in that scenario." Smoky was a multi-millionaire, in part from an inheritance, in part from his music.

Winston was doing all right financially these days. Smoky made certain his best friend profited from half of the rights from their joint musical creations. My turning Winston onto my brilliant finance counselor hadn't hurt. Along with his music royalties, my counselor forged Winston's modest VA and Social Security income into a financial portfolio that kept growing. Winston being frugal didn't hurt either.

"I don't think Winston meant it in exactly that way," I said, referencing my photographic memory for a definition of Socialism: "'A political and economic theory of social organization which advocates that the means of production, distribution, and exchange should be owned or regulated by the community as a whole.'"

"I don't know if I'm down with all that," Winston said.

"I believe Winston's referring to — correct me if I'm wrong — fair taxation across the board. The same for the rich and corporations as the working class."

"Exactly," Winston said. "A flat tax rate would do it."

"I can see that," Smoky said. I agreed.

"We'd still have a problem with tax loopholes no matter what taxation system you employ," I said. "I'm all for fair capitalism."

"What do you mean by fair capitalism?" Winston asked.

"Are you familiar with the Sherman Act," I asked my companions. They nodded. "In theory, it serves to protect us from monopolies and stimulate innovation. Two critical elements for success in any commercial society."

"Monopolies tend to breed stagnation, and innovation promotes competition," Smoky said. "Yeah, we know."

"Philosophically, it would and should work," I said. "The same can be said about socialism. I'm all for free medical and education. They should be endemic rights for every citizen."

"But?" Smoky said.

"You know a but is coming," Winston said. "C. J. has to bring the drama." Smoky and Winston had a laugh at my expense.

"I prefer to think of it as being thorough," I said.

"Can you get to your point, please?" Smoky asked.

"People," I said.

"*Excuse me*," Winston said.

"People are my point."

"Elaborate," Smoky said.

"Capitalism, Socialism, even Communism philosophically work. The problems are not the systems but the people who run them. None of those philosophies properly take into account individual motivations. Success hinges on how those in charge implement their powers. For example, greed, material, or power. An egocentric individual placed in a position of authority can and will in all probability skew the system in order to satisfy his or her own voracious end."

"Abuse of power," Winston said.

"Or misuse," I said.

"We see examples of it all over the world," Smoky said.

"The masses suffer in the meantime," Winston said.

"Depending on the infractions, possibly yes," I said. "Don't get me wrong. There are plenty of selfless people out there who are devoted to serving the public good. Making them the majority in power is a ceaseless challenge."

"In politics, campaign finance reform will help," Smoky said.

"That's a perfect example."

"It shouldn't take millions — or in the presidential race, billions of dollars to be elected into public office," Winston said.

"The flood of money that gushes into politics today is a pollution of democracy," Smoky said.

"Who said that?" Winston asked.

"The journalist Theodore White," Smoky said. "He also said, 'The best time to listen to a politician is when he's on a stump on a street corner in the rain late at night when he's exhausted. Then he doesn't lie.'"

Winston and I laughed. "That's a good one," Winston said.

"Why do the majority of our politicians resist campaign finance reform?" I asked.

"They got their hand in the cookie jar," Winston said.

"Or fear their opponents will have a spending advantage," Smoky added.

"For those absent, the fear and happy with the current arrangement," I said, "tells us something about them."

"They are not there to serve the people. They are there for themselves," Winston said.

"In far too many cases, I suppose that's true."

"How do you propose altering that trend?" Smoky said. "It's the nature of big business to dominate, for instance."

"No kidding," Winston said. "What kind of sense does it make for 99% of our nation's wealth to be controlled by 1% of the people? It places the majority at the economic whims of the few. And let's not forget how the iniquities of race and sex play into access to capital."

"I prefer gender over sex," I said.

"*Huh?*" Winston said. Both Smoky and Winston looked quizzically at me.

"To me, sex refers to physical intercourse. Whereas gender distinguishes male and female."

"Apples and oranges," Winston said. Smoky agreed with a nod.

"I'm thinking of throwing Pepper a surprise birthday party," Winston said. Pepper and Winston had been dating exclusively for a little over a year. For Winston that was a record. I had never heard Winston use the word love when he mentioned Pepper, but his actions toward her made his feelings unmistakable.

"That's great, man," I said. "I'm sure she'd love it."

"What kind of party did you have in mind?" Smoky asked.

"Something intimate, her, me, family, and close friends. I'll even invite you two if you're nice to me."

Winston was estranged from his four children and two ex-wives and didn't seem to care. We were the closest to family he had as far as I knew.

"What about a dinner party?" Smoky asked.

"That sounds perfect," Winston said.

"Yeah, it does," I agreed.

"You can use my house," Smoky offered before I had the chance. Winston lived in a small one-bedroom apartment in northeast Portland. He could afford better. As I said, he's frugal.

"I don't want to put you out," Winston demurred.

"Are you kidding," Smoky said. "I'd love to do it."

"If it's not too much bother."

"We're family, Winston. Mi casa es tu casa."

Smoky and I were all smiles. Winston looked at us, speechless. I noticed a mist in Winston's eyes before he looked away. Winston was not the type who told people how he felt. Exhibitions of affection embarrassed him. Smoky and I realized how deeply Smoky's offer touched him. Winston quickly recovered. His eyes cleared without a wipe.

"I have never had a surprise party," Smoky said in an off-the-cuff tone. Winston and I cut a sly glance at each other. We knew at that moment what the other was thinking.

The ideal crystalized when Winston stopped by my office a few days later to get the ball rolling. We were discussing venues for Smoky's surprise party when Renita popped into my office to see what we were talking about. We let her in on our plan. Renita was so enthusiastic about the idea she asked to be included. Winston playfully patted the seat next to her self-appointed uncle. Renita sat with a schoolgirl grin that wouldn't quit, and we set our plan in motion.

CHAPTER NINE

A shiny black stretch limousine rolled up and parked in front of Fullman's Restaurant. A two-story establishment styled after a Spanish bordello located in the Lombard district. A uniformed chauffeur rushed to open the rear passenger door. Out stepped Smoky and Winston dressed in pleated white cuff linked shirts, crisp classic black tuxedoes, cummerbunds, bowties, and spit-shined patent leather shoes. The men extended their hands in turn to assist their dates. Ginger accepted Smoky's hand. Ginger wore a silver short-sleeved lace evening gown with a matching clutch and shoes. Pepper followed suit. Pepper emerged wearing a sequined full-length navy chiffon evening dress with a V-neck, complete with matching shoes and clutch. Both women adorned tasteful jewelry that accentuated their elegance. The ladies took the right arm of their gentlemen as they filed into Fullman's Restaurant as if walking the red carpet, with Winston and Pepper in the lead.

"Good evening." The five-five, brown-eyed, bronze-skinned body builder greeted the couples with a warm smile. A red rose pinned to her lapel. An accessory only permitted by management and the maître d'. The young lady standing before them happened to be both.

"Hello," Winston said. "We're here for dinner."

"Do you have a reservation?" Elma Louise Washington asked.

"Of course, Winston Davis."

"Ah, Mr. Davis, table for four."

"That's us."

"Your table will be ready shortly."

Winston checked the time on his cell: 6:48. "It's almost seven now."

"Says here your reservation was made for seven-thirty."

"I asked for seven o'clock."

Elma checked the reservation again. Upside down, Winston could read 7:30 clearly penned in the time column next to his name. "Sorry for the mix-up," Elma said. "As you can see, we're full." The couples surveyed the restaurant. The place was packed with people enjoying their meals and each other's company.

"The earliest we will be able to seat you is seven-thirty," Elma said.

"How could this happen?" Winston said, starting to lose his patience.

"You could wait at the bar," Elma said. Her face tinged with embarrassment. "Drinks are on us."

"We can buy our own drinks, thank you," Winston said. "What we want is our table."

"It's okay, Winston," Smoky said.

"Yes, honey," Pepper added, patting his arm.

"We can wait at the bar," Ginger said.

"A few more minutes won't hurt," Smoky said.

Winston looked at his companions, then back at Elma, and nodded. Elma called over one of the wait staff. "Please escort this lovely group over to the bar and have them put it on my tab," Elma finished with a flourish.

"I'm afraid the bar is full," the waitperson said with a jittery grin. His body language was as nervous as his grin.

Elma's mouth twitched like a filament about to burn out. "Would you mind waiting upstairs?" she managed with an appeasing smile. "There's plenty of room in the lounge, and we'll call you as soon as your table is ready."

Winston was about to protest when he felt a hand on his shoulder. He looked at Smoky. Always the calming eye of his stormy nature in music as in friendship. Smoky gave him a reassuring nod.

"Fine," Winston said with a huff.

Elma escorted the couples along a carpeted aisle that separated the dining area from the bar up a circular stairway, offering her sincere apologies for the mix-up along the way. She opened one of two heavy oak doors and stepped aside along with Pepper, Ginger, and Winston, allowing Smoky to enter first.

"Surprise!" was blurted out in unison by a room full of people. Smoky's mouth dropped open, and his eyes went wide. Cell phones and digital cameras captured the moment. Smoky was speechless as he looked around.

"Is he in shock?" came the comical statement from the crowd. The room exploded with laughter. Smoky looked back at Pepper, Ginger, and Winston. Tears of joy ran down Ginger's cheeks. Pepper's smile was so broad it appeared it would break her face. Winston grinned. The crowd applauded, whooped, and some shouted, "Happy Birthday!" Smoky stared in awe at the scene.

"You did this?" Smoky said to Winston, still stunned.

"We did this," Winston said.

"I don't know what to say. Although I should have been suspicious when you said you were treating me to a birthday dinner. Because as many of us know, 'my treat,' are not words normally strung together in your vocabulary."

That drew a roar of laughter, even from Winston, who nodded in agreement. Smoky stepped forward and hugged his friend. "Thank you," Smoky said into his ear. Winston put up his hand, asking for quiet. Silence fell like a veil over the occasion.

"Don't thank me," Winston said, turning his friend around. "The people in this room love you and not only for your kickass music. They are here to celebrate the blessing of having a good solid person like you in their lives. I just happen to be one of them."

Smoky and Winston faced the fashionable admirers as they had done packed houses many times after great stage performances. An arm draped around the other's waist. Both grateful and amazed as they gazed out at their good fortune. To share something they loved with so many appreciative people. A gift they never took for granted. Between now and then, the biggest differences being the rapt quiet and their free hand relaxed by their sides instead of waving to an adoring crowd.

"You two want to be alone?" Another voice rang out.

Laughter lanced the moment. Smoky and Winston parted with Winston, gently shoving Smoky forward. Ginger returned the handkerchief someone had given her to dry her cheeks. She stepped to Smoky's side as Winston retreated to Pepper. Ginger hugged her man. Smoky kissed Ginger and hugged her back.

"If you would be so kind as to follow me," Elma said with a gracious smile.

"You played your part well, my dear," Smoky said. Still smiling, Elma gave Smoky an appreciative nod. Smoky and Ginger followed Elma through the parted crowd of birthday well-wishers and congratulations. Ginger held tight to Smoky's arm. Smoky gave an occasional nod as they walked. They were king and queen of the ball.

Winston and Pepper hung back so as not to intrude on their spotlight. When Smoky and Ginger arrived at the table of honor with members of Smoky's family awaiting them, the couple waved for Winston and Pepper to join them. Their friends did so in modest fashion.

Monty Holbrook. A short, powerful man with aubergine skin and an incredible smile placed a golden chalice on the table in front of Smoky.

"As the guest of honor," the half owner of Fullman's said, "you are to have the first drink."

Smoky took a drink from the chalice and smiled. "Ginger ale. The good stuff." Everyone laughed. Smoky never developed a taste for alcohol. He tried it. Didn't like it and saw no reason to press the issue.

"As the guests have been informed, this will be a dry affair in honor of Mr. Jenkins."

"*Ah man*, I thought that was a joke," someone chided, drawing smiles and a few chuckles.

Monty turned to address the crowd. "There will be plenty of non-alcoholic refreshments available. I have sampled them, and they are delicious. And that's coming from a Scotch drinker."

Everyone laughed.

"Turn on the music," Monty ordered. "Let's get this party started!"

*   *   *

While Winston, myself, Renita, Pepper, and Ginger provided ideas for Smoky's surprise party, Monty, Ernest and Elma made everything happen. Monty and Ernest also donated the venue, food, refreshments, and entertainment. Both owners were friends and fans of Smoky and Winston. They were also fans of them as men. Monty also mentioned something about the whole affair being a tax write-off. He didn't elaborate. I didn't want to know.

It was an exclusive black-tie affair with sophisticated decor. The music selections were drawn extensively from Smoky and Winston's jazz catalog. With vintage flavors of all-star fillers from jazz luminaries too numerous to mention. The guest list proved Smoky had friends in high and low places. From fellow artists, the mayor, police chief, and DEA Director to organized crime, drug czars, thieves, and killers. Even resolute reporters like Shawn

Calloway agreed to put away their pens for a night. An armistice was established. The Lair code of illegal abstinence was respected. Everything about the festivities was on point. Renita and Ernest's birthday congratulation video from Mexico went over well. Played on the big screen with the stunning Ixtapa beach in the background. Making everyone jealous and prompting Smoky to joke why we hadn't thrown his surprise party in Ixtapa.

People congregated more and more with those of common ground and comfort as the party progressed. That was everyone in attendance for Smoky and Winston. I excused myself from the stimulating company of Destini, her homicide detective partner David Liederman and his woman friend Nora Doucette, Portland Medical Examiner Dr. Blake Saba, Patrick, Carl, the Police Chief and their spouses, to have a word with the director of the Fremont Community Center, Shelly Morton. I stopped in my tracks near Shelly and within earshot of Smoky at the sight of a familiar face. Shelly was part of a group listening to Smoky educate them on why someone's comparison to his surprise party as a throwback to the legendary Cotton Club of Harlem was erroneous.

"There's no denying the Cotton Club left a legacy of trailblazing artists," Smoky said. "But there's a bleaker side to that nightclub's history that's often glossed over or romanticized. Heavy weight boxing champion Jack Johnson opened a supper club called Club Deluxe. Owen Madden, a gangster, and bootlegger took over Club Deluxe and turned it into the Cotton Club. The nightclub he created catered exclusively to white audiences. The Cotton Club applied Jim Crow and segregationist practices. Much of its entertainment featured my people as savages or plantation darkies that were common American depictions in the 1920s and 1930s. Harlem Renaissance poet Langston Hughes described his experience at the Cotton Club as 'a Jim Crow club for gangsters and monied whites.'"

Smoky paused as if personally recalling Hughes Cotton Club's experience. He raised his golden chalice. "Let us toast." Everyone within earshot raised his or her glass. The woman of my attention did as well. That was when she spotted me.

"We have come a good distance from the limitations of the Cotton Club," Smoky continued. "Look at us gathered here in celebration. Many races rich in culture and identity. A true melting pot with no restrictions or abuses placed upon this cabaret. I am grateful to each of you for sharing this blessed birthday with me. I am honored to be a member of this tribe."

The gathering chimed in their agreement then turned up their glasses. I drank half of my virgin martini. She sipped her drink, eyeing me the whole time. I eased my way through the standing crowd toward her. Her attention shifted from me to someone I knew who was talking to her. When I asked Portland Fire Marshall Zane Holloman how he was, Ms. none-of-your-business standing between the Fire Marshall and Oregon FBI Special Agent in Charge Aloisio Reis remained cool. Both men were on the guest list, plus one. Both were bachelors by divorce.

"C. J., I'd like to introduce you to Janet Proctor," Aloisio said. That answered two questions. Who she was and how she got in. I was surprised at having not noticed her earlier. Ms. Proctor was dressed appropriately for the occasion. Her dark hair a chic pompadour and bun. Modest makeup accentuated her blue eyes. She seemed comfortable in this environment. As comfortable as she had appeared tough upon our first meeting.

"C. J. is a PI," Zane said.

"Really?" Her surprise act was convincing. "Working on anything interesting?" Janet asked with a playful tone.

"Nothing worth mentioning," I said, playing along.

"He wouldn't say if he was," Aloisio said.

"C. J. is good at keeping things close to the vest," Zane added.

"Sounds as though you two are speaking from experience," Ms. Proctor said. Both men nodded. I had investigated personal matters on their behalf. I apply attorney-client privilege to all of my cases. Their secrets were safe with me.

"Good to know," Janet said. "If I ever need discretion, I'll know who to call."

"If you don't mind my asking, Ms. Proctor —"

"Please, call me Jan. Everyone does."

"If everyone does then why should I be any different?" We smiled at each other.

"What do you do for a living, Jan? If you don't mind my asking?"

"I'm an artist," Jan said.

"Interesting," I said. "What type of art?"

"Painting, sketching, sculpting, whatever strikes my interest." I didn't recall seeing any original art at the house where Jan and I first met and she refused to tell me her name.

"A visual artist," I said.

"Yes. I've been experimenting with Tilt Brush VR. It's incredible and liberating. Fire fascinates me of late."

"Digital or active fire?"

"Active. Are you a fan of fire art?"

"Some of it."

"Are you a fan of fire art?" Aloisio asked Fire Marshall Zane.

"Nope," Zane said, taking a sip of his drink.

"Me either."

"Fire is a unique and amazing creative tool," Jan said. Her enthusiasm building. "When done well it is breathtaking. I'm interested in creating visual reality representations like Steven Spazuk. He's a genius."

"I've seen his work," I said. "I agree. He is a genius."

"He uses soot from when the flame touches the paper. I don't expect to be as good as Spazuk, of course. It will be fun to try."

Monty excitedly waved me over. He was in the company of three people who could be described as those in low places. "Breathtaking, doesn't that apply to all great art," I said. I excused myself to join Monty before anyone could respond.

I had expected it to be an urgent matter. Only to discover they wanted my opinion on who would win in a boxing match between Muhammed Ali and Joe Louis both in their prime. While all parties considered them to be the greatest heavyweights of all time, they were split down the middle to the possible victor. I am not a boxing fan but I am a fan of both boxers. Ali was much closer to my generation so I had seen a number of his fights. I had only seen clips of The Brown Bomber. I chose Ali based on that evidence. My vote broke the tie but didn't quell the argument. Each side good-naturedly ribbed the other about their choice, citing what each boxer would do to the other in the ring. My back had been to Zane, Aloisio and Jan during our exuberant deliberation. I turned to look for them as the debate cooled. They had vanished. I searched for Shelly. He and his wife had disappeared too.

CHAPTER TEN

The remainder of my weekend was low key. Destini and I spent some quality time together. I tackled a couple of minor house projects. Tended my garden and tried not to think about the Epitome man in disguise or Janet Proctor.

With local DEA returning to full strength—aside from Luca Olsson being on maternity leave, Deputy Director Patrick O'Malley informed me on Saturday morning my short stint with his DEA office was ending. Patrick thanked me for my service. Besides informing Patrick he would soon receive my invoice for those services, I let him know he could call on me anytime. Not meaning I would answer being the unstated caveat of course. It would depend on his needs. Both of us knowing deep cover assignments were out. I asked Patrick how much longer he planned to run the Epitome Self Storage surveillance. He told me he hadn't decided. Patrick was still hoping to land some big fish. He would arrest those he had on a hook, try to flip them, and use them to climb the ladder.

My DEA release meant I could fully concentrate on my agency's outstanding cases. I stopped by the Fremont Community Center before heading into the office. I recognized the delicious aroma of chicken and dumplings when I entered the director's office. *Breakfast?* I thought. The chubby tan man seated in the ergonomic chair behind an artisanal hardwood desk going over paperwork was Shelly Morton. He was wearing heather gray sweats and spotless white basketball shoes. Shelly greeted me with his winning smile. The smile that could charm open checkbooks for sizable donations to The Center. He offered me coffee, tea, water and a seat. I declined the refreshments. We raved about Smoky's surprise party for a couple of minutes. Then I got down to business.

"Shelly, is there anything going on that I should know about?"

"Like what, C. J.?"

"Anything with you specifically?"

"I have no idea what you're talking about."

"Let's say for the sake of argument, I stumbled across some information that would reflect badly on you. A situation that has placed you right smack dab in the middle of a very nasty situation."

Shelly bore into me with intense brown eyes. "What the *hell* are you talking about, C. J.?"

"Two words. Drug…trafficking."

Shelly swallowed hard. His eyes darted back and forth for a moment as if he were searching for a way to escape. Shelly's reaction disintegrated any doubts of my being mistaken. He was the man in disguise I saw making a drug pickup from Locker No. 137 at Epitome Self Storage. I would have told Shelly exactly what I knew and how I had come by that evidence if I could have. There was no way I was going to tip the hand of an active DEA surveillance operation.

"I'll lay it out for you, Shelly. If you are involved, in the shady business I think you are, you need to clean it up now. You need to clean it up fast. Before it's too late."

"I don't know what in blazes you're talking about, C. J." His voice quavered as he tried to seize control. He looked scared. Shelly didn't frighten easy. Few things are black and white in this world. What Shelly had gotten involved in I could only begin to guess. My belief was he was marching down a short, dark corridor leading him directly into a prison cell.

"Put an end to it, Shelly."

Shelly started to speak. I raised my hand to stop him. I leaned forward, lowering my voice to a whisper. "I'm telling you this as a friend. Everyone makes mistakes. Take care of this before it goes too far. These young people need you. This community needs you. Whatever I can do to help remedy this situation let me know."

"You can start by keeping your mouth shut about what you think you know," Shelly blurted.

"I can do that for a minute," I said, returning my voice to normal. "I'm not the one calling the shots."

Shelly's mouth dropped open as he grasped the severity of his situation. I leaned back in my chair. Shelly dropped his eyes and gave me a quick nod. There was a knock on the door. Shelly sat there frozen. "Shut it down, Shelly." I said before Shelly said, "Come in."

The door opened. Lerone Winbush popped his head in. A gangly teen with buttery skin, baby dreadlocks, green eyes and an electric smile. Lerone had been bullied into becoming a delivery boy for the neighborhood drug gang. Shelly got involved. He somehow managed to sever the kid from the corrosive arrangement without incident. Lerone was now a regular at The Center.

"Sorry, Mr. Morton," Lerone said. "I didn't know someone was in here with you."

"No worries, Lerone," I said. "I was on my way out. How is everything?"

"Good, Mr. Cavanaugh."

"I'm expecting an invitation to your high school graduation," I said.

"That's not until next year."

"I like to plan ahead."

"I'll make sure you get one," Lerone said, grinning as if someone was tickling him.

"You do that Lerone," I said with a smile. A smile I shut down when I spoke to Shelly. "See you soon, Shelly." Shelly gave me a dismissive wave. I had delivered my warning. I left without another word.

CHAPTER ELEVEN

I dropped into my routine back at the office. Checking for Renita's emails my only variance rather than having direct dialogue with my partner. There were no recent emails from Renita. Read and responded as needed to new emails from clients. Beginning with Lunsford Insurance and rippled out to other clients in sequence and order of importance. Wrapped up a couple of written reports. One was a background check on a prospective VP for a major grocery chain that Renita had already done the investigation. He passed. The other was compiling and editing my DEA journal entries before handing them over to Patrick, excluding for the time being any incriminating information regarding Shelly Morton.

I received an email from Renita in the middle of writing the background report. I finished the report before opening her correspondence. Renita enquired about Smoky's birthday party adding their apologies for having missed the occasion. She asked how I was. Let me know she was available if I needed anything. Supplied a link to photographs of her and Ernest posing with some of the locals. Renita closed with "Having a great time!" Her photographs supported that statement. I replied with a brief overview of Smoky's surprise bash. Informed Renita I was fine. Encouraged her to forget about work and enjoy herself.

Destini phoned to invite me to lunch around one. I stopped editing my DEA journals to join her. We met at an Indian restaurant near my office. Destini vented about her heavy caseload before, during, and after our meal. That wasn't like her. Destini embraced challenges. With three of their best lead detectives on indefinite leave for various reasons and no scheduled replacements in sight, Portland Homicide had been stretched thin. Destini and David were one of Captain Williamsen's go-to teams for their toughest homicides. Destini had been going at it hard for the last few months, working overtime and weekends in order to keep pace. Smoky's surprise party was a nice break. It only made her realize she was exhausted the next morning when faced with the heap of unsolved murders on her desk.

My love sounded as though she were nearing her limit. I felt she could use a vacation, although I didn't mention it. When the going gets tough, the tough get going is a way of life with Homicide Detective First Class Destini Pendleton. Suggesting she take a vacation at a time when her colleagues needed her most was the equivalent of surrender in her book. Even the most machismo of us requires a confidant to unfurl our burdens once in a while. I was glad to lend an ear. We made plans for dinner at my place. I intended to surprise Destini with a full-body massage. Be just the thing to help dial down her stress. Might even advocate for a couple of mini-staycations if her mood was right.

I set to work on Renita's outstanding cases. Having cleared my DEA report and agency case docket. Next in line was Timothy Walker. I suspected Renita had not started her investigation, judging by the absence of comments or notes on Walker's original Lunsford Insurance file. I checked our network and Renita's PC for additional information. Provided Renita followed our agency's digital case filing protocol, there was none. No surprise, I had handed my partner the case the day before she was scheduled to leave for vacation. I could have contacted Renita and asked her about the Walker case, thereby discounting my own suggestion for her to forget about work. It was quitting time by the time I finished reading Mr. Walker's file.

*　*　*

Destini couldn't make our dinner date. Duty called. She sounded better. More relaxed. More of her confident, professional self. Destini thanked me for listening to her gripe session at lunch. "Anytime, anywhere, baby," I replied. She told me she loved me before signing off.

I would be lying if I said I wasn't disappointed. I had been looking forward to our evening together. Knowing Destini's wellbeing was on the mend helped quicksand my discontent. I packed up the rented portable massage table. Put away the tranquility natural massage oils and played with my rambunctious twin terriers, Andrew and Booker. I spent time talking and listening to my singing Zebra finches Claude, Toussaint, Coretta, and Truth. I eyed my colorful exotic tropical fish for a bit and chatted with some friends for about an hour. Ate an asparagus and scallop Alfredo dinner I'd made, especially for Destini in front of the TV while watching a Portland Trail Blazers game. I filled my home with smooth instrumental jazz from one of my playlists after a Blazers victory before settling on my living room couch in front of a crackling fireplace with a mug of steaming oolong tea and engaged with a book on the history of racist ideas in America.

CHAPTER TWELVE

2:26 a.m. Cleburne, Texas.

Tyler "Pickle" Jeffries had gotten the nickname Pickle when he was a kid. Tyler loved dill pickles. Still does. His family took to calling him Pickle as an inside joke. Tyler liked the family nickname and adopted it for himself. When asked his name, his response depended on his feelings toward that particular person. If Tyler liked the person, he would introduce himself as "Tyler, but you can call me Pickle." They would, of course, become curious about his unusual nickname. He would explain. For those, he felt indifferent or disliked, he accepted nothing less than Tyler. Not even Ty would do.

Pickle was a chubby squat child with copper blonde hair and playful blue eyes. Most females described the native Texan as cute or adorable. High school sports and the Marines had changed the adorable child into a five-ten fit man with piercing blue eyes with a face that had gone from cute to resembling a young Robert Redford.

Pickle was introduced to Firestorm by a fellow Marine Corps Infantryman. Both Grunts served together in Iraq and Afghanistan. Anytime there was a fire in their occupied territories, whether combat related or due to jarhead ignorance, Pickle knew exactly what to do to extinguish the flames. He unofficially became one of the division's firefighting specialists as his reputation spread.

His dad was a career firefighter. He taught Pickle how to extinguish all sorts of fires from the time Pickle could speak. He also gave Pickle a general working knowledge of how fires started. His father's teachings were, of course, designed to educate his son on how to avoid creating fires not starting them. The Marines made Pickle realize he wanted to follow in his father's footsteps and become a firefighter. Fate thwarted his dream.

One week after receiving his honorable discharge, Pickle was back home in Texas. His civilian wardrobe was sorely lacking. Pickle went clothes shopping at a local community shopping center to stock up. He was putting away his purchases in the back of his mother's SUV when the hostile sound of gunfire erupted in the parking lot. Pickle dove for cover behind the SUV but not before being shot in his leg. The first victim of a mass shooting that wounded twenty-seven others and killed eight. Pickle caught sight of a man dressed in black fatigues and armed to the teeth running past him toward the shopping center. Pickle assessed his wound. He was trying to block out the excruciating pain. The bullet had gone through his right knee. Four other bullets had ripped into the SUV.

His injury would not allow him to pursue. Pickle managed to pull himself upright using the SUV for support. He propped himself up on his left leg, doing his best to dispel the piercing pain from his throbbing right knee. Pickle had been loading his purchases into the SUV when shot. The lift gate was still up. He eyed the passenger cabin of the SUV. If this were his father's pickup, there would be a Colt .38 in the glove compartment. His mother did not like guns. She did not want them in her car. Pickle looked around for anything he could use to stop or impede the assailant. There was nothing within reach. He witnessed the carnage through the front windshield. His vision blurred or doubled as he fought to retain consciousness. The active shooter gunned down innocent people of the panicked, fleeing crowd with an Uzi submachine gun in one hand and a forty-five-caliber Glock in the other. Armed security guards rushed outside from four different directions. Two citizens had grabbed their firearms and hurried toward the madman. The six surrounded the assailant. Took aim and fired. All six continued their assault until the shooter was down and did not move. Pickle only wished he had a weapon so he could have been part of the firing squad that killed the bastard. This he thought before he passed out.

The forty-five slug destroyed his right knee. Pickle had to have a prosthetic knee replacement. Rehabilitation went well. Pickle recovered seventy-percent mobility in his right leg. Unfortunately, the prosthetic and limited mobility prevented Pickle from realizing his dream of becoming a firefighter. He was angry. Damage, the enemy, was unable to inflict in more than a dozen firefights on foreign soil had found him at home. Pickle hid his resentment well. "Shit happens," he would say with a snarl and move the conversation along whenever anyone offered him sympathy for his plight.

Pickle ran into a Marine buddy at Costco's, where he worked as a store manager. They met for drinks after Pickle's shift. Both men were still single with girlfriends but no children. After rehashing their shared military history of the good, the bad, and the ugly, Danny "Dan" Pearson asked Pickle if he were happy.

"Am I happy?" Pickle said with a snort. "What does that even mean?"

"Are you happy?" Dan repeated.

"With what? My life? My Job? My 401K Plan?"

"Your job?" Dan said after a laugh.

Pickle thought about it for a moment. The pay was decent. So were the hours. He knew he was there because it paid the bills if he were to be honest with himself.

"Not like being a firefighter, is it?" Dan said as if reading his mind.

"You remembered."

"How could I forget, Pickle? You were a genius when it came to anything to do with flames. All of those lectures about fire prevention and causes were nauseating at times. Enough already. Sometimes I just wanted you to shut up about that stuff."

"Some of the Grunts did tell me to shut up about fires," Pickle said. "Bollo told me if he heard one more word about fires come out of my mouth, he would throw me in one."

They laughed.

"He would've too," Dan said, still amused.

Bollo was a hulk of man but Pickle and Dan knew Bollo's was an empty threat. Like the kind parents use on their children in order to get them to behave with no true intention of bringing the threat to bear. Proof of that came a couple of days later when Pickle lectured Bollo on the dangers of leaving the cap off his canned cooking fuel. Bollo capped the fuel and with a groan walked away.

"You talked about wanting to be a firefighter like most men talked about their wives or girlfriends," Dan said.

Pickle chuckled. Dan turned somber. "I'm sorry things didn't work out, Pickle. You deserved better."

"Shit happens," Pickle said with a sneer. He turned away his gaze. Gulping down his beer and immediately refilling the mug from the pitcher, drinking half the refill down in a couple of swallows.

"How would you like to make good money?" Dan asked. "I'm talking about large coin. More money in one day than you will see in a year at Costco."

His friend reminded Pickle of a paid promotion not sounding as contrived or rehearsed. Pickle glanced sideways at Dan. "You're being here isn't a coincidence, is it?"

His friend smiled. "I'll admit it. I tracked you down. Because I know you are perfect for this job."

"What sort of job, Dan?"

"A job involving something that you love."

Pickle eyed his friend. He knew Dan better than most people know the people in their lives. They had lived, fought, and worked together. He had seen him during the best and worst of times. Pickle witnessed Dan risking his own life carrying a wounded Marine to safety during a fierce firefight. Earned Pearson the Silver Star. He trusted him. The least he could do was hear him out.

"I'm listening," Pickle said.

What Dan had to offer brought Pickle to this point.

The client wanted the Medina Building burned to the ground. The client also wanted it to appear like an accident. Pickle didn't know who the client was or why they wanted it done. With the amount of money he was being paid he really didn't care on both counts. The offer was not only sweetened by the money but by the fact no one was to be physically hurt. His friend had emphasized that was the Firestorm way from the beginning. Pickle told him that was his way as well. Pickle could see no harm in burning down a few buildings for personal gain under those conditions.

The Medina Building sat on an independent lot in the tiny business district. A four-story box-style conventional office building constructed predominately of red brick and glass. A thirty-year-old structure that had aged well. The glass was crystal clear. The red bricks shined like new in the Cleburne afternoon winter sun. Regular exterior maintenance was clearly a high priority with this owner. A healthy green space of grass surrounded the Medina Building providing a built-in safe zone. There was no chance any of the surrounding structures would be affected by the flames. Another Firestorm mandate to which Pickle agreed.

Dan had supplied Pickle with PDF copies of the construction documents for the building just as he had done for Pickle on his six previous jobs. The Medina Building fire alarm system was manual, not automated. That meant someone had to trigger the fire alarm that would, in turn, set off the sprinklers. That worked in his favor. The plans also gave Pickle ideas where best to initialize the burn. The central problem was he couldn't see any way to do it without arson being discovered. He needed to do some reconnaissance.

Pickle entered the Medina Building three times over the past five days as a fake delivery person. He didn't need to bother with a disguise. An armed, uniformed portly security guard with the nametag "Caleb" was more interested in flirting with women than security. The front desk clerk with the nametag "Cornelia" had her face glued to her smartphone. Pickle believed he could have walked in with a bomb strapped to his back, and he doubted either one would have noticed.

Pickle had an undetected run of the building once he made it through the lobby. The lobby was the only place that had security cameras. He went from floor to floor on his first two visits, gauging the best way to set the building ablaze. Not wanting to spend too much time looking around for even an inattentive security person might become suspicious as to why his delivery was taking so long. Pickle's reconnaissance missions came up empty. He still could not determine any way to burn down the Medina Building without fire inspectors discovering it was arson.

Pickle slipped down into the basement for a quick look around on his third visit. The basement turned out to be a godsend. He spotted a half-dozen fire code violations at a glance. As modern as the building interiors were above grade, its basement looked its age. A place mostly used for makeshift tenant storage. Storage units walled off by chicken wire. Stacked record boxes predominated the storage unit contents. There was a full-time maintenance workers' office currently unoccupied. A janitor storage closet for cleaning and repair supplies. One large storage unit dedicated to cleaning crew supplies. Jerry-rigged electrical wiring in some places. Pickle wondered how the wiring had passed building inspections. He speculated who the building owner paid off to make that happen. All in all, the basement was a fire hazard only in need of a match.

Pickle noticed a brand new four-pack of sixteen-ounce propane gas cylinders in one of the storage lockers tucked away in the back corner. The kind used for outdoor camping appliances. That gave him an idea. Propane is a flammable gas at room temperature. When mixed with air, it becomes explosive. He searched for jerry-rigged electrical wiring closest to the cylinders. The next locker had a shitty job of exposed wiring drooping down from the ceiling. Pickle would short-circuit the wiring at that point, creating sparks. Those sparks would, in turn, set anything flammable aflame. This included turpentine, paint thinner, linseed oil, disinfectants, aerosol cans, cleaners, hand sanitizers, and a host of other items. Common flammable products stored in the basement for use by the janitor and cleaning crews. The heat would create a pressure cooker in the cylinders. Once the pressure became great enough, it would pop the relief top off like a cork from a bottle of champagne. Releasing the propane gas into the air, adding an accelerant to the scorching mix. The brick exterior of the building would operate like a kiln. Everything inside incinerated as if it were shoved into a blazing brick oven. Brick walls and steel columns would be all that remained if his theories held. The interior would be ashes by the time the fire department could respond.

Pickle had done his homework. Studied the after-hour comings and goings of the Medina Building for a couple of weeks. Pickle watched the office building from behind the tinted windows on the driver's side of his new black pickup parked in the parking lot across the street. He was waiting to make certain the building was empty. A swing shift cleaning crew was finishing up. The security guard, desk clerk, and janitor clocked out at six sharp. Turning over what there was of building security to the unmonitored lobby cameras and security keypads at all of the entrances. Pickle had gotten the access code by simply standing behind a tenant who cared less if he saw him punch in the code. Pickle dressed in a business suit probably made the man assume he belonged. Knowing the security code allowed Pickle to slip inside the Medina Building when everyone was gone. Setting up a short circuit device in the basement that he could trigger remotely.

Pickle had gone beyond the knowledge his father had taught him. He earned his Fire Science degree online. Intrinsic within that knowledge of course was how fires started. He began to focus more on creating fires rather than dousing them. He was fascinated by the beast. He recalled one dictionary's definitions of fire as "the phenomenon of combustion manifested in light, flame, and heat. One of the four elements of the alchemists." Pickle liked both of those definitions. They embraced how he felt about fire. He was concerned he might be a pyromaniac. Until his research on the condition revealed to him that pyromaniacs had irresistible impulses to start fires. His fascination was intellectual. He enjoyed putting his theories into practice. Pickle was an arsonist. He was not a pyromaniac. Pickle had gone from the dream of being a firefighter to the reality of becoming an arsonist. The irony was not lost on him. He was even considering teaching in the Fire Science field one day. Once he retired from Firestorm.

The supervisor of the cleaning team pulled away at 2:47 a.m. Pickle had expected his departure between two-thirty and three. He waited until the supervisor's van disappeared from view. The Medina Building was officially empty.

Pickle pulled the remote out of the glove compartment of his truck. Now was his moment of truth. Would his theories pan out? He armed the remote. He took a deep breath and pressed the button. Everything about the office building appeared tranquil, like a brick Buddha awaiting the sunrise of another day. Twelve minutes later, he saw the flames. Shooting up through fissures in the floor into the lobby. The fire was gaining momentum faster than he had anticipated. He watched the flames and smoke consume the lobby. The pressure blew out the glass front of the lobby with a roar. At the rate the fire was climbing, the Medina Building would be engulfed in no time. Someone would notice and contact the fire department. The fire damage would be extensive from what Pickle could see. Enough investigators would only be able to determine the source. They would have no evidence it was arson. The short circuit device he used he had designed and built himself. It literally went up in smoke. Pickle was confident the accidental fire setup due to faulty wiring would work. Pickle pulled out of the parking lot. There was no one around. Still, he used the driveway furthest from the Medina Building to minimize any chance of being spotted. Hearing a distant siren as he drove away in the opposite direction.

CHAPTER THIRTEEN

The Berge Building, located near the Northwest Industrial Area of Portland, Oregon, was a corporate headquarters abandoned for nearly three years. The place had been cleared out but never sold. The two brothers who owned the building, Henry and Louis Berge, disagreed over what to do with their vacant property. The Berge Building had been constructed in 1947 handed down to the Berge brothers by their father. Henry wanted to sell to a supplier offering them top dollar. The buyer wanted to tear it down and build a warehouse. Louis wanted the building to be maintained and sold to another business entity that also offered them top dollar. Being fifty-fifty owners who would not sell or bow to the other, they took their battle to court. After eighteen months of contested and counter contested legal shelling from the lower to the higher courts, a final decision was handed down. The Berge brothers had to decide what was in their own best interest between themselves.

Obstinacy prevailed. The brothers remained stubborn to their positions until both mysteriously drowned. There was no evidence to suggest that either had been murdered according to the coroner's report. The only explanation the family had was that the brothers enjoyed taking their small fishing yacht out early on the Pacific to watch the sunrise and take a morning dip. What didn't figure was the drowned men were found dead on the deck of the yacht that was adrift off the Oregon coast near Yaquina Head.

Their spouses inherited the contentious property as part of their estate. The original offers had moved on. The widows wasted no time selling the building to the highest bidder, The Sickle Development Group. Sickle specialized in commercial modular buildings. Sickle decided to replace the Berge Building with a larger modern office structure after their people had a good look at the building's interior and construction. That would, of course, require demolition of the original. Going from a remodeling project to a brand new building bumped up their startup estimate by between four to six million dollars. Anywhere Sickle could save money was welcomed by the national board.

Edoardo "Ed" Longo sat on the local board of The Sickle Development Group. A tall, rangy man with calm brown eyes, a leering smile, and straight brown hair. Ed came from a construction background. He specialized in demolition, the most dangerous part of construction. Ed was a site foreman who favored taking shortcuts. Figuratively ripping out the pages of workplace safety and OSHA practices that he believed were financially over burdensome on the construction industry. Ed never cost a life with this attitude. He had cut corners that led to debilitating injuries for a few of his workers. The company did not want to part with Longo despite a couple of losing lawsuits against Longo and Sickle because of his willful negligence. His skimping practices had saved them quite a bit of money over the years. They bumped him upstairs.

Longo was familiar with the use of arson to cheapen demolition costs although he had never taken advantage of the method. His only reason from abstaining was that it was against the law. Another limitation he felt was idiotic. Why shouldn't you be allowed to burn down your own building? Longo suspected arson when he had seen the breaking video footage of the Cronus Building going up like a Roman candle a few weeks earlier. News reports verified his suspicions. He was familiar with the bitter history between the Cronus Building owners and Gerald Hayes. The man who felt he was screwed by the owners. He and Gerald were golfing buddies. What Longo discovered by being bumped upstairs to an office was that he was even better at business than he was demolition. Business afforded him an opportunity to utilize his shrewdness and cunning. Two characteristics that came natural to him.

Longo eased into a conversation about the Cronus Building while playing nine holes with Gerald. Gerald could hardly contain himself. He was so giddy with excitement over its destruction. Longo hinted at how he wished he could do the same for a current project he was working on. Before Longo knew it, Gerald gave Longo contact information for someone who might be able to help him realize his desire. Gerald was an intelligent man. He never admitted to having anything to do with the Cronus fire. Longo also knew if he were caught and decided to roll over on Gerald—

which he would very likely do—Gerald would deny this conversation ever took place. It would be his word against Gerald. Hayes' word carried more weight.

Longo wasted no time. He texted the number Gerald Hayes had given him in the country club parking lot. An automatic response instantly came back. Longo went on with his day, trying to keep his mind off what the text message had said. Someone replied to his text message as promised within twenty-four hours. One of their representatives would set up a meeting with him shortly.

*   *   *

"French fries or onion rings, which do you prefer?" Janet Proctor said. Janet had taken Longo by surprise on the corner of SW Yamhill and SW Sixth near Pioneer Courthouse Square. They were supposed to meet *in* Pioneer Courthouse Square.

"Dreams don't lie. People do," Longo replied.

"Meet me in Room 423 at The Heathman Hotel in ten minutes," Janet said. She was off before Longo could respond. He had been texted what his contact would say and what his precise response should be. A bit old school spy thriller as far as he was concerned.

The masculine "he" was used in the communication. He hadn't expected his "mediator" to be a woman. Let alone such an attractive one. Longo was married with two children but fooled around regularly on his wife without guilt or remorse. Perhaps when they were finished with official business, they could conduct business of a different nature. He had a few extra bucks he could spare.

Longo would have enjoyed Janet's invitation under different circumstances. He was concerned at who might be waiting there with her. Was this some sort of setup? Longo was able to relax once he looked around Room 423 to confirm that they were alone.

"Are you people the ones who burned down the Cronus Building?" Longo asked.

"You want us to torch the old Berge Corporate Headquarters, correct?" Janet asked, ignoring his question.

Longo was surprised at her candor. "Yes."

"How soon?"

"The sooner, the better."

"We'll need time to properly set things up."

"How much time?"

"I take it you want this to look like an accidental fire?"

"Of course."

"Two-to-four weeks."

"What will it cost me?"

"You, nothing. The people you work for one-hundred-thousand."

"I can get it done cheaper."

"I'm sure you can. Does the cheaper deal come with a guarantee that the fire will never be traced back to you? We can make that guarantee."

Longo thought for a moment. She was right. You could hire anyone to burn down a building, from a junkie to a crooked fireperson. The hardest part was not being caught.

"How do I know you're as good as your word?"

"Mr. Longo, we have been operating for years. Have you ever heard of us before now?"

"Come to think of it, no."

"That's because we are ghosts. We operate in the shadows. We go through great pains to protect our clients and ourselves. We're damn good at what we do. Someone who is equally as good at what you do should appreciate that."

Longo nodded. She was right. He was good at what he did. He also knew when he was being snowed. This Janet chick was speaking the truth.

"You're already familiar with one of our references," Janet said.

"Then you did burn down the Cronus Building."

"Half up front. The other half when the job is completed. We keep the deposit if you change your mind and decide to cancel the project. So you better be certain that you want this done."

Longo thought the price was a steal. It would cost him at least five times that much to demo the right way. Not to mention the kickback from fire insurance they had on the place. They would come out ahead.

"Deal," Longo said. "How do we handle payment?"

Janet handed Longo a phone. "Put in any of your business account numbers, the password, and the amount of fifty-thousand dollars. The software on our end will handle the rest."

Longo suddenly realized something. What if their meeting was being recorded? It was something he would have done. He thought about Gerald Hayes and The Cronus Building fire. Gerald was pleased by the arrangement. He was already in too deep. He might as well go all of the way. Longo punched in the data.

"You said this will cost the company but not me. How is that possible?"

Janet generally knew how it worked. The software on their end could tentacle throughout Sickle's accounting network once they had a legitimate in. At that point, the software could make minor adjustments to hundreds or even thousands of transaction totals by such small amounts no one would notice.

"That is none of your concern," Janet said. "All you need to know is no one in your accounting departments or the banks you do business with will notice a thing."

"Impressive," Longo said with a smile.

"We know," Janet matter-of-factly stated.

Longo looked Janet up and down while she awaited verification on the transfer.

"Transfer's complete," Janet said. "We're in business."

Longo moved in close. The hunger in his eyes reflected in the lascivious tone of his voice. "Maybe we can celebrate together now that our business is concluded."

Longo towered over Janet. He placed his big hands on her shoulders. Janet batted her eyes and looked up seductively at Longo. "Leave now before I rip your balls off and feed them to you," Janet said in a sensual whisper.

His hunger vanished like lust in an ice bath.

"We'll be in touch once the project is completed," Janet said, returning to her professional tone, forcefully sweeping his hands off her shoulders. Longo glared at her. Janet calmly stared back.

"That's no way to treat a client," Longo said with ire as he headed for the door.

"You may file a complaint with our complaint department," Janet sarcastically said.

"I just might."

"Mr. Longo." Longo stopped and turned in front of the door. Looking angry enough to take a bite out of a bull. "Do not try to screw with us," Janet continued. "It will be the last thing you ever do. From what I've seen here, we'll be doing your wife a favor."

Longo stormed out. A sense of satisfaction brought forth a smile to Janet's face.

CHAPTER FOURTEEN

Abílo Vilar inspected the chicken stew. The arsonists had given up red meat. Considered going vegan. At present, Abílo would miss chicken and fish too much to make a total commitment. One day his taste might change. When he officially retired from the business, perhaps. The hot delicious aroma made his mouth water. Abílo tasted. Added a pinch more organic ground black pepper to the organic ingredients, stirred, and sampled. He smiled. Covered the stainless steel stockpot, turned off the gas flame. Removed the pot from the burner, placed it in the flat center of the cook top, and stepped over to the table where a golden brown loaf of homemade organic blueberry bread cooled on a wood cutting board. Abílo checked it. Cut the tender loaf into thick slices, tore loose a corner from one slice, and ate it, nodding his head in approval.

His beard had been reduced to a mustache. His black curly hair barbered to half of its original length. At five-ten, narrow shoulders, barrel-chested and gangly arms, Abílo moved with grace and ease about the kitchen. Comfortable with the utensils of cookery as he was with the instruments of arson.

Finding this place had been a steal out of the way of nosy neighbors and prying eyes. Yet still accessible to his area of focus. A couple heading south of the equator to escape winter was looking for a house sitter. Abílo applied for the opportunity. His cover being on temporary assignment to a local software company that needed his specific programming skills for a few months. The company wanted everything done in-house for security purposes. Firestorm provided him with convincing essentials to pull off the ruse. Being an exceptional programmer required little tweaking in the skills department, not that it mattered. The couple was most interested in his personal references than anything else. Abílo planned to stay until the snowbirds returned as per their agreement even though his actual assignment was finished.

The doorbell rang as Abílo grabbed an earthen bowl out of one of the wooden cabinets. He set the bowl down on the kitchen counter. Abílo picked up his cell and checked the peephole camera he had installed. He answered the door when he saw who it was.

Janet Proctor wore dark jeans, brown suede ankle boots, gray padded parka with hood, a colorful wool Sherpa earflap hat, and a smile. Clothing appropriate for cold, wet weather. The smile suitable all year round. Abílo liked her smile. A lot more than he knew that he should.

The arsonist stepped aside and gestured for Jan to enter. Janet yanked off her hat as she did and stuffed it into her empty coat pocket. Her dark hair fell loose upon her shoulders.

"How was Smoky Jenkins' birthday party?" Abílo asked, closing the door and locking the deadbolt.

"How'd you know about that?" Janet's smile brightened.

"The news, paper, internet. It's big news on the social circuit," Abílo said with a grin.

"The party was outstanding. Are you a fan, Abílo?"

"Are you kidding? I love jazz. Holland 'Smoky' Jenkins and Winston Davis have put down some of the greatest music ever."

"Why didn't you go to the party if you're such a big fan?"

"I wasn't invited."

"Right, invitation only."

"How'd you get in?"

"I was someone's plus one," Janet said.

"Lucky you."

"They played jazz all night long," Janet said. "Some of it I could get into. I'm more of a rock 'n' roll girl."

"Modern or past?"

"Both."

Abílo nodded.

"I'm not here to chat about music," Janet said. Her tone remained cheerful despite her vanished smile.

"I take it your client was satisfied with the results," Abílo said.

"Oh yeah," Janet said. Her tone voiced its satisfaction. "The way the Cronus Building went up was a thing of beauty. And that's a direct quote."

"He didn't watch it burn in person, did he?" Abílo asked. A look of disapproval on his face.

"I didn't ask. Some things are best kept private."

Abílo nodded. "It's weird enough he wanted to make it look like arson. Most people go the opposite route."

"Again, don't ask," Janet said. "I'm depositing the final payment into your account."

Janet pulled her smartphone out of her other coat pocket, navigated to a site, punched in some commands and passwords. Waited as a progress bar inched toward completion. Janet showed the arsonist the completed transfer acknowledgment. Abílo went to the kitchen, grabbed his smartphone, and returned to Janet standing near the sofa. Janet had opened her coat, unveiling a pink-checkered cotton lumberjack shirt. The arsonist followed a similar input pattern as Janet steering toward a different source. Verified the fifty-thousand dollar deposit finalizing their one-hundred-thousand dollar agreement. Abílo piloted to another location and transferred twenty-five percent of the one-hundred thousand dollars over to Firestorm, thereby honoring their arrangement.

"What's your cut in all this?" Abílo asked.

"The satisfaction in knowing a job well done," Janet said, sounding playful.

"I doubt you're doing this for gold stars and attagirls," Abílo said, amused.

"You would be wise in that assertion, Mr. Vilar."

"You're not going to tell me, are you?"

"Nope," Janet said, maintaining her playful tone. "What are you cooking?"

"Chicken stew."

"Smells delicious."

"Stay for dinner?"

"Don't mind if I do." Janet handed the arsonist her coat. Abílo hung it up in the living room closet.

"Help me set the table," Abílo said. "I planned to eat in the living room in front of that big screen TV. Blazers are on."

"They're playing the Nuggets, aren't they?" Janet asked.

"Yeah," Abílo said. "Are you an NBA fan?"

"My high school boyfriend was nuts about basketball, loved the Blazers and Oregon Ducks. I guess I caught the fever from him. Are you a Blazers fan?"

"Nuggets," Abílo said.

"*Booooooo!*"

The arsonists laughed. "Alright then," Abílo said. "Let's set up in front of the TV. I don't have any beer. Is a non-alcoholic substitute okay?"

"No problem. Is that a Denver thing?" Janet mused. "Not drinking alcohol during a professional sporting event. Seems almost sacrilegious."

"It's my thing," Abílo said. "I don't drink alcohol."

Janet followed the arsonist into the kitchen. "I have another job for you. If you're interested?"

"Might be," Abílo said. "What's the job?"

CHAPTER FIFTEEN

Aidan Madigan had filed a back and hip injury insurance claim with Lunsford. The CEO of Madigan Engineering had been involved in a car accident in which both vehicles were totaled. Madigan Engineering specializes in building renovations. Lunsford's accident investigators exonerated Mr. Madigan from any wrongdoing. The accident was the other driver's fault, who had a suspended driver's license for repeated DUI offenses. The offender was operating his brother's car at the time of the accident. Unbeknownst to him, his brother had allowed his car insurance to lapse. The driver at fault was also legally intoxicated at the time of the accident. Oregon has some of the strictest DUI laws in the country. The drunk driver was sentenced to a maximum of ten years on a Class B felony. I was camped out in Mr. Madigan's neighborhood to verify the extent of his injuries.

I readied my digital camera and set it down in the passenger seat. Patience is always the most challenging part of stakeouts. You have to be ready for anything. Training and experience had stabilized my reflexes for quick responses to unexpected occurrences. I enjoyed the occasional bombshell, to be honest. Insurance stakeout surprises can be exhilarating but rarely dangerous. Stationary, mobile solo surveillance offers a different boredom challenge than an enclosed high-tech observation space. Your primary distractions are typically a curious neighbor or mundane neighborhood activities such as someone doing yard work or taking out the trash. Neither is enough to alleviate the tedium. Mind games worked best for me to stay alert.

The threat of winter rain was upon us but had not as of yet made good. I was going through a checklist of ways to con my way into the Madigan residence to have a closer look at him after two hours and no sign of Mr. Madigan. Their children were at school. That would make matters easier. Misdirecting adults is simpler than fending off inquisitive broods.

Thoughts of Shelly drifted into view. Shelly had been a recent exception to my zeal for stakeout surprises. That was the DEA, so what should I expect. I was deeply concerned about my friend. His actions were uncharacteristic of the man I knew. What explanation could he possibly have besides the obvious? Criminals of all sorts were constantly trying to infiltrate the Fremont Community Center. To take advantage of the youth and use FCC as a front. A number of the children in the community had escaped a criminal life because the center offered them haven. A few were still involved in the dark side, walking a tightrope while groping for a lifeline to set them free. Shelly and his staff served as a bulwark against the cesspool of felonious destruction of human potential. Illegal narcotics being at the forefront of that demolition.

Was Shelly being blackmailed? Had someone uncovered some contemptible secret Shelly wanted to remain hushed? Was the motivation economic? Shelly would do anything for the center. Had someone made him a financial offer he couldn't refuse? Worse yet, could someone have threatened the life of his family or the center, which to Shelly were the same? My warning to Shelly was a double-edged sword. I would tell the DEA what I knew if he didn't come clean. On the other hand, I was hoping Shelly would use my threat as an opportunity to clue me in. There was still time. I hoped my friend trusted me enough to make the right choice.

A forty-six-year-old man emerged, moving gingerly. It had been just over two months since the car accident. His clothes hung loose on him as if they belonged to a man twice his size. Mr. Madigan was stooped over at the waist, wearing a back brace and using a metal quad base cane to steady himself. I could see traces of the healed cuts from the shattered glass on his anguished face through my telephoto lens. His short brown hair was brushed back. He looked twenty years older than his age. A forty-two-year-old diminutive woman with red hair, freckled skin, and hazel eyes had to help him every step of the way. Farah Madigan managed to usher her husband down their front steps and into their luxury SUV with some effort. I recorded the whole event using video on my camera.

I followed them to Providence Portland Medical Center. Parking within a few stalls of the couple, I locked my camera in the trunk of my car. They didn't notice me then as they hadn't noticed me on stakeout. Not surprising considering their circumstances. I strolled toward the hospital entrance, keeping an eye on the Madigans. Each determined jarring step seemed to post a new level of agony on the victim's face. A faint grimace of sympathy pain accompanied Mrs. Madigan in duet, who was struggling to keep her husband from teetering over.

I jogged over to them. "May I help?" I asked.

"Thank you," Mrs. Madigan said, as did Mr. Madigan. His speech a bit slurred.

I gently placed a hand on his upper back and the other beneath his elbow opposite his cane hand for support. His body felt brittle. As if the slightest tremor would cause him to crumble. We inched our way into the hospital. Mrs. Madigan encouraging her husband every step of the way. The front desk receptionist was expecting them. A nurse and orderly took over.

I offered to wait with Mrs. Madigan while her husband was in physical therapy. The distressed mother of two repeatedly attempted to decline my offer but eventually conceded to my insistence. She appeared exhausted. During our extensive wait, Farah, as she asked I call her, volunteered the story behind her husband's condition. Sometimes the unassuming shoulder of a stranger feels like the safest harbor for which to lay down one's burdens. The car accident details Mr. Madigan had relayed to his wife were the same as those that had appeared in the Lunsford report. The accident itself had severely damaged her husband's pelvis and vertebral column. Her husband could recover to about eighty percent with more surgeries and bouts of physical therapy. The treatment Mr. Madigan was currently undergoing was to get his body in the best possible shape for what was to come.

I helped Farah support Mr. Madigan back to their vehicle. He moved with more ease and with less discomfort than before, a positive result from the combination of physical therapy and medication, no doubt. They thanked me for my assistance and drove off with a wave. I didn't have to use my cover story. Neither asked me why I was at the hospital.

Doubling back inside PPMC, I identified myself to the desk nurse and asked to speak to Mr. Madigan's physician. Dr. Darlene Wahlang met me at the front desk. A short, plump woman with smooth brown skin, and big brown eyes. I knew from Mr. Madigan's insurance file that specialists were involved in his care. Dr. Wahlang was overseeing and coordinating his recovery. I further identified myself to Dr. Wahlang as an agent of Lunsford Insurance, giving her my card and Carl Wheaton's if she required confirmation. Dr. Wahlang seemed mystified by my presence but invited me into her office for a private chat. Her confirmation was what I needed to add a period to this sentence.

In her mild Indian English accent, Dr. Wahlang spelled out Aidan Madigan's physical condition without confirming my identity with Carl, detailing what medical steps he needed to undergo to restore him to a healthy and productive life.

"I will be supplying a full report to the hospital billing department," she emphasized from behind her desk. As comfortable as a queen on her throne. "They will in turn pass that information in an itemized bill along to Lunsford Insurance. If there are any doubts or discrepancies between our two parties then it is usually handled in house. I simply don't see why hiring a detective to spy on this poor man is necessary."

Private Investigator, I thought to correct Dr. Wahlang but bit my tongue. "It is common procedure in the insurance game I'm afraid," I said. "Fraud is at an all-time high and no one is exempt. Insurance companies simply want to cross their t's and dot their i's in order to make certain everything is above board."

"Sounds more like they are attempting to worm their way out of paying. I see insurance companies doing it all of the time. Looking for an escape hatch or clause so they can stick our patients with the bill."

"Not Lunsford."

Her silence suggested she agreed.

"What are you going to do?" Dr. Wahlang asked with a bit of contempt to her tone.

"Approve the claim," I said. "It's crystal clear to me Mr. Madigan's injuries are legitimate."

The doctor smiled for a moment. A gracious smile. "Good. Is there anything else?"

"No Doctor. You've been very helpful. Thank you." I stood to leave. Dr. Wahlang stood with me.

"Doesn't Lunsford have investigators who confirm these things?" Dr. Wahlang asked. "They are a big company. Our hospital insurance is with them. So is my malpractice and personal insurance."

"They do, Doctor. Sometimes they get overwhelmed with claims. That's when they call people like me." Dr. Wahlang's comment about carrying malpractice insurance made me curious about something. There is no federal law that mandates doctors have medical malpractice insurance. Some states do. Oregon is not one of them.

"Doesn't the hospital have liability insurance on all of its employees?" I asked.

"Yes, they do. Some doctors, like myself, carry malpractice insurance as a precaution. Should the hospital decide, it is more practical to throw us under the litigation bus, so to speak. Besides sullying your reputation, a decision like that would bankrupt most doctors. This is, after all, a business, as much as it goads me to admit."

For the life of me, I couldn't figure out how this case crossed my desk. I assumed Lunsford suspected some sort of collusion to fraud the company. There had been an ambulance on the scene and four patrol officers. Mr. Madigan was non-responsive and in bad physical shape according to the police report. The EMT report generalized he suffered from severe pelvis and spine injuries, a concussion, and multiple facial and neck lacerations. All an investigator had to do was follow up with the hospital doctor as I had done and this case was a wrap. It was unlike Carl to waste resources on an open and shut case. I needed to contact Carl to see if there was something I missed.

Dr. Wahlang and I shook hands across her desk. I thanked her again for her help.

"Could you do me a favor, Doctor?" I asked. Dr. Wahlang looked at me as if I were going to ask for a free medical consultation. "Don't mention my investigation to the Madigans."

"Why?"

"I feel bad enough as it is. They're going through a terrible time. Might do them good to believe in the kindness of strangers." Dr. Wahlang appeared puzzled by my last statement. My sincerity must have resonated.

"They won't hear anything from me." I gave her an appreciative smile.

"Mr. Cavanaugh?" The doctor said as I reached for the doorknob.

"Yes, Doctor."

"I take it you also do investigations of a private nature?"

"Dependent on the case. Give me a call, and we'll discuss the matter. Everything said in discovery between a potential client and her PI is confidential in my book."

Dr. Wahlang gave me a curt nod. I left.

CHAPTER SIXTEEN

The twins barked at the front door. The doorbell rang a few moments afterward. I wasn't expecting company. I was in the middle of cleaning up after dinner. I had made plans for a cozy evening, reading a good book to the backdrop of great jazz in front of a glowing fireplace.

"Hey, C. J." I was surprised but glad to open the door and see Shelly Morton standing there. The chubby tan man looked tired. There were bags under his eyes. "Mind if I come in?" he asked barely above a whisper.

"Not at all." I stepped to the side, allowing Shelly to enter. It felt warmer outside. Weighty darkness prevailed. The rain had settled to a steady drizzle, giving the air a faint earthy smell. "Let me take your coat."

Shelly handed me his dripping coat and rain hat, unleashing his curly brown hair hinting gray. I put away his rain gear in the hall closet. Shelly bent down to pet the two balls of Scottish terrier energy circling his feet.

"Smells good in here," Shelly remarked, straightening up.

"That's the porridge yams I made for dinner. There's some left if you'd like a plate."

"Thanks but I already ate."

"Have a seat, Shelly." Shelly ambled over and sat on the sofa. "Can I get you anything?"

"Some water would be nice."

"Tap or bottled?"

"Filtered?"

"Yes."

"Tap will be fine."

I came back to find Shelly nervously rubbing his knees. I handed him a tall glass of cold water and placed a sandstone coaster with a sea turtle design on the wooden end table next to him. The coaster being part of a handcrafted set given to me as a birthday present by Portland Medical Examiner Blake Saba's daughter Shayla. Shelly gulped down a third of the water, gripping the glass with both hands.

"When is the last time you had a vacation, Shelly?" I asked after making myself comfortable in my reading chair. The Director of the Fremont Community Center let out a weary, brittle laugh.

"Three years ago. I took my family to the Bahamas. I remember because we left the day before Adrian's birthday." An awkward silence followed. Adrian is Shelly's oldest son.

"What can I do for you, Shelly?" Shelly sucked in some air then let out an audible sigh.

"I need your help, C. J." His voice cracked with anxiety. His typically intense brown eyes rippled with deep concern. This was not the Shelly Morton I knew. Shelly is the type of person who could be concerned without worry. He saw problems as challenges. Difficulties that could be overcome if given the right incentives.

"I'm listening," I said.

"Lerone Winbush was caught with some PCP and Ecstasy in his backpack, enough to get him serious time under current drug laws. The cop who busted him said he received an anonymous tip. Lerone said he was setup and I believe him. I know Lerone. He's no saint. He'll occasion a little alcohol or marijuana now and then but he is definitely not a drug dealer. Not since I was able to get Lerone away from that bullying drug gang."

"How'd you manage that?"

"Trade secret," Shelly said with a nervous laugh.

"Who made the bust?"

"Thompson."

"Chris Thompson?"

"Yes." Shelly took another long drink of water. "You know him?"

"More than know of him. Any idea who called in the tip?" I asked.

"I know who made the call. Thompson won't confirm it."

"Who?"

"Quentin Drayton."

"The drug dealer?"

"Yep, not him directly but someone who works for him called in the tip. I'm sure of it."

"What makes you so sure Drayton's behind this?"

"I had some gang members busted for attempting to deal drugs at the center. They threatened retaliation. Framing Lerone was their way at getting back at me. Lerone was the seventh child I was able to liberate from his drug dealing operations in the last six months. Drayton's probably fed up with my interference. He set up Lerone to get back at me. Drayton denies knowing anything about drug dealing at the center or any setup, but I know it was him."

"Drayton knew you would come to Lerone's defense?"

"Which I did. I made a deal with Thompson. Me in exchange for Lerone."

"You're an informant for Thompson?"

"You could say that."

Shelly wasn't telling me the whole story. None of what he said explained why he was wearing a disguise, making a narcotics pickup and driving a rental car. I decided to approach the problem from a different angle rather than pressure Shelly.

"I'll see what I can do on my end to alleviate your situation."

"I really appreciate it, C. J."

"That's what friends are for, Shelly."

Shelly took a sip of water, still clutching his near empty glass. "How'd you find out about my involvement in this mess?"

"Trade secret." Shelly let out a tired chuckle. I hesitated before speaking again. I wanted to assure Shelly of my sincerity. "Don't worry. We'll straighten this out."

Shelly smiled. It was the first time he appeared relaxed since he had arrived. Booker and Andrew barked at each other. I glanced over to see the twins wrestling on the carpet in front of the fireplace.

"I love the Fremont Community Center, C. J. I love the work we do. Sometimes I feel like I'm fighting an uphill battle and the hill keeps getting steeper. Dealing with someone like Drayton makes me wonder if it's worth it."

"It is worth it," I said, "and you know it. Think of all the good you've done. The lives you've saved and changed for the better."

"I don't know how much longer I can go on," Shelly said. All life draining out of his voice.

"You're not alone, Shelly. I'll be glad to step in and take over running FCC until you feel up to it again."

"What about your PI business?"

"A little hiatus won't hurt. I could use the break. Renita can take over for a while."

"You're okay with that? With Renita taking over I mean?"

"Renita already thinks she runs the place."

That got a genuine chuckle out of Shelly. "Your partner can be a handful," Shelly said. "I can't tell you how many times I've had to step in and mediate disputes between Renita and other counselors and team leaders at the center."

"I'm going to tell Renita you said she can be a handful."

"You'd better not," Shelly said, allowing a smile. "I can hear Renita loudly proclaiming to me in no uncertain terms why she is not stubborn or bossy and how I'd better not forget it."

"After she let me have it for not defending her."

We both laughed.

"My partner can be outspoken, persistent, and judgmental at times," I said. "Which are some of the things we love about her if we're being honest. Don't tell her I said that last part."

"You keep my secret. I'll keep yours."

It felt good to go back and forth with Shelly again. Ease the sense of dread we were both feeling about what lay ahead.

"Renita is something else," Shelly said, on the tail end of a teetering laugh. "I appreciate your offer to step in and run The Center, C. J., but I'm going to pass. So you know. I have a short list of people who I consider perfect candidates to take over FCC if something happens to me. I've even included the list in my will."

"Am I on the list?"

"No, and for good reason. We appreciate you, C. J. The Center owes part of its success to your selfless contributions of time and money. You're always there when we need you. The person who takes over the reins of the center has to know in their hearts that it is their life's priority. The Center is not where your passion lives. You may gripe about the work sometimes. We all do about the things we care about most. You love being a PI. You know it. I know it."

Shelly was right. His revelation disappointed me. I had come to consider myself on par with Shelly when it came to community, equally resolved to his salvation commitment. Which brought to mind the question? If there was no Shelly Morton would I be as involved with the Fremont Community Center? The simple answer was yes. I couldn't be sure as to what degree. I regarded Shelly and FCC to be one in the same. Inseparable. What would be my outlook on The Center if something did happen to Shelly?

"You plan on checking out anytime soon?" My question was deliberately sober. The strongest of us will consider suicide given the right circumstances.

"I'm not going to take my life if that's what you're implying, C. J."

"Do you think someone means you harm?"

"That danger is always out there. I've accepted it. If it's God's plan then I will receive it as my destiny."

"God's plan is for you to be around to spoil your grandchildren."

"You know this how?"

"I know it as well as any man."

"I pray you're right, Brother."

Shelly and I both knew fate was often beyond our control. Shelly needed a life raft to steer him away from the darkness and bring him back into the light.

"You're growing a beard?" Shelly asked.

"Thought I'd try something new."

"Not bad," Shelly said, nodding approval.

"I see you're letting your hair grow," I said.

"Yeah."

"Considering an afro, cornrows or dregs?" I asked.

"Afro," Shelly said with pride.

With an understanding nod I said, "Cool. You up for a game of chess or checkers?"

"What's the matter? You afraid I might beat you at Scrabble again?" Shelly asked. A hint of cockiness in his voice.

"One lucky game and you're the Scrabble king?"

"Only one way to find out. Set 'em up."

"How about something stronger than water to drink?" I asked.

"Some coffee would be nice."

"Did you have dessert?"

"No," Shelly said.

"I'm having a slice of apple pie," I said. "Picked one up fresh from the bakery."

"Pie à la mode?" Shelly asked.

"Not my style."

"Mine either," Shelly said. "Let me have a slice of that apple pie with coffee, black."

"Coming right up."

I felt a bit guilty as our evening of entertainment was set in motion. I knew I was going to use the occasion to see how much more truth I could pry out of Shelly on his situation before our night was through.

CHAPTER SEVENTEEN

"C. J."

"Chris."

"Thanks for stopping by. Have a seat."

"That's alright, you have something for me?"

Portland Narcotics Detective Christopher "Chris" Thompson was a muscular man with a thick neck, meaty hands, square fade hairstyle, goatee, and mean brown eyes. While Thompson and I shared the same caramel complexion, we did not frequent the same social circles. I learned about Thompson from the Portland Drug and Vice Division head Carlton Richardson who did. The forty-five-year-old, twice-divorced native Northwesterner was by all accounts a great detective. Thompson had several accommodations to go along with his stunning conviction record. The only gripes came from members of the communities he served. He was unconscionable, according to some. Thompson had a reputation for being unscrupulous when it came to using people in order to make arrests. It wasn't uncommon for ruined lives and dead bodies to be found floating in the wakes of his convictions. I was not one to judge. I had done my share of damage in my time with the DEA. This matter was personal. I had arranged for a private meeting at my office with Detective Thompson baiting the hook with information about a drug shipment. We knew each other well enough to be on a first-name basis. Still, I considered Thompson more of an acquaintance than a friend. I was confident he felt the same.

"There is no tip," I said in a cold tone.

"Then why are you wasting my time?"

"I want you to cut Shelly Morton loose."

We were standing in my office. Chris took a seat. "You know about that, huh? It definitely didn't come from Destini. She's not plugged into Narcotics."

"The kid you have something on as well. I want you to cut him loose too."

"Kids."

"There was more than one?"

"Two teenagers to be exact."

I wondered who the other child was and why Shelly neglected to mention him. "According to Shelly he—or they—were set up."

"That's their story," Thompson said. "We hear that lie so often perps should lay it down with a backbeat."

"Did you look into it?" I asked.

"Are you trying to tell me how to do my job, C. J.?"

"What did you find, Chris?"

"That's none of your business."

"Maybe I'll do my own investigation," I said. "See if their accounts check out."

"Interfering in an ongoing police investigation could land you in a tub of hot water. Could get your PI license suspended or worse."

"The teenagers have not been charged," I said. "You wouldn't have anything to hold over Shelly if they were."

"Not yet they haven't been," Thompson said. "It could still happen."

I had been fishing with my last statement. Thompson confirmed what I suspected. I knew Chris Thompson had been trying to recruit Shelly as an informant for some time. Shelly coming to the defense of those teens afforded Thompson a way in. It should not surprise people that a number of those involved in law enforcement are not nice people. Veterans of the trade often develop cruel, callous, and vicious streaks. Catching and convicting criminals is not a polite business, especially for offenders of the die-hard variety.

"You're asking a lot, Cavanaugh. What do I get in return?"

"A clear conscience."

Chris gave a snort of a laugh. "Nothing's wrong with my conscience."

"You know what Shelly means to that community," I said.

"He offered up the deal. I didn't."

"You framed the terms of the agreement, Chris."

"That's the way it works. I don't have to explain that to you, C. J. You were in the trenches. You know what it's like. You do what you have to do to cross the finish line."

The reasons people deal drugs are generally straightforward. Some do it to survive. Others do it for power and wealth, control, and status trappings. A few do it because they enjoy the thrill of the hustle and find it easier than an average job. Dealing complicates lives, no matter the reasons. Add our legal system's treatment of narcotics to the mix. You have ignited an already volatile situation.

"I'm not going to try and play high and mighty with you, Chris. I do know what it's like. Been there and done that. Shelly's my friend. He made a mistake. I'm asking you to wipe his slate clean."

"Which brings us back to what am I getting in return, C. J."

I thought for a moment before I spoke. Chris Thompson was not the kind of man you could intimidate. To be good at what he does you can't be. He wanted quid pro quo. Something worthwhile in trade for releasing a valuable asset like Shelly. That's where he and I were going to have a problem.

"I can derail your professional life if you know what I mean," I calmly said as if mentioning I was going to the store.

"Are you threatening me?" Thompson asked, appearing openly surprised by my statement.

"Not at all, simply offering you a preview of coming attractions. Blackmailing tactics such as the one you're using on Shelly in exchange for his cooperation are typically frowned upon by the brass. Not to mention what the press would do with that information." The resolute reporter for the *Willamette Times*, Shawn Calloway, came to mind. "Should such coercion come to light, who knows what long-term effects that could have on your career?"

"You are threatening me," Chris said, recovering with a sneer shaded more with amusement than hostility. "My bosses know what I do. Some of them have been there. As far as the press goes, I could care less. You've got nothing. Should you happen to involve the press. I'm sure the media would have a field day with a story about an ex-DEA agent's attempt to blackmail a Portland Narcotics Detective into letting one of his friends walk on a drug charge."

"Shelly did not commit the crime," I said. "The teenagers did."

"Like sensationalized modern media cares about such minor details when it comes to a hot topic headline."

Thompson was essentially trying to determine if I was bluffing. I would leave it up to him to make the first move. If he decided to follow through on his threat, damage would be done to both our vocations. While I wouldn't go as far as ruining his career, I could and would make things unpleasant for Chris. Jaded and cynical, Thompson reminded me of what I might have become had I continued along my course with the DEA.

I could read in his eyes that Thompson was being honest regarding his concerns about the press and his method for revenge. Still, he knew how things worked. His superiors wouldn't be so flippant. In the back of his mind, he was mulling over what disciplinary actions would be taken against him to appease the public and media outcry. Whatever those disciplinary actions were, they would be placed in his evaluation jacket, which in turn could hurt his assured promotion. My DEA career was rock solid. Thompson's threat could damage my PI practice. My threat could derail his professional future.

"We both know people, Chris. We can both pull strings. My people, my strings go higher and are more powerful than the ones at your disposal."

"You're not DEA anymore, C. J. You're a civilian."

"With a whole lot of top shelf connections. Once a member of the club, always a member. I don't have to tell a narc that."

Chris leaned back in his chair a bit. His sneer morphed into more of a bemused look. "I'll think about it," he said.

What I believed Thompson really meant was he was going to check me out. See if I could make good on my threat. Chris was no fool. He didn't make detective first class by forging enemies in high places. Word had it that he was next in line to head Portland's Drug and Vice Division when Richardson retired. The twist was Thompson obviously wasn't afraid of a fight. He welcomed conflict, judging by his body language and composed expression. Detective Thompson smiled. His eyes lit up when he did. "I like you, Cavanaugh. We're cut from the same cloth."

"I guess that's true. Except I do have a conscience. I don't deliberately place innocent people in jeopardy without reservation."

Thompson removed an engraved silver cigarette case from his inner jacket pocket. "There's no smoking in here," I said before he opened the case. "This is a smokeless building, in fact."

Thompson stared at me for a moment. The glinting case dwarfed in his big hand. "Right," he said. "Sometimes I forget. Need to give them up anyway." He put the case back into his pocket. "What's with the beard?"

"Trying something new."

"Humph," Thompson said as if he had no opinion regarding the beard matter one way or another. "How'd you find out about Shelly's predicament? I know for a fact that's not the sort of information he'd broadcast."

"I hear things," I said.

"Yeah, I bet you do, C. J. I bet you do. Hear this. Stay out of my operations."

"No can do."

Thompson thought for a moment, his gaze elsewhere. "I know the general consensus is that I don't give a damn about the people of the communities I serve," he said with conviction. "Nothing could be further from the truth. I keep my eye on the big picture. If it takes a few casualties along the way to bring down a drug dealer or supplier, then so be it. The community is better off in the end. That philosophy extends to the Fremont Community Center. Consider me the serpent of temptation in the Garden of Eden. If I can find a way to weed out the bad apples at the Rec Center then the FCC is better off for it."

"Not if you lay waste to the community you're trying to protect," I said.

"Picking up the pieces is not my job," Thompson said. "Family and friends, counselors and social workers, people like your Shelly Morton are tasked with keeping someone on the straight and narrow. My job is to bust them when they stray off the path. My job is establishing and maintaining order."

"What if someone shoves them off the path?"

"Not my problem."

Thompson was a hard ass despite his humanitarian protest. Whatever sympathies he had for those involved or victimized by the drug trade had evaporated. He was all about catching the perps. Thompson was willing to lead lambs to slaughter to make that happen. His exploiting Shelly was not mean-spirited or malicious from his prospective. He saw an opportunity to burrow deeper into the wasp's nest and he took it. The normal course of doing business as far as he was concerned.

I knew where Thompson was coming from. I was no boy scout. During my undercover days with the DEA, I had set plans in motion or allowed events to occur that had gotten people killed or seriously injured. Some lives were irreparably destroyed. All in the name of justice. Did I feel bad about it? That depends. For those who were neck deep in the game. No. For those who stuck their toe in the water and were sucked in. Yes. Did those feelings of guilt prevent me from doing my job? Not for a second. My compassion and broader vision returned once I stepped away from deep cover life in the DEA. Little is simple or black and white when it comes to people, even criminals. Crossing the line and sacrificing lives had to be done with caution. The long view had to be employed. They were still human beings in the end no matter what they had done. Remembering that helped me maintain my humanity in most instances.

"When you were a special agent with the DEA," Thompson said, "you could flash your ID and probably make the whole Shelly thing disappear. You have no government clout. No legal muscle."

"I wouldn't test that theory if I were you, Chris."

"Shelly Morton means that much to you, huh?"

"Shelly Morton means that much to his community."

"You might want to tell your buddy, Shelly, some people can't be saved."

"I'll pass. You and I may believe that. Shelly doesn't."

"Then I'll educate him myself."

"After you cut Shelly loose?" I asked.

Thompson gave me a wicked smiled. "I'll think about it." We were back to square one.

"You do that," I said. "I expect to hear from you soon."

Thompson left without saying another word, still grinning.

CHAPTER EIGHTEEN

I phoned Shelly on his office landline from my landline after Thompson left. I would prefer to do this sort of questioning in person. In this instance, I wanted to give Shelly room for cover.

"Hey, C. J. How's it going?" Shelly sounded like his old self. Our evening of trash talking, Scrabble, pie and coffee must have done him good.

"I just spoke to Thompson," I said. There was a pause. The background noise on his end deadened as if Shelly had closed his office door. I could hear a slight creak from his office chair as he sat.

"Did you get him to soften my deal? Even drop it altogether?"

"Not yet. Thompson said he busted two teens. Lerone Winbush was one. Who was the other?"

"Didn't I mention that?"

"No you didn't. I would have remembered. Who was the other one, Shelly?"

Shelly groaned. "I didn't know how to tell you."

"No time like the present."

There was a pregnant pause. "My son." He spoke so low I wasn't sure I heard him correctly.

"Who did you say?"

"My son," Shelly said, as if addressing his son rather than me.

"Did you say your son? Adrian?"

"Yes."

That's why Shelly made the deal with Thompson. He would go to bat for Lerone. Offer him and his family support, counseling and legal aide, but not to the extent of self-betrayal. Shelly would sell his soul to protect his family.

"Adrian and Lerone are good friends," Shelly said.

"You believe Adrian was the setup target?"

"I do," Shelly said. So did I. Lerone was probably both victimized for his association with Adrian and as an act of revenge for deserting the gang. My mind was racing on how to get ahead of this situation. How could I exonerate Shelly, Adrian and Lerone without any fallout? I needed to get Shelly straight on something in the meantime.

"The next time anything like this goes down you call me, Ernest or Monty. We're with you in this fight to save young people. We'll make certain the situation gets handled."

"I didn't want to burden anyone else with my trouble," Shelly said. I could hear the shame in his voice.

"Hey man, we're family. We look out for each other. Understood?"

"Understood."

"And another thing, the next time one of those young people gets into this type of scrape, help them in any way you can, but never, ever, make a self-destructive deal like the one you made with Thompson."

"Not even to save your own child?" I didn't know how to answer Shelly's question not having a child of my own. Something my dad was fond of saying came to mind. *A relative is someone who shares your bloodline. Family shares your life.*

"What's your deal with Thompson?" I asked.

"To inform him if I see or hear of any illegal drug related activity."

"Have you told him anything yet?"

"I've given him a couple of kids who attempted to sell drugs at the center. Other than that I haven't heard anything to tell."

"Nothing out of the usual?"

"That's right."

Shelly had a strict drug free zone at the center. Reporting people who attempted to sell or use drugs at the center was standard procedure at FCC. Thompson was after bigger game. Playing dumb on grapevine matters was only going to work for so long with Thompson before he would begin to apply pressure. There was no way of knowing as of yet whether my warning would make Thompson back off or had exasperated the situation. I needed to work fast.

"Let me know if the situation changes."

"Will do—and C. J., no matter how this plays out. I appreciate everything you're doing."

"I haven't done anything yet. Talk to you soon." I hung up.

My conversations with Shelly and Thompson filled in some of the holes in Shelly's story. They still hadn't explained what Shelly was doing at Epitome Self Storage making a drug pickup.

CHAPTER NINETEEN

The Fremont Community Center, often referred to as The Center, Rec Center or FCC, was bristling with youthful energy. Everywhere you looked was evidence of healthy, positive, vibrant activity. A Community Center teeming with the bright sounds of collective interaction. From the basketball and volleyball court to the weight room and game room. All except the heated indoor pool that typically received little use during the winter months. I had shown up just before seven, ready to play basketball. I would have to wait a while. Five people had games before me. All of whom had already chosen their teams. Not at all a surprising development. A number of those same ballers would be playing on outside courts in the summer. Portland winter weather made basketball a strictly indoor sport.

There were always trained volunteer uniformed security personnel roaming around the FCC, keeping a watchful eye on things. They were armed with pepper spray, expandable batons, and walkie-talkies. They were discreet, friendly, and fit. All were members of the Fremont community. Their presence was there to protect people, not to intimidate or harass them. The Center was a hotbed for attracting those with illicit intentions. The security force was there to assure they did not succeed. When they saw something, they either nipped it in the bud or reported it to the director or acting supervisor. Their services were not often needed. Most times, talking got their point across. They were no nonsense if they needed to get physical. They knew how to subdue an unruly person with swift efficiency and skill. They also had no qualms about calling the police when necessary with permission from the acting person in charge, of course. Everyone in the neighborhood knew about FCC security. Even the thugs respected The Center security enough to behave themselves. FCC had weapons detection at all entrances. For legal reasons as much as for security. In an age when random shootings were commonplace, rather safe than sorry had become a mandate.

I was there to gather whatever information I could about Shelly's circumstance. Shelly was usually home with his family by six. His house was only three blocks from the center, which was why I showed up when I did. I talked with the swing shift supervisor, aides and security personnel.

I asked a few people about Chris Thompson. Insinuating in my tone I had some suspicions about the detective. One of the security guards summarized the consensus of the people who knew Thompson.

"The narc?" He spit out as if Thompson's name put a bad taste in his mouth.

"Yeah," I said.

"He's an asshole."

"Besides that," I said.

"He's clean as far as I know other than that. He just doesn't give a damn about people. All he cares about are making busts."

My presence wasn't suspicious. Besides my regular volunteer work, I often played basketball at The Center. Even Shelly wouldn't consider my presence as dubious if he heard about it. I made my rounds keeping my conversations casual without ever mentioning Shelly, hoping to mine some nuggets on what was going on with the Fremont Community Center Director, also keeping an eye out for any unusual activity that might contain a clue. Three hours later, I had played a few games of pool and ping-pong and a couple of games of basketball. I didn't see or hear anything out of the ordinary. I found that to be a good thing. It suggested to me whatever chaos Shelly was mixed up in. He had managed to keep The Center uncontaminated. Thompson's hold over Shelly didn't involve the FCC from the information I had garnered so far.

CHAPTER TWENTY

Edna Paxson was a high school chemistry teacher. It was a career, as Edna put it, that chose her. A profession proven far more fulfilling than her initial career path. Edna graduated at the top of her class with bachelors' in both Biology and Chemistry from her hometown University of Kentucky. Then went on to earn a Master's in Pharmaceutical Sciences at the University of Pittsburgh. A line of big, small, and medium pharmaceutical companies made her offers to join their pharmaceutical research labs. Edna chose one of the big pharma companies located in southern California. She had been led to believe she would have the opportunity to follow her dream. To focus on unraveling the mysteries behind the genetic makeup of diseases. Instead, Edna was teamed with scientists charged with developing drugs for seniors. There were no available positions in her desired field of study.

It's all good, Edna told herself. Diving into her work with the enthusiasm you would expect from a newbie. Theories were plentiful. Advances were far fewer and came at a tortoise pace. Edna knew quality research took time. Once there was a breakthrough, then testing was mandatory to prove the drug was safe. That could take years. Most drugs have side effects. Some are minor. Others come with major health risks that can only be justified for use when there is little to no other choice of medical treatment. Everyone in the pharmaceutical research business recognized what they did was a gamble. There was no guarantee a new drug would receive FDA approval. Edna was patient. The shine wore off the apple after seven years and a couple of patents under her belt.

Edna was a team player. She did all that was asked of her without complaint. Contributing her own ideas whenever appropriate or called upon. The hours were long, the pressure was constant for results and staying within budget, and the competition was fierce, with many of her colleagues jockeying for prestige, promotions, and patents. The constant backbiting and snarky behavior of too many of her coworkers took its toll on her positive can-do attitude. She wasn't sleeping well. Work consumed her life. Regular exercise and a healthy diet were displaced by working around the clock and fast foods. When Edna mentioned to one of her associates that their research seemed more focused on treatments rather than cures, he chuckled. "Treatments are where the money is, Edna," he said as if talking to a child naïve in the ways of the world. Whether he was correct or simply jaded did not matter to Edna. All she knew was she was not happy. Edna had to move on for her own wellbeing.

Edna applied for a number of pharmaceutical positions online. Every position she applied for made her an offer after her interview. Edna accepted one from a general merchandise store. It paid almost as much as what she was making at big pharma. Part of her big pharma employment package had paid off her student loans. Not having that debt hanging over her head made her pharmacist paycheck more than enough for a comfortable lifestyle. Bringing along her 401K and Roth IRA made money the least of her concerns. The best perk for Edna was that she was returning home to Lexington.

Edna was surprised at the turnout for her going away party. Everyone was there, from the newbies to the head of the department. They were warm, affectionate, and sincere in their good wishes. Edna had not spent much time with her colleagues off the clock. That could be said of anyone in her position, she was certain. It was in that relaxed venue, laughing, joking, and reminiscing with her fellow scientists and researchers, that Edna realized something. They were good people with the best of intentions. Not unethical sheep as some outsiders had them portrayed. They really were working hard to try to make the world a healthier place, using their knowledge to the best of their abilities in that effort, making the most of what the system had to offer. Edna wished she had taken more time to get to know her coworkers. Her decision would not have been altered. Memories of vicious competitiveness were not lost to her during their revelry. It would simply have made for more pleasant memories of their time together.

More free time meant time for a personal life. Edna had boyfriends in college but never anything serious. Her studies always came first. Her time at big pharma allowed little time for dating. A relationship was not even a consideration. Most of her colleagues had found their partners before starting work at big pharma. The few available male colleagues held no attraction for Edna. All signals from them suggested they felt the same. Edna was juggling a couple of men she enjoyed spending time with since switching jobs but saw no long-term benefit in either.

Edna had returned to jogging. Her favorite path was the Arboretum Trail. A popular botanical garden trail featuring hundreds of native species near the University of Kentucky. That was where she met Mason. A tall, fit man with brunette hair dyed silver on top and a trimmed beard shaped like dollar signs. Mason caught up to Edna on the path and introduced himself. They chatted while finishing their run together. They exchanged contact information and planned their first date while cooling down in the parking lot.

Edna found Mason handsome, charming and clever. He liked to laugh. She imagined it was in part to show off his perfect smile. Mason also knew when to turn serious, welcoming a thoughtful conversation with a sharp focus contrary to his sometimes offbeat humor. Mason returned an unfettered joy to her life that Edna had not experienced since she was a child. Not at all the personality, you would expect to find in a corporate tax manager. Edna stopped seeing anyone else. They became exclusive. This went on for a year before Mason asked Edna to marry him. They were married in an elegant spring church ceremony surrounded by family and their closest friends.

Married life agreed with them. They bought a two-story three-bedroom home in an upper middle class Lexington neighborhood and settled into a life filled with fun activities and travel. They had talked about having a family during their dating period. Both had agreed they did not want children. Mason did a variety of volunteer work from helping out at homeless shelters to tutoring children and adults in math. Edna had never found time to volunteer. It seemed as though her life was overrun with school, work or both. Edna accompanied Mason during some of his volunteer work. For Edna, tutoring teenagers in biology and chemistry was most fulfilling. She loved seeing their faces light up when they grasped a concept they had previously believed was beyond their reach.

Edna had gotten to know Principal Gillian Bedford of Rufus E. Clement High School through her tutoring sessions at the community's public library. The high school was located in a poor working neighborhood infested with gangs and drug activities. Clement had trouble attracting and keeping qualified teachers. Not only because of its location and reputation for having difficult students but lower pay. Poverty begets poverty, even in institutions created to uplift. Science and math teachers were particularly hard to acquire. Principal Bedford let Edna know how much she would love to have her join their faculty. Edna's father was a high school math teacher. Her mother was an aeronautical engineer. Edna had followed her mother's example. She felt the time had come to step into her father's shoes.

Mason was all for the idea of Edna becoming a high school teacher as long as it made her happy. Their monthly expenses amounted to less than one-week's pay of their combined incomes. Edna's dip in salary would not be an issue.

Principal Bedford was able to fast track Edna's teaching credentials. Alternative certification enabled Edna to reduce the time it took her to earn her standard teaching certificate. Since Edna already had college degrees in Pharmaceutical Sciences, Biology and Chemistry, with GPAs over 3.0, her required teaching course knowledge was covered. Her work related experience and volunteer tutoring in Chemistry and Biology lessened Edna's required teacher preparation program hours. What surprised Edna was how nervous she was when taking her state educator exams. While she aced the tests, her anxiety at taking them proved to her how badly she wanted to teach. Edna accepted a vacated full-time Chemistry teacher position at Clement. The vacating teacher had accepted a position with Goldham Middle School. A private school in Edna's own upscale neighborhood.

The transition was not as easy as Edna had envisioned. Most students did not embrace her as the ones she had tutored. Most were indifferent, in fact. A handful was downright belligerent, turning her classroom into a test of wills. Edna was able to gain control over her classroom situation with patience and perseverance, utilizing helpful tips from her colleagues, the principal, and her dad. She won their respect by being stern but fair. Most minds followed. A tragic few whose personal problems were clearly so dire not even casting her deepest net could reach them.

Mason and Edna changed their minds about having children. Edna gave birth to a girl three years into her teaching career. Agnes Louise Kingston. Edna took a leave of absence to become a stay-at-home mom. Rufus E. Clement High School was struggling to survive. The public school's troubles had escalated within the first year of her tenure. The same old story of school funding disparities along school district lines. Since local property taxes dictated how much funding was received by each school wealthy districts trounced poor.

There had been a push by certain members of the city council whose motivation was reputed to be financial and not racist to close the school. The student body of Clement being predominately minority was mere coincidence according to those same resistant members. The principal, faculty, staff and especially the parents of Clement students were against it. Closing down their community school would mean their children would be forced bus elsewhere. The school board had agreed. Redistricting aided the cause of the advocators. The past election results gave a majority to those who wanted Rufus E. Clement High School closed. They wasted no time making it happen. Arrangements were made for Clement students to be bussed to the nearest district schools the following year. Gentrification plans for the community had been on the table for some time. Homes and small businesses were being gobbled up by developers and corporate interests. Rufus E. Clement High School was slotted to become a mixed-use development. A development that had yet to happen.

When the school was officially shut down Edna was heartbroken. Not only for herself but the students and people who had given so much of themselves to make Clement work. There were teachers who had been there for over fifteen years. Principal Bedford and a third of the cafeteria staff had been there for over twenty. Most faculty and administrative workers were offered similar positions in theirs and other school districts throughout the state. Unions helped a great deal. Most of the displaced would survive financially. It would take some time for the shattered spirits of the Clement High faithful to mend.

The winter following the school closing, Edna had settled into being a stay-at-home mom. Mason was leaving his office one night when an armed mugger forced him into a dark alley. The man did not look well. He was sweating profusely and shaking. Mason suspected he was a drug addict suffering from withdrawal. Mason remained calm. The robber told Mason to give him his wallet, watch, and jewelry that included his wedding band. Mason cooperated, offering no resistance. The mugger checked the wallet. There were only twenty-two dollars in cash. Mason carried very little cash. He didn't see the point in our e-banking, e-commerce world. The mugger became furious claiming Mason was holding out on him. The more Mason denied the robber's claim, the more irate he became. The mugger shot her husband four times. Mason was dead before the ambulance arrived. Edna was six months pregnant with their second child.

Mason had taken excellent care of their personal finances. A topic Edna found boring. Mason made Edna attend a once-a-month meeting held in their study in order to educate her about everything regarding their personal financial portfolio. Edna would feign dozing off during his tutelage. It was one of the few times Mason was firm with her.

"Money is not a laughing matter, Edna," he would lecture her to gain her full attention. "It's hard to come by and must be handled with care. That's what I do professionally and personally. I expect the same of you for the sake of our family if something happens to me." Edna always thought Mason was being melodramatic but she settled down and listened. If it was that important to him it was the least she could do.

Edna tried to take over their personal finances. She could not clear her mind long enough to concentrate on what needed to be done with the distress of Mason's murder and a new baby on the way. The police found her husband's murderer a month after his death. A nineteen-year-old overdosed on heroin in an abandoned home in a rundown neighborhood in Louisville. Locating Mason's killer did not soothe her pain or buoy her sense of justice. Edna simply wanted her husband back. Her younger sister, Skylar, was an economist who became a financial advisor. Skylar volunteered to step in as her sister's personal finance manager. Edna was happy to accept her offer.

The new baby arrived. Owen Hunter Kingston. Edna had elected to keep Mason's last name. Edna had considered naming her son after Mason. The thought of carrying the name of his dead father might be too big a burden for him to bear. Mason had opted out of the standard company life insurance policy and selected one of his own. The two million dollar payout along with their amassed savings and investments would provide Edna with a lifetime financial security blanket barring a cataclysmic financial meltdown.

Edna loved her children. She cherished their time together. It wasn't enough. She was a career woman. Having a career gave her a sense of purpose outside of motherhood. Edna needed to return to work. Teaching had lost its attraction since Mason's death. Returning to the world of scientific discovery lacked luster. She had kept her pharmacists license up to date. Finding a position would not be a problem. Working at a pharmacy would be stable and fulfilling. She would hire a nanny rather than opt for drop off childcare. Edna had not yet decided when she would return to the work force. She only knew that she would.

Her children were spending a couple of weeks with Mason's parents. Edna was clothes shopping for herself. She had put away her purchases in her family SUV and was considering where to have a late lunch.

"Mrs. Kingston!"

Edna stopped and turned to see a muscular, caramel-skinned baby faced man with long wavy brown hair wearing designer clothes jogging toward her. It took Edna a moment to recognize the young man as one of her former high school students. She hadn't seen or spoken to him since the funeral. Carter Gordon hugged Edna without a word. His embrace was comforting like an old friend. Carter had been one of Rufus E. Clement High School's honor students. Carter had expressed an interest in banking and investment while at Clement. Principal Bedford asked Mason if he would give Carter some insight on what it meant to be an investment counselor. Mason was happy to do so. Even though her husband was a corporate tax manager, Mason knew a great deal about investments. What began as a request to help one student turned into a presentation for the entire Consumerism Class. A presentation that was video recorded. Becoming a class teaching tool staple. Edna had a copy of that recording at home. She watched it on occasion after her husband's murder. It made her ache for Mason every time.

"How are you?" they asked in unison after their hug. They laughed before answering they were well.

"And please call me Edna, Carter. We're not in school anymore."

"Alright," Carter said. Edna did not remember his voice being so deep.

"I was about to grab a bite to eat," Edna said. "Would you like to join me? Give us a chance to catch up."

"I would love to," Carter said, offering Edna his arm. Carter had always been a gentleman. Edna was glad to see that hadn't changed. Carter was a member of the last graduating class from Rufus E. Clement High School. Edna had occasioned a run-in or conversation with an alumnus, worker, or former student of Rufus E. Clement High School. The alumnus and workers weathered the storm best. The outcomes of the former students were a mixed bag. Some had plowed through and made a productive life for themselves. Some maintained treading water. Others had been swallowed up by crime. For those, Edna wondered most if Clement High School would have made a difference in their lives. She felt confident that for most the school would have.

They complimented each other on how well they looked. Grazing their shared high school history as they strolled. They happened upon Coralee's Pizzeria a couple of blocks from where they ran into each other that tickled their taste buds. The place was half-full. Cozy with décor that reminded them of a family-friendly Red Robin rather than a local pizzeria. The young server's smile broadened when she saw Edna and Carter enter arm in arm. A look of approval on her face with a hint of jealousy in her blue eyes. Edna started to explain they were only friends, then thought, why bother. If the server wanted to believe there was something more than friendship between them, then where was the harm. Edna had to admit. It certainly gave her ego a boost.

The server escorted them to a booth by a window, and they accepted. Carter helped Edna off with her coat. He hung hers, then his coat on brass coat hooks mounted on wood posts framing the booths. They made themselves comfortable. The restaurant was brimming with delicious aromas. The window was frosted with winter chill. The young server handed them menus. Her nametag read, "Honey."

"Would you like anything to drink?" Honey asked. With more of an eye toward Carter than Edna.

"Hot tea," Edna said.

"I'll bring you hot water," the server said in a rehearsed warm but professional tone. "Help yourself to any of our teas." Honey pointed with her silver ink pen at a black metal caddy crafted like a bird nest on the wooden table containing sugar packets, artificial sweeteners and a limited selection of teas.

Lingering her gaze and smile on Carter longer than necessary Honey finally said, "And what would you like to drink, *sir*?"

"I'd like a hot chocolate," Carter said.

"*Very good*," Honey said, as if Carter had solved her riddle. "Would you like whipped cream on top?"

"I'll take mine straight."

"I'll give you both a few minutes to look over your menus. In the meantime, your drinks are coming right up."

"Thank you," Carter said. Edna nodded to the server. Honey left. A young man with a faint smile deftly deposited a glass water bottle on their table. Edna let out a small chuckle when he was out of earshot.

"Do you believe her?"

"What?" Carter uncorked the bottle, offering to fill Edna's glass first. Edna accepted.

"Our waitress was flirting with you."

"Really?" Carter filled his glass, recorked the bottle and placed it back on the table on his side near the window.

Edna looked at Carter in disbelief. He really did not appear to know what Edna was talking about. "You mean to tell me you didn't notice anything?"

"She seemed nice. I assume that's part of her job. Increases her chances for a better tip."

Edna let out an amused laugh. Carter smiled. A bashful smile. The same smile he had back in high school. Edna remembered Carter had the same high school girlfriend for the entire time he was there. Zadie Dixon. Another honor student. Girls flirted with Carter all of the time at Clement but never got anywhere. At the time, Edna thought Carter was only pretending not to notice. So not to lead them on out of love and respect for Zadie. Carter was a book nerd although he certainly never looked the part. He was gangly but handsome. He didn't wear glasses. Was always dressed in the popular teenage fashions. Even had a bit of swag to his game—as the teenagers would say. Edna was just now coming to realize that Carter was oblivious to the effect he had on some women.

"Never mind," Edna said. "What have you been up to, Carter?"

Carter was living in Charleston, South Carolina. He had become a CPA working from home. He served a select list of small to mid-size businesses. His family was well. They had left Lexington the summer following the school closing to settle in Jackson, Tennessee. Zadie and he tried to make a go of it. The distance proved too much. They officially broke off their relationship in their freshman year of college. Zadie had married a professional basketball player. He and Zadie remained friends. His college roommate introduced Carter to bodybuilding. Said it would help fill out his skinny frame. Carter never competed but discovered he enjoyed the workout and continued. Carter became engaged to a young woman that he met at the University of South Carolina. Chiamaka Okafor. Edna could not help but beam as Carter showed her pictures of them together on his phone. A lovely young woman with the gentlest brown eyes Edna had ever seen. The wedding was in September and Edna was invited. Edna was proud of Carter. Edna knew Mason would be too.

"Do you do any personal investment counseling?" Edna asked. She had no plans of switching over to Carter from her sister who was doing an excellent job. She was simply curious.

"Only for family and close friends. You're family, Edna. Anytime or in any way I can help, please let me know."

Edna suspected Carter meant that outside of her financial needs as well. Edna smiled and thanked Carter, giving his hand a gentle squeeze. Carter glanced away with a bashful grin. It was clear to Edna he had not outgrown his crush on her. If his shy behavior around her when they were alone at school were not enough of an indicator, Edna had overheard other students teasing him about his feelings for her. Carter never denied their incriminations. Carter and his family were amongst the disenfranchised Clement High multitude that had attended Mason's funeral. Carter was one of the shoulders to cry on offered Edna. She never took Carter up on his offer. It always felt inappropriate to her even in her time of sorrow. As if she would be leading a child toward expectations that would never be realized.

"I can't tell you how sorry I am about, Mr. Kingston," Carter said. "I still think about him all the time."

"Thank you," Edna said. Hoping Carter would say no more about her most painful memory. Honey returned with their drinks. Honey smiled approvingly at the sight. Edna realized she was still holding Carter's hand and released it.

"One tea setting for the lady," Honey said, placing a gleaming white cup and saucer and silver teapot in front of Edna.

"Thank you," Edna said. Honey had already turned her attention to Carter.

"Hot chocolate straight for the gentleman."

"Thank you," Carter said.

"You're more than welcome, *sir*," Honey said. Again with the lingering smile and gaze. A wave of recognition swept over Carter's face. For Honey, it must have seemed like acknowledgment that her flirting was working. Edna knew exactly what it was. Carter was realizing—perhaps for the first time in his life—what flirting was like. It clearly made him uncomfortable.

"Have you decided?" Honey asked. The question was meant for both of them but she hadn't taken her eyes of Carter.

"Give us a few more minutes," Edna answered.

"I'll be back in a few." Honey bounced away.

"Now do you see?" Edna asked in a whisper.

"I guess—I mean—I suppose I do," Carter stammered.

"This is not the first time a woman has flirted with you," Edna's voice returned to normal now that Honey was out of earshot. "Is it, Carter?" Edna knew it wasn't but wanted Carter to realize it for himself.

"I don't know. It's inappropriate if she was flirting with me. I have a fiancée."

"I don't think Honey cares. Didn't you see the way she looked at us when we walked in?"

"Not really."

"She thought we were a couple."

"Why would she think that?"

"We walked in arm in arm."

"I was being a gentleman."

"Honey didn't know that and she's still flirting with you. I would have knocked her on her butt by now if you were my fiancé."

"Chiamaka's not like that. She's not a violent person."

"I meant that figuratively. I would have verbally dressed her down by now for flirting with my man."

"Really?" Carter was grinning.

"Haven't you had to make a man step off from making a move on your girlfriend or fiancée by confronting them?"

"On a few occasions. Especially in high school with Zadie."

"I had to do that a time or two when some women tried getting their hooks into Mason."

The conversation nosedived from the trajectory of humor to gloom with the mention of Mason's name. This time Carter reached over and squeezed Edna's hand. Honey returned for their order. The server seemed to sense something was wrong. Her smile dipped sharply to tight lips. Carter removed his hand from Edna's.

"Sorry to interrupt," Honey said. Her voice faint and gentle. "Are you ready to order?"

Honey took their orders without any more flirtations aimed at Carter. Their server was pleasant and professional for the rest of the afternoon. Edna had not realized how much history had passed since last they saw each other. They caught up on the latest news and gossip during the course of their meal. Both agreed it was possibly the best pizza they ever had.

"The closing of Rufus E. Clement High School represented the epicenter of the dispersion of a community," Carter said. Edna concurred. Prisons were getting fatter amongst his peers. College graduates were shrinking.

"I hope you two have a nice evening," Honey said with sincerity as she left the check on the table. Carter insisted on paying. Edna could not deny Carter something he regarded as a privilege. Carter left Honey a large tip.

Carter escorted Edna to her car, arm in arm. They had exchanged contact information with promises to stay in touch. Promises both knew they would keep. Edna and Carter gave each other a friendly hug. Carter held the car door open for Edna. She got in and rolled down the window at his beckoning.

"Watch the local news tonight," Carter said. "You'll see something very interesting."

"What?"

"Watch and you'll see."

Carter walked off. Edna rolled up her driver's window. She thought for a moment about what Carter could be referencing. It was a thought that kept popping up for the remainder of the day.

"Breaking News!" announced the dashing news anchor in a dramatic voice leading off the late news as if World War III were upon us. "For a live report, we go to Amy Park on the scene. Amy."

"Thanks, Brad." The young reporter's tone mimicked his. "I'm standing here in front of what used to be Rufus E. Clement High School. As you can see behind me, the abandoned high school is immersed in flames."

The shot switched to the burning building with Amy as a voice-over. A blazing inferno with flames bursting out of every opening. Water cannons and manned discharge hoses shooting water from a distance appeared to have little effect on the unquenchable pyre.

"At 10:16 p.m., a civilian reported a fire at this location. Local fire fighters responded to discover a raging fire engulfing this building. The fire was immediately upgraded to a five-alarm fire which is why you see fire personnel and equipment from various stations."

The shot returned to Amy. Standing next to her was a spokesperson for the fire department dressed in full protective gear.

"I'm here with Fire Chief Ace Connors, whose unit was first to arrive on the scene. Chief, what can you tell us about this fire?"

"The building is a total loss," Chief Connors decisively stated. "Right now we're looking to contain it."

"Any chance of it spreading?"

"None. There is no wind and with these cold damp weather conditions containing it won't be a problem."

"Then there is no need for anyone to evacuate?"

"None whatsoever."

"I've noticed none of the fire fighters have attempted to enter the building. Why is that?"

"Good question. It isn't safe at this time for any of our people to go in. Once we're confident the flames are out and things have cooled enough, we'll send in a clean-up crew to extinguish any hotspots."

"Was it arson?"

"That would be my guess. The fire inspectors will be able to confirm that for certain."

"Thank you, Chief."

The Chief gave Amy an affirmative nod and went back to work. Amy looked over her shoulder at the blazing inferno then back at the camera.

"According to local police officials the former high school had become a known hangout for vagrants, drug dealers, gangs and addicts. It's a miracle no one was hurt. This is Amy Park reporting live for WKYT, Lexington. Back to you, Brad."

The broadcast returned to the studio.

"Thank you, Amy," the dashing news anchor said. "As Amy said, it's a miracle no one was hurt." The anchorman handed off to his equally dapper female partner.

"A miracle indeed." Her dramatic tone and expression identical to his.

The news team went on to give background on Rufus E. Clement High School. Edna had zoned out. She had been fixated on seeing the high school going up in flames. The video footage repeatedly playing in her mind. Rufus E. Clement High School had been a nexus in her life. A bond had emerged between her and the people of that community. One Edna had not fully realized until that moment. At the center of it was Mason. He had been the one who introduced Edna to a more fulfilling life. A life she believed she had before they met. Mason had expanded her heart beyond familial love and draped it in the world, taking Edna from the optimism that she could make a difference to the certainty that she would.

Her phone notified Edna that she had a text message.

"Did you watch the local news?" It was from Carter.

"Yes," Edna replied.

"Did you see RHS going up in flames?"

"I did."

"A beacon of light toward the heavens. We were here. We deserved better."

Had Carter burned down Rufus E. Clement High School? Edna could never condone such a thing if he had. Not that she didn't understand. Edna had a fleeting thought or two of destroying the place once the school was closed. Especially after Mason died, she considered asking Carter directly if he had anything to do with the Clement fire. The obvious answer was yes since Carter had told her to watch the news. No one was hurt, a miracle indeed. How did Carter manage to clear Clement out to burn it down? Did he have help? Was anyone else from Rufus E. Clement High School involved?

"Where are you?" Edna texted.

"Home in Charlotte."

Edna thought for a moment before she responded. "We did deserve better. Stay safe, Carter. Keep in touch."

"I will. You too."

"In other breaking news—" Edna switched off the television.

CHAPTER TWENTY-ONE

Dr. Blake Saba invited me to dinner with him and his family. Blake and I had dinner as often as we could, alternating between his place and mine. His invitation, by default, extended to his friend and colleague and my woman friend, Destini Pendleton. An invitation Destini attempted to decline due to her exorbitant workload. When Portland's Chief Medical Examiner learned from me, Destini would not be able to join us. He took immediate action. Blake paid Destini an office visit to express how saddened he was by the news. Blake also enlisted his wife, Alivia, and their children Desmond and Shayla in phoning her to express their disappointment. Destini had little choice but to make time to attend by the time the Blake family finished guilt tripping her.

It had been a while since I had spent quality time with Blake. Even longer since I had seen his family. We occasioned a lunch, or Blake would pay an impromptu office visit. I rarely repaid the courtesy at his job for obvious reasons. The business of corpses may sometimes worm its way into my line of work. That didn't mean I wanted to see them when I was off the clock.

Blake and I had regular non-work-related phone conversations we called "checking in." Both of us preferred talking as opposed to texting. Like every responsible spouse and parent I know, Blake's life was brimming with time demands. Our phone conversations were usually brief, doused in the topics of family and mutual friends, politics, and sports, possibly nudging into our chat a few stray subjects like books or movie recommendations or a play or art exhibit worth seeing. Getting together for dinner afforded us an opportunity to indulge in one of our mutual passions. Blake was an authority on Native American history and culture. Dinner always afforded

Blake a chance to deepen my education on the First People, enriching my knowledge and bolstering my pride in a third of my genetic heritage.

The Saba family resided in the King neighborhood. A gentrified section of Northeast Portland that at one time had some of the highest crime rates in the city. Blake and Alivia had purchased a three-story, four-bedroom fixer-upper for a steal as a wedding gift to themselves back in the day. After two years, four months, and fifteen days of renovation, their dream house materialized. Every aspect of their home proudly exhibited their culture and heritage with Klamath, Modoc, and Yahooskin décor as their main themes. Some of which were of Alivia and Blake's own creations. The Saba's maintained a strong connection to their Klamath Tribal roots and community. One thing I didn't know was what drew Blake and Alivia away from southern Oregon to Portland in the first place. They never volunteered that information. I never felt it my place to ask.

Four years after the christening of their new home, Desmond was born. His sister Shayla joined him three years later. Both children inherited their parent's walnut-colored skin. Desmond was the spitting image of his father, both physically and in manner. Minus the slight paunch. Average height, lean, and fit with an aquiline nose, pitch-black hair that he wore in a ponytail, and alert brown eyes that appeared to miss nothing. Desmond excelled at sports. Soccer being his favorite. Shayla inherited her mother's radiant eyes, luxurious black hair, and stout figure, along with her father's nose and mother's dimpled smile. Shayla's outgoing personality came predominately from her mother with a healthy dose of Blake's cutting wit.

Universities and colleges nationwide had offered Desmond both soccer and academic scholarships. He chose Portland State University and academics. PSU because he liked the faculty and campus. They also offered everything he wanted in his chosen fields of study and were close to home. Sports were recreational fun for Desmond. He had no desire to take it beyond that pleasure. He enjoyed watching sports, especially soccer, basketball, track, field hockey, baseball, and lacrosse. Desmond teamed with friends on a regular basis to play pickup matches of soccer, basketball, and lacrosse that satisfied his craving for physical competition. I had played basketball with and against Desmond at the Fremont Community Center. Everyone respected his game. He had mad skills.

The eldest Saba was now a third year student at Portland State University. He was majoring in Environmental Science with a minor in Music. Desmond lived at home by choice. The family loved having him home. Having a doting mother was an additional benefit. A talented musician and singer, Desmond was wise to the economic pitfalls of such a career choice. Even though his parents emphasized he should select his vocation based on his passion and not his wallet. His major and minor choices were a win-win as far as Desmond was concerned.

Shayla was a high school senior who had received early acceptance into Reed College undergraduate program. The Portland private liberal arts college was the only institute of higher learning she was interested in attending. Shayla was a straight A student like her older brother. Also, like her brother, Shayla had weighed in on the economic realities against a more fickle pursuit. For Shayla those two waffled between two passions. A talented performing and visual artist, Shayla was drawn to the light of Liberal Arts. Science was her other beacon. More specifically, stem cell research. Shayla was leaning toward science as her major and art as her minor. She had yet to finalize her decision.

Mealtime was family time. There was a strict no phones policy around the Saba dinner table. Phones were turned off and left on a handsome lamp table set in the corner of the dining area out of reach. The table was hand waxed and made from oak. I know all of this because Blake shared with me the details. A Blake Saba original like a number of their wood furnishings. Including the rustic wood dining room set we were seated at.

The conversation around the dinner table was lively and spontaneous. We enjoyed a delicious meal of grilled salmon, vegetable stir fry and wild rice pilaf with sautéed mushrooms and roasted garlic. We were having my homemade pumpkin pudding topped with a sprinkling of fresh ground cinnamon and a modest dollop of fat free non-dairy whipped topping for dessert. The Sabas are lactose intolerant. Blake was explaining the process of grounding "wocas" or water lily seeds into flour or meal. Once a staple in the Modoc diet. I found the process fascinating. Destini was mildly interested. The rest of the Saba clan respectfully listened. The topic of tribal and native history was nothing unique to the Saba offspring. Such knowledge was matter-of-fact to them. Desmond and Shayla had been home schooled on the subject since they could talk. It was a solidly embraced tradition. One they would carry on with their children.

"You should write a book," I said to Blake. "Several in fact."

"I do," Blake said. "Every day."

Blake was referencing the oral teaching and storytelling tradition of native peoples.

"Don't let my husband kid you, C. J.," Alivia said with a playful smile. "Blake has written a number of manuscripts on our culture and history. He's simply waiting to retire before publishing any of them."

Alivia works as an associate curator of Native American Art at the Portland Art Museum. I had no doubt she had a book or two lined up on her equally beloved subject of Native American Art. The couple had more than once mentioned they planned to retire simultaneously, returning home to the Klamath Basin when the time was right. After their children completed college and settled into careers for themselves, I would miss my friend when Blake made good on his plan.

"*We* are waiting for *us* to retire, my love," Blake said to Alivia. His voice as soothing as a kitten's purr. "Alivia has already drafted drawings and illustrations for my manuscripts. She has even created some great book cover design concepts."

"Why wait?" I asked both Alivia and Blake. Like someone anxious to open their gifts.

"Exactly what we've been saying," Desmond said.

"We've read most of what father has written," Shayla said. "As far as we're concerned they're great and important works."

"We'd be glad to help," Desmond said.

"In any way we can," Shayla chimed in.

"Count me in," I said. "I'll do whatever I can."

Everyone looked at Destini, who was quietly enjoying her dessert. Destini noticed she had suddenly become the focus of attention.

"Sure," Destini said with a shoulder shrug.

Everyone laughed except Destini, who scooped up another spoon of pudding.

Alivia and Blake looked into each other's eyes, engaging in the telepathy that accompanies couples that have been together for the long haul. Alivia reached out her hand to Blake. They held hands on the table: a firm, gentle grip of assurance. I've got you. Their hands seemed to say to me. I will never let go, no matter what. Alivia gave her husband a reassuring nod. A mental elbow, if you will.

"I want to spend my retirement years devoted to documenting the ancestral history and culture of indigenous people from our point of view," Blake said. "My focus must not be divided in order to accomplish my goal. I will not shortchange my people. They deserve my best, and I will give it to them."

"You already are giving your best," Alivia said. Everyone nodded in agreement.

"Thank you for saying that my darling," Blake said. "Thank you all."

"Don't get sentimental on us, father," Desmond said.

"It's my party, and I'll cry if I want to," Blake said.

We all laughed.

"And don't think I won't take all of you up on your generous offers here tonight when the time comes," Blake said.

"Let us toast," Alivia said. We raised our water glasses. The SABA family did not drink alcohol. "To family, friends, history and traditions."

We air clinked our glasses across the table and drank deep.

* * *

The rain was coming down in buckets on the drive home.

"I needed a break more than I realized," Destini said, seated snugly in the passenger seat of my car.

"Glad you enjoyed yourself," I said.

"Do you think our children will be anything like Blake's?" Destini asked.

"If we're lucky."

"And if we're not?"

"We'll love 'em just the same."

Destini chuckled. "Speak for yourself."

"There will be one difference I can foresee," I said.

"What's that honey?"

"I'll be a stay at home dad."

"Why do you get to be the stay at home parent?"

"You're the one with a career, sweetheart."

"You don't consider what you do a career?" Destini asked.

"I consider what I do an option. My careers were with the military and DEA. I do what I do now because I enjoy it."

"Do you miss working for the DEA?"

I had to think about Destini's question. I was done when I left the DEA. I felt burned out and disheartened, believing that all of my best efforts had only resulted in extinguishing a few fires of an uncontrollable inferno. The kicker was I felt rejuvenated after working on the Epitome Self Storage stakeout. The way I had felt near the start of my DEA career. "I don't know," I said. "Maybe?"

125

"Have you ever considered going back to the DEA?" Destini asked. "As an undercover operative, I mean?"

I detected a touch of concern in Destini's voice. "Would you mind if I did?"

Destini sighed. "Yes."

"Why?"

"Because I believe if you were to return to the DEA, I would lose you. To the job or maybe even worse."

The worse being death, I assumed. I could relate. I felt the same way about Destini's homicide work.

"And don't try comparing my being a homicide detective with your DEA undercover assignments," Destini said as if she read my mind. "There is no way what I do on a daily basis comes close to putting yourself in front of a buzz saw and hoping it stops before it cuts you in two. I see what our undercover officers go through. How deadly the game is they play. Thompson told me himself that what they do only scratches the surface of what undercover DEA agents face."

Thompson probably mentioned his take on DEA undercover ops to Destini because he knows we're a couple. I wish he hadn't told Destini that albeit true.

"You have nothing to worry about. I'm not going back."

"Who says I was worried?" Destini kissed my cheek. Drawing back with a crinkled nose as if she were about to sneeze. Destini told me she didn't care for my beard. She did not like the feel of facial hair against her face or body. Above all else, Destini disliked that the beard hid my scar. "Still, I'm glad to hear you say it," she said.

I parked in Destini's driveway. Her car was tucked away in her garage. Her single story Craftsman style home appeared dark and docile with the twinkling of a corner living room lamp its only star. I walked around and opened the passenger door. Breaking out my compact pushbutton umbrella that I kept in the car and rarely used in an attempt to shield Destini from the onslaught of rain. A gentleman's privilege I had fought for early on in our relationship. Making it clear this was who I was and had no intention of changing. Destini argued such archaic gestures were not necessary for a modern, healthy, independent woman such as herself. I refused to surrender. Destini acquiesced, nudging me with a barb on occasion about my Old School manners. Always with a glint in her eyes and often a smile.

I escorted Destini to her front door. We kissed. She unlocked the door and entered the foyer. I waited for her to close and lock the front door before leaving.

"Aren't you coming in?" Destini asked as I stood there waiting. I collapsed my umbrella and stepped inside the foyer. Destini turned on her hall light, taking off her wet coat as she headed toward the living room closet. I placed the dripping umbrella in the brass openwork umbrella stand inside the entryway. I closed and locked her front door behind me. I followed in Destini's wet footprints on her polished hardwood floors, feeling like a lottery winner as I unbuttoned my coat.

CHAPTER TWENTY-TWO

Janet had taken an Uber from her place to the Watershed. A popular downtown Portland dance club near the Dirty Pie Pizza she loved so much. The Watershed was electric with energy. A diverse, dynamic crowd from twenty-one to early thirties, engaged in the art of socializing or dancing to a combination of modern pop and club music hits. Janet was swept up in the magic from the moment she entered. She danced for a bit, met two players and a nice guy, drank three cranberry spritzers compliments of each before letting them down easy. Janet received a text message while in the middle of dancing with her fourth dance partner. "I'm here," was all it read. Janet politely excused herself, explaining to Arnesh that she had to leave. Arnesh pressed her for her phone number. Janet told him the same thing she had told the others.

"I have a boyfriend, and I don't fool around."

Janet left the exhilarating comfort and bright lights of Watershed feeling exuberant for a required business meeting a few blocks away. The temperature was expected to dip near freezing with light rain but no snow in the forecast. Janet elected to wear a short rain jacket rather than one of her three-quarter length choices. The shorter jacket matched better her rainbow spirit desert printed rain boots. Greeted by slicing wind and icy sheets of winter rain, Janet rushed through what felt like an arctic blast. Streetlights were gauzy beacons in the murky darkness. The wind had driven the cold through her damp blue jeans uncovered by her insulated jacket by the time Janet arrived at her parking lot rendezvous.

Janet jumped in on the front passenger side of a dark green panel van, relieved to be free of the brutal weather. The heated van revealed a chill that had crept into her body. Four unoccupied vehicles shared the self-park surface lot. Gerek Choinski had chosen a parking space furthest away from the four. Choinski stared at Janet for a moment. Gerek had turned off the headlights but kept the van running. Janet's coat was dripping wet. Her oversized chunky baggy winter beanie hat had kept her head warm. Janet realized how good a job her beanie had done when she removed her hat. It felt like a water-saturated sponge. She dropped it on the floor near her feet. Choinski reached behind him and brought forth a blue cotton hand towel. Janet hesitated.

"It's clean," Choinski said. "I grabbed a couple out of the utility closet when I saw where the weather was headed."

Janet accepted his offering, drying her face. Her bout with the unexpected winter rainstorm might not have happened had Janet not believed it necessary to take certain precautions. Janet felt as though Firestorm was watching her. She couldn't say why she felt that way. It was only a feeling. Like when you have an uneasy sense, someone is staring at you. You turn to look to discover that they are. Janet didn't like being spied on. She was good at her job and didn't need anyone breathing down her neck. Her dance club detour was her attempt to throw her spies off her trail. A maneuver that made her feel better whether her suspicions were real or imagined.

"How do you like this weather?" Choinski quipped.

"I don't," said Janet, placing the towel on the dashboard, fighting a shiver that threatened to overtake her body. Choinski had his parka open and the heat on low. He was wearing a safari rain hat. Janet thought the hat was overkill even in this weather. Why would he need a hat with the fur-lined hood attached to his parka? Janet turned up the heat full blast.

"Not many do," Choinski said to Janet's response with a playful grin.

"You look warm and dry," Janet said almost accusatorily.

"The van was parked inside when I loaded it," Choinski said matter-of-factly. "I got in and drove straight here."

"Lucky you."

Choinski uttered a humph. "I wouldn't go that far," he said with a smirk.

Choinski turned serious. He handed Janet a folded sheet of paper. Janet unfolded the paper and took a good look. It was a printed list of the items Janet had emailed him a couple of days prior. The same list of essentials Janet had gotten from Abílo Vilar that he would need for the Berge Building job.

"I've gotten everything you asked for," Choinski said.

"Any problems?" Janet asked.

"None."

"Good. I'll let you know if we need any additional materials."

Choinski's expression changed without warning. His face went from playful to depressed in the snap of a finger. Janet noticed. Choinski suddenly looked like a brooding child. As if someone had given him the worst news of his life. That was unlike the Gerek Choinski she knew. The man who was tough, cautious and professional.

"Something wrong?" Janet asked.

"What did you make of that Cavanaugh guy?" Choinski asked. They had not discussed C. J. Cavanaugh since the incident.

"I think he is what he claimed to be," Janet said, confirming what they had agreed upon at the time. "An insurance investigator checking up on your back injury claim, which reminds me. Call in sick whenever you need to take time off from your job to conduct any of our business. Don't use the back excuse from here on out. Make it the flu or a cold or something. Be creative. We pay you enough that missing a day or two's pay won't hurt. We don't want a heavy weight like Lunsford Insurance snooping around asking questions."

Choinski nodded. Janet was convinced what she said about Cavanaugh was true. Her running into Cavanaugh at Holland Jenkins' surprise party had made her anxious. Janet made discrete inquiries about Cavanaugh at the party. She discovered he was an exceptional private investigator and ex-DEA before their introduction. Janet tried avoiding Cavanaugh, moving around the crowded room, using people as human barriers. Cognizant of his line of sight. Janet had not realized Cavanaugh spotted her until he was standing in front of her. Cavanaugh never let on they had met, never hinted at the circumstances by which they had. She had wondered why. What was his angle? Gerek did not know about her attending the party. Janet felt no need to share information about Cavanagh's second run-in. Or that she attended the party with FBI Agent Aloisio Reis. The less Choinski knew about such matters, the better.

"You don't think he knows anything about Firestorm?" Choinski asked. "Or our connection to them?"

"I seriously doubt it. Firestorm will handle him if he does." Janet didn't know if her last statement was true. She simply assumed Firestorm would take whatever necessary measures to keep their organization a secret.

"I don't feel good about this," Choinski said. His tone as sour as his expression.

"What's the problem?" Janet asked. "You're making easy money and nobody's getting hurt."

"There's nothing easy about stealing from people who trust you."

"Where was this remorse when you were stealing from these people who trust you to cover your gambling debts?"

"It was there," said Choinski, shifting uneasily in his seat.

"That didn't stop you from stealing."

Choinski had nothing to say.

"You agreed to be our supplier. If you want to terminate this arrangement, say the word, and we're done."

Choinski remained silent. The van heat had chased away Janet's chill and was drying her jeans. Choinski was sweating. Janet had unfastened her jacket. Janet turned down the heat halfway. She reached inside her jacket and unzipped a concealed pocket within the lining.

"Here." Janet handed Choinski a dry as a bone, sealed manila envelope with forty-thousand dollars in it. "Maybe this will help drive away your blues."

Choinski had insisted on receiving his payments in cash. He took the envelope and shoved it into one of the inside pockets of his parka.

"This van is clean?" Janet asked, her tone dipping back to professional.

"Yes. The registered owner has been dead for a couple of years."

"You arranged for the phony vehicle registration papers yourself?"

"Yes."

"With no guilt?"

Choinski looked away. "Some crimes are victimless."

"Like the one you're committing right now," Janet said. "Remember that."

There was a pregnant moment of uneasy quiet between the shady business partners. Janet's brought on by irritation. Gerek's influenced by shame. The rain beat against the van like BBs being dropped from heaven. Choinski got out. The rush of cold he let in was like opening a freezer on a warm summer day. Janet slid over into the driver's seat.

"Maybe you should take a break," Janet said, sounding and feeling more sympathetic. "Go on a vacation with your wife and kids. We'll be here when you get back. I'll understand if you still want to quit."

"But will *they* understand?"

Janet knew Choinski was referring to Firestorm. She had no idea how the organization would react to his desire to quit. That was beyond her scope of knowledge or influence. Their arrangement was simple. Choinski was her supplier. Janet made certain Choinski filled her order to the letter. Janet delivered the materials to her arsonist. Choinski had been excellent at maintaining his end of their agreement. It made Janet wonder. Was his stealing from his employer the source of his newfound guilt? Or was the sudden emergence of this unknown element C. J. Cavanaugh rooted in his distress?

Choinski didn't seem to notice the weather. He stood there. His parka still open. He hadn't even bothered to flip up his fur-lined hood.

"Button up before you catch your death of cold," Janet said, quoting her mother's advice to her on many occasions. Janet wasn't into giving out motherly advice to adults. This situation seemed to merit an exception to that rule. Choinski blankly stared at her.

"Take it easy, Gerek."

"I'll take it any way I can get it."

Rather old school for a man Gerek's age, Janet thought. A reply one of her uncle's often offered when given that advice. It always made Janet laugh when he said it, delivering the line with the right amount of zeal and hint of mischief, sometimes following up with his sidesplitting laughter, reacting as if it were an impulsive response. Over time, Janet realized it was the joy behind his clichéd retort that made her and others laugh. No matter how many times they heard him say it.

Janet saw none of that joy in Gerek Choinski's attempt at humor. She could not recall Choinski saying or doing anything before that she could classify as old school. Maybe she didn't know Gerek as well as she thought. Janet stared at Gerek for a long moment. Gerek attempted a smile that resulted in no more than a nervous tick. The wind had ceased, but the cold rain was still coming down. Gerek closed the driver's door and took a step back away from the van. Janet turned back up the heat. She adjusted the driver's seat forward. Janet checked her side view mirrors. Gerek was looking in her direction, but Janet doubted he saw her. Janet put the van in drive and eased away. She checked her driver's side view mirror out of curiosity as she took her time exiting the parking lot. Gerek Choinski hadn't moved. Shoulders slumped, head drooping as if unhinged with rain pouring off the brim of his safari hat. A statue of a broken man. In search of his soul in the frigid puddles of water pooling at his feet.

CHAPTER TWENTY-THREE

I resist taking Andrew and Booker with me in inclement weather on my morning runs out of concern that my twin terriers might get sick. Most times, I dressed appropriately and still did the runs on my own. This morning I did not. The torrential rain was cold and a threat to freeze. As the saying goes, the type of rain that chilled you to the bone. I hit the office treadmill for my morning jog instead.

I was anticipating a low-key next few days. All of my outstanding investigative work involved routine background checks, mostly online research, phone calls, and emails accompanied by paperwork with no fieldwork I could foresee, checking them off one by one as I closed them. That was fine by me. I didn't mind staying put in this kind of weather. While I was still reading and responding as needed to Renita's daily emails, I was becoming accustomed to working solo, rediscovering my PI roots, if you will, finding my old rhythm. My focus was sharp and clear, with fewer distractions and teaching sessions, as was my efficiency. I still missed Renita handling the virtual paperwork, which was the original reason I hired her. I had returned to plowing through such necessities as quickly I had done before.

I was eating lunch, enjoying the piano genius of Smoky Jenkins, reading an online article on the dire effects of the Amazon Rain Forest fires upon the environment when the front door opened. I looked up to an odd surprise. Fire Marshall Zane Holloman dressed in civilian clothes, FBI Special Agent Aloisio Reis, and the artist known as Janet Proctor walked in together. I turned off the music. I greeted my guests in the reception area and instructed them to deposit their dripping rain gear on the coat rack. Once again, no umbrellas. A northwest thing.

After we dispensed with the pleasantries, I served each hot coffee of their choosing. We sat in my office, where we got down to business.

"Sorry to disturb your lunch, C. J.," Zane said.

"No problem." I closed the plastic container containing my lunch and set it off to the side. A homemade salmon salad. "What do I owe the honor of this visit?"

"First of all, allow me to introduce you to FBI Special Agent Sarah Nelson," Aloisio said.

I smiled as I reached across my desk to shake Sarah's hand. "A pleasure. Is that your real name or another stage name?"

"It's genuine," Sarah said. "You don't seem surprised to discover I'm an FBI agent."

"I would be if I had only met you at Smoky's party. Having encountered you before with Gerek Choinski, I figured something was up. What's the deal with you and Gerek Choinski?"

"Gambling debts," Sarah said. "Cards mostly."

"To whom?"

"Here and there. Aidan Madigan enlisted Gerek Choinski. Had Firestorm pay off his gambling debts and placed Choinski on their payroll. Without their financial intervention, Mr. Choinski was on a steady decline toward self-destruction that awaits all gambling addicts who don't find help. Choinski is their local supplier. Anything an arsonist needs, he provides with no paper trail. I was just getting to know him better when you barged in."

"Sorry about that. Just doing my job."

"We both were," Sarah said.

"Excuse me," I said. "Firestorm? Gambling debts? Arson? Local supplier? Aidan Madigan? Someone want to tell me what this is about?"

"We want to hire you, C. J.," Aloisio said.

"For what?"

"We want you to go undercover."

"*Excuse me?*"

"We know you worked undercover with the DEA," Sarah said.

"We want you to put those skills to use for our operation," Aloisio added.

"What operation?"

"We'll get to that if you agree to take the job."

"Why not use one of your people, Aloisio?"

They looked uneasily at each other. Aloisio spoke. "We may have a leak or two in our departments regarding the people we're trying to capture."

I eyed the three of them. They appeared embarrassed by the admission.

"I don't do undercover anymore," I said.

"What we're proposing is simple and straight forward," Sarah said.

"Sounds too good to be true, Sarah."

"It isn't, C. J.," Sarah said.

"We just need someone to make first contact," Aloisio added.

"Like aliens from another planet first contact?"

"Like arsonists," Zane said.

That got my attention. It also explained why Zane was involved. "Go on."

"You've heard about the recent rash of building fires in our area?" Zane asked.

"Half of which were arson according to the press."

"All of them were arson, in my opinion," Zane said. "Only half we could prove. The provable cases were unique because the arsonist did not attempt to cover his tracks. They wanted it known it was arson."

"As some sort of extortionist scheme?" I asked.

"No," Sarah said to my question. "The owners of those buildings were fully reimbursed. It didn't matter whether it was arson or not."

"As long as the owners are innocent of collusion," I said.

"Collusion is difficult to prove," Zane said. "Most fires involving the people we're after are revenge or clearance arsons."

"Clearance arsons?" I asked.

"In some cases, it's cheaper for an owner to have the building torched than to pay demolition and disposal costs," Zane responded.

"Sarah, was your fire artist ploy at Smoky's party some sort of deliberate hint at the truth," I asked, "or were you simply winging it?"

"A little of both, I suppose."

I'm always curious how other undercover operators think when forced to improvise. Sarah's answer was what I would expect from a good agent.

"We've come to learn that these arsonists are recruited through an organization," Aloisio said.

"Local, regional, national or international?" I asked.

"National from what we've been able to determine," Aloisio said. "We can link their involvement with arsons in New York City, Philadelphia,

Atlanta, Cleburne, Miami, L. A., Lexington, Denver, Seattle, Portland, and another forty locations across the country."

"And those are just the ones we know about," Zane said.

"Why not set a trap?" I asked.

"You mean like hire them to do a job then arrest them," Aloisio said.

"Exactly."

The three of them laughed.

"Tried and failed four times," Sarah said.

"Five, actually," Aloisio corrected. "Don't forget about the Baltimore bust."

"Oh right," Sarah said.

"What happened in Baltimore?" I asked.

"Nothing good that's what made it a bust," Sarah said.

"A new agent on his first infiltration mission," Aloisio said. "He was made in less than five minutes."

"Sounds more like four and a fifth," I said.

"If that," Aloisio said.

"Any organized crime affiliations?" I asked.

"None that we can see," Aloisio said. Sarah and Zane shook their heads.

"They have an interesting mandate we only discovered recently, thanks to Sarah," Zane said.

"No one is to be physically harmed due to one of their fires," Sarah said.

"Have they been able to keep that mandate?" I asked.

"Far as we know," Sarah said.

"They value human life but have little regard for property," I said.

"Has an anti-capitalist ring to it, doesn't it?" Zane said.

"I disagree," Sarah interjected. "The arsonist I have been working with has not breathed a word against capitalism. He approaches what he does like a regular job. No different from a laborer reporting for their nine to five. Arson happens to be his skillset. He is very good at it. He's plying his trade for maximum profit. He's more of a hardcore capitalist than any of us, if anything."

"Is he a pyromaniac?" I asked.

"Not in the least," Sarah said.

"Where did he learn his trade?" I asked.

"Some in the military," Sarah said. "Other than that he's not saying."

"He works for an organization that connects their clients with their incendiary needs," Zane said.

"And he's not alone," Sarah added.

"A professional staffing agency for arsonists?" I said.

"Precisely," Aloisio said. "They call themselves Firestorm."

"Nothing subtle about that," I said.

"Operating exclusively on the dark web," Aloisio said, "they don't have to be."

"We know the arsonist responsible for the Cronus fire," Sarah said. "And who was behind it."

"Thanks to the stellar undercover work of Agent Nelson," Aloisio beamed. "We've gotten closer than ever before."

"I can't arrest him, of course," Sarah said. "He's our rope ladder to people at the top. I haven't been able to win enough trust from upper management for that final push."

"Did you know Aidan Madigan is involved with Firestorm?" Aloisio asked.

It turned out Carl Wheaton had not intended for us to look into the Aidan Madigan case. That item had already been cleared. The assistant who forwarded our agency that batch of assignments accidently mixed the Aidan Madigan case file with the rest. Carl had apologized. He said he would personally vet what cases we received from here on out. I appreciated Carl's vigor, although I was grateful it was a mistake.

"The same Aidan Madigan who is suffering from a horrific car accident?" I asked.

Sarah and Aloisio nodded. "We had him under surveillance," Aloisio said.

"Madigan was on his way to a meeting with an arsonist," Aloisio continued. "The same one who torched the Cronus building when the accident happened. We used the unfortunate incident to interject Sarah into the picture."

"I took Madigan's place as the intermediator between Firestorm, arsonist, and contractor."

"Does Mrs. Madigan know what her husband is involved in?"

"She hasn't a clue," Aloisio said. "Madigan Engineering was hemorrhaging money. Aidan Madigan became involved with Firestorm to save his company. His primary function was to provide Firestorm with building layouts. Aidan Madigan was recently promoted to a Firestorm intermediary as well.

We were able to enter Madigan's residence and tap into his computer and laptop to find everything he had on Firestorm while his family was awaiting Aidan's fate at the hospital. It was quite a coup."

"Talk about kicking someone when they're down," I said.

"Take it up with the universe," Aloisio said. "We saw an opportunity and we took it."

I could not disagree.

"There's no face or voice time with these people," Sarah said. "They deal in data streams and text communications. Except when it comes to recruiting their fire talent."

"That's where you come in, C. J.," Aloisio said.

"You can help stamp out Firestorm," Zane said.

"That's as far as we are willing to go," Aloisio said. "Until we know you are all in."

"What do you need me to do?"

"We need you to make a solid connection with the people running the show," Aloisio said. "Once you're in, we'll take it from there."

The three of them stared at me as if they were waiting for permission to breathe. I thought about how this decision could affect Shelly's situation. I thought about Destini and our conversation on the way back to her place after our dinner with the Sabas. I assured Destini I would not return to doing DEA undercover ops. This was different. The FBI needed my help. Shelly needed me more. I was leaning toward a soft no when a thought reoccurred to me, *surveillance*. I couldn't go to Patrick without raising a red flag. The last thing Shelly needed right now was the DEA sniffing around his already dicey situation. Thompson would be of no help after our last run in. That left Aloisio.

"I'll think about it. How soon do you need this to happen?"

"Last week," Aloisio said.

I looked at my computer monitor. Staring at the background report almost made me yawn. "Give me twenty-four hours."

"Mind if I ask why you need the twenty-four?" Aloisio asked.

"There's something I need to take care of before I can give you a definite answer."

Aloisio nodded. Zane and Sarah stared at me as if attempting to will me into changing my mind.

"We'll see you back here in twenty-four hours then," Aloisio said.

They showed themselves out looking like three moping teenagers having been assigned a month's detention. Smoky and I picked up where we left off. I returned to reading the Amazon Rain Forest article and enjoying my salmon salad.

CHAPTER TWENTY-FOUR

Aloisio Reis is the FBI Special Agent in charge of the Portland office. That means he has unencumbered access to all information generated under his command. In under an hour after Aloisio, Zane, and Sarah left, I texted Aloisio, asking him to circle back to meet with me alone in my office. Emphasizing it was urgent and urging him to keep my request confidential. Aloisio was seated across the desk from me in less than ten minutes.

"Have you come to a decision about our offer?" Aloisio asked before his butt hit the seat.

"That depends," I said.

"On what?"

"Am I right in assuming the FBI is keeping tabs on Quentin Drayton?" I asked.

Aloisio leaned in. Wary but captivated, he asked, "Quentin Drayton? What does he have to do with anything?"

"Drayton's involved in a very sensitive case I'm working on. I could use as much information on him as I can get in a hurry."

"I see," Aloisio said. "What exactly is this case you're working on, C. J.?"

"Confidential."

"And I thought I was tight-lipped."

"Sorry, Aloisio. I can't tell you who my client is. Their reputation depends on my ability to be discreet."

"Without that information, I can't even consider helping you, C. J." Aloisio leaned back in his chair. I was in no position to make demands. Aloisio would find a way to make his operation happen without me if push came to shove. It all hinged on how badly he wanted me on the Firestorm case. Bargaining was still my best option.

"I will say this about this particular case," I said. "The person I'm trying to free from Drayton's tyranny means a lot to his community and the city of Portland."

"I don't care if it's the mayor of Portland. I still can't help you, C. J."

"Another way of putting it, my friend, is that without that information, you'll need to find someone else for your undercover op."

I was all in. Aloisio thought long and hard. He was sizing me up in the process. We had known each other long enough that at least he believed he knew when I was bluffing. I wasn't.

"Drayton's bad news, C. J. You sure you want to tangle with him?"

"No choice," I said. Aloisio didn't budge. He needed another push. "The worst that will come out of my proposal is that you get me for your undercover operation *and* possibly Quentin Drayton off the streets. That's a win-win in my book."

"You can do something the DEA, FBI, and local narcotics can't?"

"I have some ideas that might work." My ideas were long shots at best. The question I was expecting Aloisio to ask himself was, what did he have to lose?

"Exactly what do you need from the FBI?" Aloisio asked with the glint of intrigue in his eyes.

"Copies of everything your surveillance teams have gathered on Quentin Drayton and his associates. I mean video, photos, audio, transcripts, the works for the last few months. Not the redacted versions either."

"That information is classified, C. J. I can't go handing it out to any civilian who asks for it like they were Halloween treats."

Yet you have no trouble asking this same civilian to go undercover on a possibly dangerous FBI operation, I thought but didn't say. There was no sense rocking the boat. "Do you want me on this case, Aloisio?"

"Of course."

"Then all of the surveillance information you have on Quentin Drayton for the last few months has to be part of our deal."

"You're asking a lot, C. J."

"I wouldn't be asking if it wasn't vitally important."

"How do I know I can trust you? If I hand over this information, it won't come back and bite me in the nuts?"

"I give you my word that it won't."

"Your word is good. Will it be for your eyes only?"

"Yes."

Aloisio nodded. "In exchange, you're on-board for as long we need you on this case."

"I'm fine with that arrangement," I said.

There was a long pause. Aloisio's hard stare returned. I had been where he was several times with various players on both sides of the law. So had Aloisio. His mind was racing through as many scenarios as he could fathom. He was attempting to determine the most likely developments and consequences on how this might play out.

"You drive a hard bargain, C. J."

"This is a tough business, my friend."

"I'll have the information ready for you by this evening," Aloisio said.

I suppressed a rush of excitement. "Drop it by my place no matter the time," I said.

"I hope this person is worth it."

"They are in my book," I said. *Yours too if you knew who he was*, I thought. "This agreement goes no further than this room."

"Understood."

"No one else is to know about this, Aloisio. Not even Karen and Zane."

"I have no problem with that C. J. My ass is on the line here. I hope you grasp the gravity of what you're asking me to do. If I'm found out, it could cost me my job, my career, and possibly land me in prison."

"Believe me, I know. You can trust me, Aloisio. You know from personal experience that I am the soul of discretion." I was referring to a case I had done for Aloisio that required the utmost secrecy. Until this day, only he and I knew anything about what was involved.

"Show up with Karen and Zane as planned tomorrow," I said, "and I will make my joining your Firestorm team official. You can pretend this is the first you've learned of my decision."

"I will. Don't let me down, C. J. If any of this leaks…."

"It won't," I said.

"If this does go south, I'm throwing you under the bus. Just so you know."

"You won't have to, Aloisio. I'll lay down on the street in front of it." I said it and I meant it. This gamble was all mine. Nobody else was going to get hurt from my roll of the dice if I could help it.

"As long as we understand each other," Aloisio said.

We shook on it. Aloisio left. I was confident he was still hashing over what we had discussed. There was a chance Aloisio would change his mind about our agreement. My faith was teetering on the fact that Aloisio needed me for the Firestorm case enough that he would take the gamble.

That evening Aloisio dropped off the information I requested. He declined my invitation to stay for dinner.

CHAPTER TWENTY-FIVE

Aloisio and his team had generated a believable background for me. They placed the particulars into the system: my tax returns, employment history, military record, school transcripts, birthday, and social security number. They weren't kidding when they said they wanted it done last week. I only had three days to prepare.

Jarrett Cameron Holton, an only child, was born, bred, and educated in Harrisburg, Pennsylvania, to Hank and Regina Holton, an office worker and manual laborer. Joined the Army after graduating high school. I specialized in incendiary devices as a member of a field artillery brigade. After an honorable discharge from the Army, I found work in a stockyard before becoming a fireman in the Campbell County Fire Department in Gillette, Wyoming. Never married or fathered children. I was discharged from the fire department and accused of torching an office building for money. I was set up, my punishment for having an affair with the Fire Marshall's wife. I fought the charges, sued the city for wrongful termination, and won a settlement of five million dollars. I was never offered back my job. I took the money and left Wyoming.

I moved around the country, never settling in any place for more than a few years. I made good use of my settlement and didn't need to work. A string of unsolved fires arose every place I lived. They were suspected arsons but could never be proven. No arsonist was ever connected to the fires. I was never a member of any suspect pool by local authorities. I did the fires for profit. No one was hurt, and I enjoyed it.

Aloisio grilled me on my cover, listening for slipups. No problem; my cover was simple and solid. That was the easy part.

Zane gave me a crash course on arson. Arson is the malicious and intentional burning or scorching of property. There are six motivations for arson. Revenge, insurance claims, exhilaration, vandalism, crime-concealment, and pyromania. All of which fall under the category of an arson crime. The majority of arson crimes involve damage to buildings. Arson is typically classified as a felony due to the potential to cause injuries or death. States handle arson cases in different ways. Most states classify arson into different categories factoring in intent, the value of the property, along with resultant injuries or loss of life. Conviction on a more serious degree could result in the death penalty. Lesser infractions may result in minor punishments.

Zane also broke down the various methods in the professional arsonists' handbook. Meticulous methods I will not go into detail here. It is sufficient to say. Their techniques combined a working knowledge of physics, chemistry, and engineering to be applied in a controlled fashion to achieve a precise incendiary outcome.

After my arson tutelage, I could recite details from the arson handbook almost verbatim but had little genuine grasp of their content. In other words, I knew the jargon. I would have no trouble convincing my targets on the verbal and written exams. I was a wash if it came to any sort of real life demonstration.

CHAPTER TWENTY-SIX

Firestorm made all of my travel arrangements. They booked a one-bedroom at the Four Seasons Hotel in downtown Denver, Colorado. I was to text them once I had settled in, which I did. There was a knock on my door moments after I sent the text. I asked who it was.

"Room service," a male voice said. I hadn't ordered room service. I checked through the peephole. A uniformed bellhop stood there holding a covered plate in his white-gloved hands, white male, around thirty, thick mustache, short brown hair, brown eyes, and a deadpan expression. I doubted he was planning to kill me. Why bring someone all of this way simply to murder them? I checked my 92F Beretta in my concealed shoulder holster just in case before letting him in.

Five-eight and lean like a long distance runner. He immediately closed and locked the door behind him before he spoke. "Mr. Holton?"

"Yes."

Aloisio had cleared overseeing this operation with the FBI Denver office. He had his people fit me with an invisible micro earpiece and a pin camera that appeared no different from any of my other shirt buttons when I arrived in Denver before I checked in. "Audio and visual are working perfectly," I heard the crystal clear voice of Aloisio confirm through my earpiece.

"I'm your Firestorm contact," Deadpan said.

"Your name is?"

"Contact will suffice."

"Your name is Contact?"

"As far as this meeting is concerned, yes. My name is Contact."

"Is that your first or last name?"

"It's my only name," Contact said, maintaining his deadpan expression. I noticed a couple of tattoos on his neck. Contact didn't seem to mind my noticing. He removed the plate cover. On the plate was a large screen smartphone. I picked it up.

"We'll be in touch," he said. Then left.

"Nice meeting you," I wanted to say as he exited but kept my sarcasm to myself.

"Looks like you're in," Aloisio said. I did not respond.

"Can you hear me?" Aloisio asked. I put the Firestorm smartphone on mute, depositing it into an empty dresser drawer, nonchalantly leaving my room.

I exited the Four Seasons and headed southwest on 14th St. toward Lawrence St. I strolled around the area, appearing to be window-shopping and taking in the sights. Sidewalk footing was tenuous. There were short barriers of firm powder shoveled off to street side. The sky was clear. Cold but not windy. I came prepared for winter's worst with a fleece-lined parka, wool gloves, and trapper hat. All the while ignoring Aloisio's badgering me to respond. The irritation in his voice slid into concern. I double-backed, picking up my pace, heading along 16th St. onto Arapahoe St., dog-legging southwest onto 17th. Within ten minutes, I was in Room 403 at the Magnolia Hotel.

"They probably have eyes and ears in my hotel room," I said to Aloisio. "That's why I didn't respond."

"Roger that," Aloisio said, sounding relieved. "That may be where our agents made their mistake."

"Possibly."

"That's why you wanted another room under a different name."

"As a precaution. Why else bother picking out the room? Didn't I mention that?"

"No, you said booking another room would give us a safe rendezvous place if needed."

"That too. I didn't spot any tails. I'm betting we're safe. You heard what was said?"

"And saw it too. Looks like we're in."

"Contact said 'we'll be in touch,'" I said. "That probably means some sort of clearance or approval is still required."

"Makes sense," Aloisio said. "I put a tail on Contact. He headed straight for a van in the hotel parking lot, took off heading east. We have a car following him."

"Sounds good."

"What now, C. J.?"

"I'll grab a bite to eat then head back to my hotel room."

"Why not head straight back? Eat in your room."

"If I'm right about my room, I'm going to need a good excuse why I left."

"We're not dealing with hardcore drug dealers here, C. J. As far as we know, they haven't physically hurt or killed anyone."

"As far as you know, Aloisio. Drug dealers aren't the only people killing people out here. Attention to detail has kept me alive this long. I don't plan on changing now."

"Understood. Will you be radio silent except for the Magnolia hotel room?"

"For the time being. That doesn't mean you can't continue to listen and watch, of course."

"Of course."

"I'd better go. Leave a fish dangling on the hook for too long, and they're bound to slip away."

CHAPTER TWENTY-SEVEN

3:14 p.m. Portland, Oregon, Saturday

Torching the abandoned Berge Building was going to be easier in one respect than the Cronus Building for Abílo Vilar. Clearing out squatters represented the biggest challenge. The last thing he wanted was to be responsible for loss of human life. A police presence was not constant. As long as none of the squatters posed a general safety risk to the public or themselves, they were left alone.

Abílo had been posing as a squatter for a few days to discover the hiding places the actual squatters and vagrants used. Early in the day, when all vagrants and squatters were out scavenging, Abílo sprayed the interior of the building with mercaptan, the rotten egg odor added to natural gas. Upon returning and smelling the foul stench, most squatters evacuated. A stubborn few remained, possessing a death wish or foolish determination to take their chances against the apparent gas leak threat.

Abílo marched through the building wearing a natural gas employee uniform, hardhat, reflective yellow safety vest, and phony ID dangling from around his neck, announcing through a bullhorn that there was a reported gas leak in the building. Everyone had five minutes to clear out. Anyone still occupying the building after that would be arrested. That was enough of a warning for even the staunchest to heed. Abílo doubted any of the occupants suspected his ruse. It was a risk. One he was confident would pay off.

The client preferred the fire to look like an accident. The client was adamant about it not leading back to him if arson was to blame. "Didn't they all feel that way?" Abílo told Janet Proctor when she relayed to Abílo that fact. Janet laughed. Abílo liked her laugh even more than her smile.

With everything in place, Abílo made a final pass through the Berge Building with a high beam flashlight and wearing a gas mask. The gas mask offered Abílo a perfect disguise while lending legitimacy to his ploy. Graffiti was everywhere. If any of it was gang-related, Abílo couldn't tell.

Abílo saw a leg sticking out of a partially open closet door on the first floor, no socks, tattered shoes, and pants. Abílo walked over and opened the door. A man was passed out, slumped down like an abandoned marionette on the floor. Abílo recognized him. Other vagrants called him Dolt. Abílo never found out why. Somebody who fell on hard times and never got up. Dolt would drink just about anything. Whatever intoxicant would anesthetize his burdens. Dolt never used drugs. He would curse anyone out who offered them to him. Threaten to beat them senseless even though he couldn't beat a rug.

Abílo kicked Dolt, not hard but enough to wake him. Dolt didn't move. He looked closely at the drunk. *Was he asleep or in a coma?* Abílo thought.

Abílo removed his gas mask. Dolt smelled like shit. "Dolt!" Abílo slapped Dolt's face. "Dolt! Let's go, buddy!"

Dolt still did not move. Abílo checked his vitals. His skin was rough as sandpaper, grimy and ice cold. There was no pulse. Dolt was dead.

Abílo's immediate reaction was sadness. He knew very little about Dolt. He had watched Dolt talking to himself or to anyone who would listen throughout the abandoned Berge Building about incomprehensible events and people in his life, frequently blubbering as he did. Abílo had felt sorry for him. Dolt seemed tortured. Abílo had wondered what personal tragedies Dolt carried that forced him down this wretched road in his life. Abílo never provided an ear. Staying clear of people like Dolt was necessary for his cover. Being around people like Dolt would draw undue attention to himself. He hoped Dolt's soul found peace in death this world had not allowed.

Abílo could leave him. It would look like he perished in the fire. It might also direct the blame for the fire on Dolt. Abílo threw Dolt over his shoulder and carried him out fireman style. Abílo had put back on his gas mask. He would have smelled the stench of cheap whiskey and wine reeking from Dolt's open mouth had he not. The corpse farted.

"I should leave you here for that you bastard," Abílo said as much to himself as to the dead man.

Abílo carried Dolt outside and laid him to rest a safe distance away from the impending destruction. Dolt drooled on his safety vest. It wasn't raining, but the weather was cold and damp. Abílo ran back inside the building. He found a weatherproof tarp and wrapped Dolt in it. *That should keep the rats away until help arrives,* he thought. Finding a dead man outside a suspicious fire was nothing but trouble. Abílo knew the discovery would draw unwanted police attention. Abílo couldn't explain why he did it, only that it seemed right. Abílo believed that as long as he stayed clear of the matter, all would be well in the end once the smoke cleared. *Who knows?* He thought. *Dolt still might be blamed for the fire.*

The back of the Berge Building was out of sight. It was where he parked and laid Dolt to rest. The main gas supply was in the back as well. The gas had been shut off and access to the valve locked. The natural gas supply lines remained in place for future tenants. Abílo cut the lock and used a crescent wrench to reopen the long lines enough to fill the building with the accelerant. Fire inspectors would uncover the source of the fire. Squatters were resourceful. They would take the blame for reopening the lines.

Abílo ran over to an unmarked panel van. He removed his gear, including the safety vest smelling of Dolt, and tossed them along with his tools into the back of the van. Abílo jumped in on the driver's side. He grabbed a panel of toggle switches from the passenger seat. While posing as a vagrant, Abílo had placed miniature charges throughout the Berge Building to create enough sparks to ignite the gas. Abílo switched on the panel. A green light glowed above each toggle. The micro explosives were receiving their signal. Abílo was not concerned about evidence from the explosives being discovered by fire inspectors. Whatever tiny fragments remained after ignition would be consumed by the flames.

Abílo flipped the first toggle after one last quick visual check to ensure all was clear. A muffled explosion followed by a huge black and orange ball of flame erupted from the top floor. Abílo waited ten seconds between detonating the remaining charges, one at a time. The place went up like a tinderbox. Flames burst from lower floors in sequence, bulldozing from front to back and top to bottom. In minutes there would be nothing left of the building. The way Abílo had arranged the triggers, he expected the Berge Building to collapse inward. The fire department should have no problem keeping the flames from spreading. The gas would burn off quickly, aiding firefighters in their goal.

Abílo drove the van to the partially covered Lloyd Center Garage about ten miles away, passing two speeding fire trucks with sirens blaring in the opposite direction. He parked the van in a vacant spot farthest from the

Lloyd Center mall entrance on Level D. He grabbed a couple of Lloyd Center shopping bags from the passenger floor. They were filled with men's clothes he purchased at the mall a couple of days prior. Abílo jumped out and took a picture of the van. Leaving the van unlocked and the keys in the glove compartment. He texted the picture and location to Janet. Someone would be along to pick up the van and dispose of it soon.

Abílo took his time making his way down to Level B. Carrying his shopping bags and pretending to be preoccupied with his phone. Janet had texted him a picture of his getaway car an hour before he torched the Berge Building. The three-year-old, burgundy, two-door sedan was parked exactly where the text message said it would be. Abílo had wanted a motorcycle. Janet nixed that idea. She thought it might be too conspicuous. Abílo got in the burgundy car and headed for home. He would anonymously drop off his purchases later at a homeless shelter.

CHAPTER TWENTY-EIGHT

I retrieved the Firestorm phone from the dresser drawer upon my return. I had an incoming call. I answered.

"Where were you?" I recognized the voice as Contact. He sounded angry.

"I stepped out for a bite."

"You need to keep your phone with you 24-7!"

"Sorry. Carrying around two phones didn't make much sense to me. I figured you'd leave a message. I could get back to you."

"That's not how it works! You're on call. This is the only phone you will need from now on. That's part of our arrangement. It's non-negotiable! Are you alone?"

"Yes," I answered. Suspecting he already knew the answer.

"Turn on your speaker."

I turned on the phone's speaker.

"Take a look at your phone."

I looked at my screen. "Okay?" I said.

"You will notice apps popping up like popcorn right now."

"What's that about?"

"Not your concern for the moment. We will notify you which apps to use and when."

"When?"

"When we're ready. Go about your life as normal in the meantime. We'll be in touch when your services are required."

"Don't you want to know anything about me?"

"We already know everything we need to know about you, Mr. Holton. We wouldn't be having this conversation if you hadn't been cleared."

"Thanks, I think?"

"Do you have any questions, Mr. Holton?"

"Yes. How do I get paid?"

I heard a faint chuckle. The kind some people give when they are feeling satisfied by a response. "All will become clear when the time comes," Contact said. "From here on out, all of our communication will be text or email. Is that clear?"

"Yes. How did you find out about me?"

Contact hung up without an answer.

They were watching and listening all right. I securitized my new phone. I was confident they saw this as a common reaction from all of their new recruits. After a few minutes of examining the smartphone, I unmuted the phone and put it down on the sofa table behind the sofa.

I sat on the sofa and turned on the big screen TV. Found an interesting—yet disturbing—Nat Geo report on Animal Extinction.

"The last mass distinction, which did in the dinosaurs some 66 million years ago," the somber voice of the narrator intoned, "followed an asteroid impact. Today the cause of extinction seems more diffuse. It's logging and poaching and introduced pathogens and climate change and overfishing and ocean acidification."

I took a good look around the room. There were several places they could have placed hidden audio and video surveillance devices. I pulled out my FBI secure phone. I was confident that they could not see my FBI phone home screen from where I was sitting.

Renita had been educating me more and more on modern technology. My partner prefers texting to phone conversations. I have become adroit at texting working with Renita. My texting had spilled over from my professional to my personal life. Once word got out, I was on board. Friends and family were now texting instead of calling. I don't care for that. I still favor face-to-face or phone conversations, in that order. My sweetheart Destini feels as I do. I don't read or respond quickly enough to texts outside of work in most cases. Most of my texters will follow up their text message with a call if it's important, usually leading with complaints about me not responding to their text. So be it. The texting tidal wave I was the initial recipient of has been receding into the pool of old-school phone conversations or personal. I was adapting the modern world to my whims instead of the other way around.

I reacted as if reading an amusing text message I had just received. I texted Aloisio to ask if he overheard my phone conversation with Contact.

He had heard every word when we were on speaker. I filled him in verbatim on the conversation that preceded. He thanked me but had nothing to add. Anyone watching me would see a person alternating between being engrossed in the National Geo report or texting, which is normal behavior these days.

I put the FBI phone down and gave my complete attention to the TV report when I was done texting. Now came the waiting, the hardest part.

CHAPTER TWENTY-NINE

I didn't have long to wait. Firestorm booked my flight home for the following morning. I was landing at PDX by early afternoon. The FBI had set up a condominium for me in Vancouver, Washington, just across the northern border of Oregon. The place was clean of any bugs or surveillance and under constant FBI protection. Aloisio, Sarah, and FBI Undercover Operative Horace Chandler were waiting for me when I arrived. Horace was my clone minus my chin scar, new beard and a few years.

"Horace will be taking over your end of the operation, C. J.," Aloisio said.

"I figured as much," I said.

"A pleasure to meet you, Mr. Cavanaugh," Horace said as we shook hands. I couldn't help staring at him. The resemblance was remarkable. My brothers didn't look as much like me as he did.

The one-bedroom condo was tastefully furnished with a charcoal living room set that I wouldn't mind taking home with me. We took a seat. Sarah and Aloisio sat on the sofa. Horace sat on the love seat. I sat across from them in the armchair. I had handed over the Firestorm smartphone to Aloisio without being asked.

"Horace and I had a chance to check out your surveillance footage," Sarah said as we made ourselves comfortable. Horace smiled and nodded. "Impressive," Sarah continued. "The way you improvised. Not many agents could have pulled that off."

"You could have," I said.

"Probably," Sarah said.

We gave each other knowing smiles. I am never offended or intimidated by confident people. That's your choice if you choose to flaunt it. Those who talk the talk but not walk the walk are the ones who annoy me.

"Is there anything more you can tell us about their organization from what you observed?" Aloisio asked me.

"Nothing you don't already know: well organized, precise, thorough and high tech oriented was my impression. Contact had a couple of tattoos on his neck. A charging bull on one side. A matador on the other. Do those mean anything to you?" I asked Sarah.

"Nothing comes to mind," she said. "My mark has an Aztec warrior tattoo on his right arm. Nothing on his neck."

"I think we can rule out tattoos being any sort of group insignia," Aloisio said. "If that's what you're getting at, C. J."

I was. Horace was quiet. He was staring at me. I knew the look. He was studying me, gathering nuances of my body language, behavior, and speech. Smart. He was embracing his role. I didn't think he needed to bother. My only personal interaction with Firestorm was with Contact. I doubted very much Firestorm would be comparing surveillance footage they had of me against Horace.

"You're a handler right, Sarah?" I asked.

"Firestorm calls us mediators."

"Any ideal who my—I mean, Horace's, mediator is going to be?"

"None," Sarah said. "They only tell me what I need to know, strictly target and arsonists information. With all communication texting, email or routed through ever changing websites. There's no way to probe for additional information."

"Horace has been filled in on how the whole process works," Aloisio said. "We expect someone will be in touch with him shortly."

"Which means I better get out of the way," I said standing. "Unless you had something else in mind for me?" I asked Aloisio.

"Not for the moment," Aloisio said. "We'll let you know if we do."

"I'll leave you to it," I said. "Good luck."

"Thank you," they said in unison, turning their full attention to each other. I showed myself out.

CHAPTER THIRTY

I arrived at Fullman's Restaurant a little after twelve. A place where waiters wear black double-breasted suits, white shirts, and burgundy bow ties. The downstairs restaurant was half-full and filling fast with the lunch crowd. Understandable. Fullman's built its reputation on having some of the best southern cuisine in Portland. Their menu has expanded over the years to include Jamaican, African, Cuban, and Haitian dishes. Downstairs' diners consisted mostly of honest citizens. Upstairs was a private club. I wasn't only there for lunch. I was there to see someone, a person who might be able to shed light on the Shelly Morton mystery.

I headed upstairs. I hadn't been to The Lair since Smoky's surprise party. Everything about it had returned to normal. The well-lit, spacious second floor had the same layout and amenities as downstairs. With the addition of smoking and after-hours drinking allowed, all conversation ceased when I walked into the place Detective Pendleton and her partner referred to as The Snake Pit. All eyes were on me, a reflex from regular patrons at this time of day when the place was relatively quiet from the usual din of the evening and night crowds. I looked around the room. Drug dealers, thugs, thieves, hustlers, pimps, madams, swindlers, and con artists rounded out the pack. Portland's criminal class was congregating. The place was a quarter full. Typical for this time of day. The crowd who frequented the upstairs of Fullman's Restaurant were late sleepers. They recognized me. I recognized most. A few of the underworld veterans greeted me with a quick nod, a clear indication to all that I was okay. Conversations resumed in hushed tones. Returning in some cases to discussing business of a nefarious nature, I was certain. I stopped drawing that line in the sand once I left the DEA. They don't step on my toes. I don't step on theirs, respecting the mantra of the club. What goes on in The Lair stays in The Lair.

Elma Louise Washington rushed over to greet me. "Hey, C. J. How's it going?" Fullman's Assistant Manager and maître d' said with an upbeat tone, sounding different from her normally gracious, professional welcome.

Elma had no beef with me. She hated my partner Renita Harris. Elma blamed Renita for stealing her man. That was not the case. Elma and Ernest had never been romantically involved. Although their relationship was more than professional. As far as I knew, Ernest considered Elma a friend in the platonic sense. No one could convince Elma otherwise. I wondered why Elma was upstairs and not downstairs overseeing reservations and managing Fullman's lunch staff. Normally, a senior wait staff member would have been seating customers at The Lair.

"Good, Elma," I answered. "How are you?"

"Couldn't be better," Elma said with a bright smile. A smile I had seen far too little of since Renita had hooked up with Ernest. I had forgotten how lovely Elma's smile was, lighting up her face like an angel's halo.

"Private or social?" Elma's question was the equivalent of business or pleasure. If I were here for the last, then anywhere would be fine. Business meant I wanted to be seated as much out of earshot of all other customers as possible. Noticing the spacing between customers business was the prevailing choice.

"Business."

"Are you expecting guests?"

"Only one."

"Right this way, Mr. Cavanaugh," Elma said with a playful giddiness. Elma led me with a spring in her step to a table for two out of earshot of most. Tyrone Hamson, Karyn Newton, and Wayne Wright were seated at the table nearest me. A hustler, madam, and thief. They could hear what was said at my table if they strained to listen. The same could be said of me if I tried. I sat facing Wayne's back with Tyrone to his left and Karyn to his right. None of us acknowledged the other. Elma handed me a menu. Light instrumental jazz played through a top-of-the-line sound system giving The Lair a mellow ambiance. The Lair did not have a virtual personnel assistant provided by Amazon, Google, or Apple responding to their musical requests. The management regarded the voice recognition systems as another form of listening device that could not be trusted. Wi-Fi was as good as it got when it came to electronically connecting to the outside world.

"Good to see you, C. J.," Elma said.

"You just saw me at Smoky's surprise party."

"I know. Can't get too much of a good thing," Elma said with a wink. Her execution was smooth. I didn't know Elma had it in her.

"Good to see you too, Elma."

"I like the beard," Elma said, grinning as she examined my face.

"Thanks," I said. Slightly taken aback by Elma's flirtatious behavior. "Thought I'd try something new."

"It's working. Can I get you anything to drink?" Elma asked as a clean cut, lean young man with light brown skin, who seemed to appear out of nowhere, filled my water glass.

"Hot tea," I said.

"Any specific kind?" Elma asked. Her warm smile distracted me. Made me momentarily forget what we were talking about. The young man left as stealthily as he came. I began looking through the hot beverage section of the large, colorful, waterproof, tri-fold menu.

"We have a variety of special house blends," Elma said with a well-honed elocution.

I was aware of their house blends but said while perusing my choices, "They all look delicious."

"I recommend number four, Winter Retreat, with a dollop of blueberry honey. Just the thing to knock the chill off your bones." I read the description: ginger root, spearmint, cinnamon, Calendula, and elderberries. Elma is a tea drinker, too, so I trusted her judgment.

"Sounds good. I'll have the number four house blend."

"Coming right up.

"I'll give you a few minutes to look over our lunch menu. Is there anything else I can get for you in the meantime?"

I looked over at Monty Holbrook's open office door. He wasn't inside. "Monty if he's available."

"Didn't you see him downstairs when you came in?"

"No I didn't."

"Four of our servers are out sick so we're a little shorthanded. Monty volunteered to take care of the downstairs. As you well know Ernest and I normally handle the downstairs restaurant. Monty said he needed the practice. I think he's worried about overworking me while Ernest is on vacation. I'm sure Monty will make time for you, C. J. I'll let him know you're here.'

"Thanks, Elma."

"My pleasure."

I was unaccustomed to seeing Elma gregarious. Elma was usually polite yet reserved even before Renita and Ernest happened. Our conversations rarely lasted more than ten minutes. I always assumed Elma did not trust herself around me. She may have been concerned she might let something slip with her knowledge of The Lair's secrets. Her feelings for Ernest may have also figured into the mix in some strange way. Today Elma was cheerful, beaming even. With no signs of the Ernest and Renita funk hovering over her whenever she was around Renita or me. Maybe she got a raise or promotion or both.

The same lean young man who had filled my water glass returned. He deftly placed my cup and saucer in front of me, a silver teapot filled with steaming hot Winter Retreat and a glass dispenser of blueberry honey to my right. I hadn't seen him before.

"Ms. Washington has been called away, sir. My name is Garrett and I will be your server. Are you ready to order?"

"I'll have the Oha soup and a strawberry spinach salad."

"What sort of dressing would you like on your salad, sir?"

"Vinaigrette?"

"Will there be anything else, sir."

"You can stop calling me, sir."

His smile made him look like a teenager. I doubted he had started shaving. "Your order is coming right up."

"Thank you." Garrett reached out his hand. I handed him the menu. He walked briskly away. His footsteps did not make a sound.

Monty Holbrook strutted into The Lair with a bright smile of perfect white teeth as if he owned the place, which he did. His dark skin shining. His face and head as hairless as a bowling ball. Everyone glanced at Monty then looked away. No one stopped talking. Monty was his usual dapper self, impeccably dressed in a two-piece dark blue sharkskin suit, light blue shirt with matching pocket square, navy blue rep tie, and brown leather shoes. Monty's workout regimen included boxing and judo, keeping him fit and strong. Everyone allowed membership or entrance to The Lair knew Monty Holbrook. They would soon learn if they didn't.

There was no need to concern themselves. The Lair was Monty's kingdom, created by Mr. Holbrook in his own former image tailored for the present clientele. Why? In part because Monty preferred the company of criminals. That was his nature. One could say he embraced and even celebrated those who freely broke the law. Even though he no longer participated in that life. Yet he admired good people like Smoky and Winston, Shelly Morton, and perhaps myself. If he had a single vice outside of his love for family that would be money. Monty loved money. Criminal cash spent like any other as far as he was concerned. Monty intended to profit legally from every ill-gotten dollar that he could.

Monty sat in the seat across from me after we shook hands and gave each other a brief hug. His smile disappeared. His face calm and relaxed.

"Elma said you wanted to see me?" Monty asked after making himself comfortable.

"What's the deal with Elma?" I asked. My curiosity having gotten the better of me. "She's floating around here like she's on Cloud 9."

Monty huffed a laugh. "You noticed."

"Who wouldn't?"

"I think Elma's got herself a man," Monty said.

"Yeah, Ernest."

"Ernest is yesterday's news from what I'm hearing."

"Who is this mystery man?" I asked.

"And they say women gossip," Monty said with an amused humph.

"Don't hold out on me, Brother."

"Don't know yet. I'm confident it's not anyone who works here."

"Less drama that way," I said.

"Tell me about it."

"Think Elma's new man is legit?" I asked after a moment's thought on the matter.

"Elma wouldn't have it any other way under normal circumstances," Monty said.

"Love and infatuation put the pitchfork in normal," I said.

"True," Monty said. Monty and I smiled. An insightful grin only life experiences can put on your face.

"What are you two talking about that's got you so happy?" Elma surprised us.

"You," Monty said. "I thought you were taking care of business downstairs."

"I popped up to grab some take-out boxes." An armload of said boxes bore out Elma's claim. "The ones I asked you to order yesterday. We're running short downstairs."

"Sorry about that Elma," Monty said. "I'll take care of it first thing."

"Don't bother, Monty. I saw the order still sitting on your desk this morning and phoned it in. The boxes will be here this afternoon."

"Thanks, Elma," Monty said with sincere appreciation.

"You're welcome and don't try changing the subject. Why were you talking about me? Don't go getting up in my personal business." Her threat was more humorous than ominous.

"Who is he?" Monty asked. "You might as well tell us because you know we're going to find out sooner or later."

"We have our ways," I said.

Elma leaned in close. "You two keep your noses out of my personal business. You'll meet him if and when the time is right. The last thing I need is a couple of overprotective, self-appointed father figures scaring him off."

"Fair enough," Monty said. I said nothing. I took a long sip of my tea that was as good as promoted, avoiding eye contact with Ms. Washington.

Elma shook her head in mild frustration and walked away. The hustler, madam and thief finished their meals. Karyn and Wayne extracted cigarettes. Tyrone, better known as "Ham," pulled out a cigar. They lit up with Karyn accepting the proffered light from Wayne. Each enjoyed a deep satisfying drag from their cancer sticks before continuing their conversation.

"Well that confirms it," Monty said with a wry smile once Elma had exited The Lair. "Elma's got herself a man."

"At least she's working on it," I said. "Are you going to keep your nose out of her personal business?"

"Would you if it was a member of your family?"

"Dependent on the person," I said. "If I thought they could take care of themselves. Elma is capable from what I know about her."

"On an intellectual and physical level, I agree, C. J. Elma can handle herself. She hasn't had much experience with matters of the heart. Elma has been an education and career-minded woman most of her life. Hasn't spent much time getting to know the opposite sex."

"She'll figure it out."

"Of that I have no doubt," Monty said. "If I can minimize any emotional damage in the interim then I will."

I wondered how Ernest fit into Monty's heart protection program but didn't bother to ask.

"Do you want me to find out who he is?" I said.

"I'll keep you posted, C. J. Elma's love life is her own business, like she said. Having said that I feel about her the same way you feel about Renita. She's like a little sister to me."

I nodded in agreement.

"If I think anything untoward—"

"Untoward?" I said. "Really."

"Yes, untoward," Monty said. "You're not the only articulate brother up in here."

"Never thought so—but *untoward*. That word is archaic. Old school for us are words like buggin', crib, and fly."

"How about unseemly?"

"Even more outdated than untoward."

"Whatever, you get my point."

"Elma doesn't strike me as the type of woman who goes for the bad boys," I said.

"I agree," Monty said. "Elma's seen and heard enough around here not to be fooled by the bad boy hype. You never know. The heart wants what the heart wants."

Says the man who has broken a few of those hearts in his day, I thought. *So had I if I were being honest.*

"It takes people who care about a person," Monty said, "to run interference when the heart blots out common sense."

"Elma's family," I said. "I get that. Does Ernest know about this new development?"

"Nah. This situation just popped up after Smoky's surprise party."

"She met him at Smoky's surprise party?"

"That would be my guess."

"Ernest will be relieved," I said.

"Maybe," Monty said with a twist of his mouth.

"What makes you say that? I would expect Ernest to be happy Elma's moved on."

"Ernest has more feelings for Elma than he is willing to admit."

"Then why didn't he date her?"

"Ernest has this hang up about professional boundaries, C. J. He believed if he and Elma dated and it didn't work out, we might lose the best employee we've ever had. One of the best restaurant managers in the city as far as we're concerned. I forced the issue for employee freedom to date whoever they choose as long as it didn't affect their work."

"You're not suggesting Ernest might be jealous when he finds out Elma is seeing someone."

Monty shrugged.

I let out a low whistle. "Reality show in the making."

Monty chuckled.

"The young man who brought me my tea. Is he new?"

"First week," Monty said, matter-of-factly. "What did you want to see me about, C. J.?" Monty's tone shifted to serious on a dime.

"What can you tell me about Quentin Drayton?"

Monty squinted at me for a moment. Rubbing his chin before he spoke. "Quentin Drayton. What you asking about him for?"

"He may be involved in one of my current investigations."

"May be? You're not sure?"

"Nope," I flippantly said. "My client's kid was busted dealing PCP and Ecstasy. My client claims Quentin Drayton forced him into it. I want to gather the facts before deciding whether to move forward or leave his son to the law."

The cat and mouse game had begun. Monty knew I was not being totally forthcoming. We've known each other too long for him not to. The question was would he take it personally, or would he brush off his suspicion like pesky shoulder dandruff.

"I doubt his kid was dealing for Quentin Drayton," Monty nonchalantly said.

"What makes you so sure?"

"You've been out of the narcotics loop too long, C. J. Drayton doesn't deal drugs anymore."

"He doesn't?"

"Not in the conventional sense. Drayton is strictly a distributor these days. He supplies dealers up and down the Oregon I-5 corridor with whatever they need. Heroin, coke, meth, crack, opium, LSD, Ecstasy, opioids, mushrooms, PCP. You name it, and Drayton probably has a slice of that pie."

"I thought Kellen Westmore was the biggest narcotics distributor in Oregon."

"Not anymore," Monty said. "In fact, Westmore works for Drayton."

I thought of Louise Westmore's ownership of Epitome Self Storage and wondered if Drayton was actually behind it all. "Sounds like Quentin Drayton's moved up to the big time," I said.

Monty nodded. "Drayton's *the* major player in the Oregon drug trade these days. He doesn't get caught up in any turf wars or power struggles. He controls the distribution network. The only time he resorts to violence is when someone tries to rip him off or invades his distribution territory."

"You mean the various criminal gangs and organizations throughout this state all go through Drayton for their product?"

"Pretty much."

"And they're cool with that?" I asked.

"As far as most dealers are concerned, that's a sweet deal," Monty said. "Having a reliable supplier gives them one less major headache for them to worry about. The ones who don't feel that way are typically phased out. I know what you're thinking. How does Drayton acquire product when it comes from so many different sources?"

"You read my mind."

"Consolidation," Monty said.

"Brief me."

"He employs people from different networks. Set up a fair equity payment plan, and guess what. You're a narcotics corporation. Without an official state license, of course."

"I hate to admit it, but that's brilliant," I said, honestly impressed.

"Ain't it though," Monty said, sounding the same. "I'd want a piece of that action if I was still in the game."

"Good thing you're retired."

Monty looked around for a moment. Monty was clean. He made certain the people who worked for him were as well. The only reason he wasn't still in the life was due to a promise he made to his mother before she died to stay free and clean. Monty had done neither up until her passing. "Yeah, good thing," Monty said with a touch of nostalgia flowing off his tongue. "What's this about, C. J.?"

"Wish I could tell you more, Monty, but I can't."

"Client confidentiality."

"Yep."

Monty eyed me for a long moment. The wheels were turning. He was going through a series of possibilities regarding my sudden interest in Quentin Drayton. I needed to be cautious. Monty would figure it out if I gave him enough clues. That would not be such a bad thing. Shelly Morton was his friend too. Monty considered him family. Monty would want to help if I told him the whole story about Shelly. I needed to keep Shelly's name clear for as long as possible. Long enough to clean up his mess. One thing was certain. Monty might not allow my client's confidentiality claim to rest. If curiosity got the better of him as it had with me regarding Elma, Monty could decide to do some digging. Ultimately, he would learn the truth. Monty would probably decide to help Shelly in his way. That could lead to bloodshed and possibly murder.

"If your client tries to put the finger on Quentin Drayton," Monty said, "he won't live long to tell that tale."

"I know."

"What you going do, C. J.?"

"First, I'm going to find out if my client's lying to me to try to get his kid off," I said.

"That's what my money's on."

"In case he isn't, does Drayton have any weaknesses I might be able to exploit?"

"One. His baby sister, Carol."

"Have you ever met her?" I asked.

"Of course," Monty said.

"What do you make of her?"

"Smart, beautiful, reminds me of Elma minus her gullible streak in men."

"Think she has anything to do with her brother's business?"

"Not that I'm aware of. Quentin would go through hell and high water for Carol. He bends over backward to make certain Carol's not involved in what he does."

"They're tight, huh?"

"Tighter than a swim brief."

"Interesting metaphor." It's not unusual for those who make their living from criminal activity to want to keep those they love away. Try to protect them from a life they wish they could change. I thought for a moment. To my surprise, I knew next to nothing about Quentin Drayton except that he was a Portland drug dealer. I didn't know he had moved up. I didn't even know he had a sister.

"What's Quentin Drayton's story?" I asked.

"What makes you think he has one?"

"Don't we all?" I said.

"Quentin showed up on our northwest doorstep shortly before you arrived," Monty said. "I was a full-time hustler back then. I made it my business to know anything worth knowing about what was happening on the streets. He came in from St. Louis. According to my sources, a small fish in a big pond in St. Louis. Smart, tough, mean as they come when he had to be. You didn't want to be on his bad side. I can tell you from personal dealings that he's a stone-cold businessman. A diamond-hard motherfucker who gives four times as much as he gets. He rarely allows personal feelings or emotions to cloud his judgments. Except when it comes to his baby sister."

"What's the deal with him and his sister?"

"They lost their parents when they were young, home invasion. Armed thieves broke in killed their parents. The kids weren't home, thank goodness. They might have wound up in the morgue if they were. They bounced around between different relatives, settled in with grandparents who raised them. Quentin fell in with the wrong crowd and remained a member somewhere along the way. One of many stories of woe in the human jungle. Anyway, that's as much as I know."

Monty glanced away. There had been sentiment in his tone as he delivered Quentin Drayton's brief bio. One of sympathy and understanding. Monty had told me that some choose this life on more than one occasion. For others the life chooses them. I'm confident Monty had several personal conversations with Quentin Drayton. Many of The Lair faithful saw Monty as their confidential therapist. Whatever Monty learned from those unlicensed sessions must have instilled empathy for Quentin Drayton in him. There was nothing more to be learned for the moment. I shut it down.

"Thanks, Monty. I appreciate your help."

"Help; is that what you call it?"

"What do you mean?" I asked.

"C. J., you are badass, but you're not Superman. You go up against Quentin Drayton, and you are asking for more than an ass-whipping if you get where I'm coming from."

"Read you loud and clear, Brother."

"I hope you do," Monty said.

"Trying to ferret out the truth on my client is all I'm doing, Monty. Determine fact over fiction."

"I hope this client of yours appreciates the risks you're taking on his or her behalf." Monty was fishing for client details.

"All I require is payment in full. That's thanks enough for me."

"Be careful, C. J."

"Always am."

"Quentin Drayton is a very bad dude. He's also smart. May be even smarter than you."

"That doesn't take much in the IQ department."

"False humility's not going to help if you tangle with Drayton."

"Then I guess the key is not to tangle with Mr. Drayton," I said.

"You're joking, but that's good advice," Monty said.

"I appreciate you taking the time to fill me in, Monty."

Monty stared at me. He knew me well enough to know when I would not budge on a commitment.

"Not a problem," Monty said. With the defeatist tone of a parent unable to dissuade his stubborn teenager from a self-destructive choice.

"Bill me," I said. I was referring to our payment plan for vital information.

"Will do, C. J. I'd better get back to work. Elma can't do it all by herself. Though she thinks she can."

No sooner had Monty left than Garrett lightly placed a strawberry spinach salad in front of me.

"If you don't mind, Mr. Cavanaugh, I feel more comfortable calling you sir," Garrett said with a twinge of nervousness. He knew my name. I suspected Garrett had been instructed not to deliver my meal until Monty and I were done with our conversation, probably when Elma ordered him to take over her tables.

"No problem, Garrett."

"Thank you, sir," Garrett said with clear relief. "Would you prefer I serve the Oha soup now, sir, or wait until you've finished your salad?"

"After I'm done with my salad."

"Will there be anything else, sir?"

"That should do it, Garrett," I said.

Garrett made himself scarce. An excellent quality when you waited tables at The Lair. I enjoyed the delicious meal. Digesting the Quentin Drayton information Monty had given me as I ate.

CHAPTER THIRTY-ONE

My front office door opened. I looked up from the Lunsford insurance report I was typing. A man walked in, about six-foot, husky build, rust-brown skin, short boxed neat black beard, wearing modern hip hop gear. He closed the door behind him, looking around the office from where he stood. Satisfied we were alone, he turned and locked the door. My knuckles tingled, my mortal sense there was danger. I reached into my drawer, grabbed my 380 Glock, and shoved it into my belt. The man walked into my office like a military officer. Shoulders back, chest out, head erect, and eyes straight ahead staring fixed at me. I stood to greet him, not caring if the intruder saw my Glock sticking out of my waist. He stopped in front of my desk. Stood at parade rest. His shoulders relaxed. His hands calm by his sides. I couldn't make out if he was armed under his double-breasted sheepskin trench coat or had any weapons in his coat pockets.

"I'm Quentin Drayton. Heard you were asking about me? Here I am. What do you want to know?" His voice was deep and commanding. His demeanor was calm as his stance. All the earmarks of a person confident they could handle themselves. Poised and ready for action, accustomed to confrontations and violence. I had not seen Quentin Drayton in years. The beard, added muscle, and his fashion style was new. The biggest change was in his brown eyes. From what I remembered, they were vicious and fiery, as if he was furious at the world and would stomp anyone who got in his way. The man who stood before me exhibited none of those qualities. Nor were his brown eyes soulless as I had seen from other narcotic empire leaders. Rather they seemed tranquil. As if he were a man who had come to terms with his fate. Drayton arriving alone, strongly suggested he wanted to keep private whatever he suspected we were about to discuss.

I couldn't say I was shocked by his visit. After discovering how big a player Drayton had become in the drug game, he probably had snitches everywhere. Monty didn't say anything. I'd bet my life on Monty. I suppose I had, in a way. Having private conversations with Monty Holbrook was as safe as being locked up in Fort Knox. Elma and Garret Morgan, the new waitperson at Fullman's, weren't privy to our discussion, not that Elma would have said anything. Garret, I knew very little about. That left Tyrone Hamson, Karyn Newton, and Wayne Wright. The hustler, the madam, and the thief. My money was on Ham peddling information being part of the stock and trade of a hustler. That and the fact Ham hated me.

"Thanks for stopping by," I graciously said. "You saved me a trip. Would you like to have a seat?"

"Why don't we get to the point?" Drayton didn't intimidate me but I did appreciate his candor.

"A client of mine—"

"Who's your client?" he asked.

"That's confidential."

Drayton nodded. His immediate capitulation made me believe he already knew to whom I was referring, or he would have no trouble finding out on his own.

"My client claims you set up a frame to get at him," I said.

"Framed him how?"

"By planting drugs on his teenage son."

Drayton gave me what can be described as a mirthless puff of a laugh. "First of all, I don't have anything to do with drugs. I'm a legitimate businessman."

"And I'll bet you have the financial portfolio to prove your claim."

"I do," he said with calm confidence. "Not that it's any of your business."

"Let's say for the sake of argument, my client's claim is true," I said.

"If—for the sake of argument, what your client said was true—then what would I stand to gain from such a venture?"

"This particular person may be creating problems for your alleged drug enterprise."

"Speaking as a businessman," Drayton said, "this situation sounds as though it would be more trouble than it's worth. The risk factor of exposure and uncertainty is too great. Personally speaking, I would never use a *child* to accomplish my end game—if I were involved in such a business."

Something wasn't adding up. What Drayton said made sense. I would not involve children in my business if I were in his position. There are enough variables to juggle when dealing with adults. Mix in the impulsive nature of—in this case teens—and you're asking for trouble. More drug busts are made of adolescents than adults. The tone of disgust in his voice when he said the word *child* was unmistakable. It made clear his attitude on the subject. Was Drayton a father? Did his revulsion come from being a parent, personal life experiences, or both? The consequences of his narcotics business destroy the lives of children in every imaginable way, intentional or not. Which in part is while I may appreciate his entrepreneurial genius, I do not respect or forgive what he does.

"What you're saying—hypothetically—is that my client is either lying or mistaken," I said.

"That would be my assessment, hypothetically speaking," Drayton replied. "Also, if I were in the position of the man you claim me to be, and your client went to the police with such an accusation, I would not hesitate to silence such false rumors."

"Silence as in how?" I asked.

"I'll leave that to your imagination, Mr. Cavanaugh."

We eyed each other. Monty was right. Drayton was tough and smart. His cell vibrated. He checked the screen. Texted something then returned his attention to me.

"I have business to attend," he said in a dismissive tone. "Anything else on your mind?"

"Not for the moment."

Drayton gave me a knowing nod. His eyes were cool and calculating. This man had killed and would kill again if the need arose. I could imagine Drayton taking life with no more emotion than placing a live lobster in a boiling pot of water.

"How can I get in touch with you, Mr. Drayton, if I have more questions?"

Drayton pulled out a different cell phone. He probably had multiple cells for multiple purposes. My cell chimed almost immediately. I checked the message. It was a text message from Drayton leaving me his cell number. I was banking the phone number he texted from was separate from one of his normal business lines. My office number was easy to come by. I was listed. My cell is private. Drayton stared expressionless at me after I read the text. This man was accustomed to delivering jackhammer blows with the softness of a feather. We both knew he was sending me a warning along with that text. Letting me know that he could get to my client and me anytime he wanted. He probably knew about my relationship with Homicide Detective Destini Pendleton. Quentin Drayton gave me a smirk of a smile before turning to leave.

"One last thing," I said to his broad-shouldered back. Drayton lent an ear without bothering to face me. "You and I are going to have a problem if you lock my door the next time you visit my office."

"Duly noted," Drayton said. Oregon's number one illegal narcotics distributor unlocked my door and exited in the same bold manner he had entered. There are times I consider myself a fool, usually in retrospect. Destini, Renita, Patrick, and Monty would consider me one at the moment. Most people in their right mind would have been shaken by Quentin Drayton, knowing what destructive power he has at his disposal. Why was I dug in like someone getting to the juicy part of a well-penned mystery?

CHAPTER THIRTY-TWO

Shortly after my visit from Quentin Drayton, I was on my way out to see what else I could learn about his connection to Shelly Morton when an urgent text message came in from Carl Wheaton. A Lunsford Insurance claims case requiring my immediate attention. I could not ignore my professional duties. No matter how troublesome at times they might be.

This better be good, I thought as I pulled up Carl's urgent email on my PC. Carl was confident the claimant was a fraud. None of his people could prove it. Carl was hoping that I could. I only had three days to verify Carl's intuition. A payout of ten million dollars was riding on my efforts.

Carl had added a personal note: *There is a lawsuit attached to this claim. The man targeted in the lawsuit is Matteo Akraka. Matteo is a close personal friend of mine. I have known Matteo since grade school. He owns a successful pizza shop in Gresham that he is on the verge of franchising. Matteo has worked extremely hard to get to where he is today. Everything he has worked for will be taken away if this claim is upheld.*

Ronnie Levers is the claimant. Levers has nicked Lunsford in the past on a couple of occasions. Small potatoes. A few grand each. Nothing worth wasting valuable resources to prove false. This time Levers is swinging for the fences. Our people tell us the ruling will favor Ronnie Levers to the tune of about ten million dollars rather than the outrageous fifty million he was asking for in damages. Matteo's insurance policy will only cover a third. The rest will have to come out of Matteo's pocket. Lunsford defended Matteo. We didn't expect to lose this court case. Matteo's assault on Levers was too much to overcome. My friend will lose everything. Final deliberations are in three days. My people can't crack Levers. Neither could I. I'm hoping you can.

I read the case summary. Levers claimed to have cut his hand on a water glass that suddenly shattered while he was taking a drink. Photos of a nasty gash across Levers' right palm bore out his allegation of a cut. How it occurred was debatable. It was the other photos that made matters worse.

Levers had numerous facial injuries. The results of an assault by Matteo Akraka, according to eyewitnesses. The pizzeria security video supported their testimony. According to Matteo Akraka, he was attempting to treat Levers' cut hand while the paramedics were on their way. Levers would not cooperate. The injured man staggered around the pizzeria, making a show of his bloody hand, exclaiming to the full house how it happened. Akraka probably saw his franchise future in jeopardy. He panicked. Akraka attempted to restrain Levers. Somehow his efforts escalated to Matteo Akraka physically assaulting Ronnie Levers.

All indications were that Ronnie Levers was a nickel and dime con artist. He probably didn't expect to gain more from the cut hand scam than to have his medical expenses covered and a few grand from a personal injury claim. Levers would have made cash an option to forget the whole ordeal. The assault escalated the affair. Levers saw an opportunity for a big payday and leaped at it.

I was on my way to see what more I could learn about Ronnie Levers when Thompson confronted me in the lobby of the Stevens Building. "What did you and Quentin Drayton have to talk about?" Chris asked, invading my personal space.

"I don't know what you're referring to, Detective."

Detective Thompson flipped opened his police notebook. "At 10:43 a.m.," he read aloud, "Quentin Drayton entered the Stevens Building alone. Dropped off by three of his bodyguards in a blue SUV with the vanity plate DRAYDOG. At 11:17 a.m., Mr. Drayton exited the Stevens Building alone. The same SUV, occupied by the same bodyguards, picked up Mr. Drayton moments later."

"And?" I said.

"You're the only person Drayton would have a reason to have a conversation with in this building."

"You know this how Detective?"

"Your connection with the local drug industry, Mr. Cavanaugh."

"I have no connection with the local drug industry."

"I'll buy that. But you do have extensive knowledge of the local drug industry."

"This is not about my knowledge of the narcotics business. This is all about Shelly Morton. And we both know it."

"Not at the moment it isn't," Thompson said. "What did you and Drayton discuss?"

"In case you haven't noticed, there are twelve stories to this building, with a wide variety of tenants. Drayton could have gone into any one of these offices for various reasons. He could have been using the first-floor bathroom if he had known the code. Or maybe he stopped off to buy a toy at Finnegan's here on the first floor."

"He didn't do any of those things," Thompson said decisively. "He came to see you."

"How do you know?" I asked.

"I already told you."

"You told me what you suspect, Detective. I'm asking you. *How do you know?* Did someone follow Drayton into the building? Verify where he went when he came inside. In short, do you have any eyewitnesses to corroborate your story?"

"Don't need an eyewitness. We knew where he was going."

"Facts hold up in court, not speculation. If you question Drayton on his whereabouts this morning, what do you think he will say? That he stopped by to see me."

Thompson's momentary silence answered for him. "That's your story, huh?" Thompson said.

I shrugged. "How do you expect me to be straight with you? When you won't be straight with me?"

"We have some arrangement I don't know about?" Thompson asked, taking a step back as if sizing me up for a haymaker.

"Working on it. By the time you haul Drayton in for questioning," I said, jumping ahead to Thompson's next logical step in my interrogation. "He'll have his alibi lined up like a perfect bowling strike. Visiting me won't be anywhere in the mix. Let's cut the bullshit. How'd you know Drayton came to this building?"

"Happenstance," Thompson coolly replied, as if amused. "My partner and I were on our way back to the precinct when we noticed Drayton being dropped off at the Stevens. Your building. Coincidence?"

"It's not my building. I don't own it."

"Keep hanging out with Quentin Drayton, and you might one day."

"What do you know about Carol Drayton?" I asked, changing the direction of our conversation, hoping to find out from a reliable source, information much harder to come by on the street.

"Drayton's sister?" Thompson eyed me for a moment before answering. "She's a dead end. Carol Drayton's as clean as her brother is dirty. Big brother has made sure of that."

Thompson was proving useless for the kind of immediate info I needed. It was time to put an end to this pissing contest. "It's been interesting chatting with you, Detective, but I have pressing matters to attend to."

"Mind if we tag along?"

"I do."

"Would those 'pressing matters' have anything to do with Quentin Drayton?"

"Again, I ask, how did you know Drayton came to this building?" I looked past Thompson. An undercover vehicle was parked across the street. It was raining. A typical winter Portland rainstorm coming down in buckets. I could only make out a form seated on the driver's side through the rain blurred lobby glass front and car windows, Thompson's partner, I presumed. Thompson followed my line of sight. "You were following Drayton," I said.

Thompson involuntarily raised his eyebrows. A tell. I wondered if Quentin Drayton knew Thompson was following him. How could he not? Portland Narcotics and the DEA probably kept running surveillance on Oregon's number one narcotics distributor. What was Drayton's end game to lead Thompson to me if Drayton knew Thompson was following him? Could Thompson be on Drayton's payroll? Did Drayton come out of our meeting and tell Thompson to force me to back off? Another possibility was Thompson was sitting on me. That consideration was doubtful since I believed Thompson was not that foolish. Anything was possible. The trick was to separate the possibilities from the probabilities and create reality.

"If I find out you've been holding out on me, Cavanaugh. I'll have your ass in a jail cell, so fast your head will spin."

I laughed. His face was angry, but his eyes didn't sell it. This was one of Thompson's tricks to get a spineless perp to flip. "Go ahead. I'll be out in a blink. If you even get me in a cage."

I decided to spell it out for Thompson. "I know you've done your homework on me by now. This tough cop bit trying to squeeze me for information is not going to work. I'll tell you what I want you to know. When I think you should know it. I expect—"

"You expect!"

"I *expect* professional quid pro quo on anything you uncover that may affect my client."

"Shelly Morton is your client?"

"He is."

"I thought Shelly was your friend?"

"He's both."

"Did you ever think your friend Shelly may be guilty as Satan, and he's using you to try to get him off?"

"I think with my brain and not my heart, Chris."

"You won't be the first sucker who believed that."

"If you can't handle working together, then we can continue along on our investigative paths and see who gets to the finish line first."

Thompson laughed. He nodded before he spoke. "Alright, Cavanaugh, you win this round. This fight isn't over. Not by a long shot."

"I thought I made my point. We can cooperate on this rather than fight, Chris."

"I'll stick to partnering with Portland PD."

"Separate ways it is," I said.

"If I find out you're in any way connected to that scumbag Quentin Drayton, I will bring you down."

"Likewise," I said.

Thompson looked stunned. "What are you saying?"

"You've been after Quentin Drayton for some time. Yet he keeps slipping through the net. Maybe someone has been snipping the mesh, allowing him to swim away. Maybe he has some inside help. Drayton could buy plenty of influence in the Portland PD with his kind of money. I'm sure he already has. Certainly would make life a whole lot easier than getting by on a paltry detective salary. Wouldn't it, Thompson."

"You shut your dirty, lying mouth!" This time there was a match to Thompson's expression. Rage flickered in his eyes. Thompson got in my face. The smell of black coffee and tobacco was on his breath.

"Or what?" I said. "You'll shut it for me."

"I might. Someone needs to."

"That someone won't be you, Thompson. Not today, not ever."

Fear and intimidation did not cause Thompson to back away. The detective had been in the trenches too long to surrender to those predators. Thompson succumbed because he believed getting into a physical altercation with me would not bode well for his career.

"Two can play the insinuation game," I said. "Doesn't feel good when someone tries to besmirch your reputation. Does it?"

"Don't get in my way, Cavanaugh."

"You won't even know I'm there. Now, unless you're planning on hauling me down to the station for further questioning, Chris, I'm going to be on my way."

Thompson left without another word. I exited the Stevens Building for the light rail to head home. I preferred to arrange what I was planning for my latest Lunsford case from there. The last thing I had wanted was to make an enemy of Detective Chris Thompson. Not for my sake, I could handle an irate narc. For what it might entail for Shelly. Thompson might turn small-minded and exact revenge on my friend. The narc left me no choice. My primary concern was to liberate Shelly Morton from a wasp nest without him being stung. Thompson was as much of a problem as Drayton in that regard. The bigger issue still loomed. I had very little to go on. How was I going to get Shelly out of this mess?

CHAPTER THIRTY-THREE

I have been taking Light Rail to work for the last few weeks. Very convenient from work. A bit of a walk to and from home, but it was worth it. Rain was steady, heavy overcast. Like someone had lined the clouds with lead. I was lost in thought between Shelly Morton and Carl Wheaton when four men jumped out of a parked blue SUV a couple of blocks from my house, dressed for the rainy season in what I would term as casual varieties of blue-collar to suburban and urban streetwear. A clear indicator to me thugs were bred from all walks of life. Solidly built men with the hostile demeanors of enforcers who enjoyed their work. Had I not been preoccupied with formulating a plan to extradite Carl's friend, Matteo Akraka from his current circumstance, then I would have noticed the unfamiliar vehicle and been prepared for what happened next. The one with a Soul Patch dressed in what I considered casual suburban stepped in front as his associates surrounded me. My mind raced as to how to best defend myself against the inevitable assault.

"You, Cavanaugh?" Soul Patch asked. I looked to the man on my left then right, sizing them up. I could only guess what the man behind me was doing. Playing it cool, I waited for a signal to strike. I shoved my hands in my coat pockets before staring back at Soul Patch.

"Who wants to know?" I said.

Soul Patch looked at a picture of me on his phone. "Yeah, you're Cavanaugh, alright," Soul Patch said, showing me the picture. The picture was recent. I recognized it. A clip from a photo of me at Smoky's surprise party, his copy probably lifted from Fullman's website, where numerous photos of the event were posted.

"I'm here to deliver a message," Soul Patch said.

"You could have called, texted, or emailed. I would have gotten back to you at my earliest convenience."

I heard the other three men chuckle. My eyes set on Soul Patch. He was the leader. He called the shots. These were professionals. They did what they were paid to do and nothing more. They would follow orders, unlike an unruly gang who were often unpredictable, where an attack could come at any time from any direction.

"Cute," Soul Patch said with a smirk. "He said you had a smart mouth."

"You'll have to be more specific," I said. "I hear that a lot. Who exactly is 'he'?"

"Back off, or we'll close that smart mouth of yours…permanently," Soul Patch said.

"Did Quentin Drayton send you?" I asked.

Soul Patch grinned. "Just so you fully comprehend how serious we are here's a taste."

Soul Patch stepped back as the others closed in. I had armed myself for the streets after Quentin Drayton's visit, not knowing how Drayton would react to our conversation. I had shoulder-holstered my 92F Beretta. Hip holstered my .380 Glock. No chance of getting to those weapons. Fortunately, I had coat pocketed my Colt 32 and stiletto switchblade. I was shoved from behind, momentarily freeing me from their human mousetrap. Perfect. Before Soul Patch realized what happened, I had my switchblade at his throat. Maneuvering quickly around behind Soul Patch with my stiletto tickling his Adam's apple. The men froze, not knowing how to react. I yanked out my Colt 32. and aimed it in the general direction of the three thugs.

"After I slit his throat," I said. "Who's next?"

I could feel Soul Patch attempting to reposition himself to disarm me. I slide the blade over to his right carotid artery, applying enough pressure to make him uncomfortable but not enough to draw blood. One swift arc across Soul Patch's throat with my razor-sharp stiletto would slice through both his carotid arteries. If they thought I was bluffing, they would soon find out how wrong they were. The other thugs spread out as if telepathically ordered, reaching inside their coats, packing a basic business requirement. Soul Patch blurted, "Don't bother."

"Tell them to stand down," I said.

"Do as he says," Soul Patch said. They raised their hands in mock surrender. I let Soul Patch go and shoved him toward the others, pointing my .32 at the group. My stiletto hand relaxed but ready at my side. Soul Patch adjusted his clothing as if recovering from a heated make-out session. His cold gray eyes stared expressionless at me.

"The next time, you won't see us coming," Soul Patch said with calm confidence.

"You forgot to say if I don't back down," I said.

"You get the picture," Soul Patch said, showing no ill effects from his near-death experience. I believed Soul Patch. I hadn't seen them coming. Sneaking up on me would not be as easy the next time.

Soul Patch gave a quick jerk of his head, and they all piled into the SUV. Soul Patch coolly eyed me from the front passenger seat as they pulled away. I pocketed my weapons. It was daytime. Dark clouds and steady rain made it appear more like dusk. I looked around. No one was about. In this weather, hibernating was the norm in my neighborhood, unlike in summer when there would be people everywhere. Soul Patch and his crew would not have attempted a daylight assault in the summer. Maybe someone witnessed what occurred from their home. Maybe someone had phoned the police. I walked briskly toward home, not wanting to have to explain myself if and when the police arrived. There was no time for that. Hoping if the police had been notified, they would not be directed to my door. Thinking on the way how this day just kept getting better and better.

I kept an eye out for Soul Patch and his crew circling back on my way home. It was obvious they knew where I lived. How else did they know where to lie in wait? I looked around the grounds before entering my house. Nothing appeared disturbed. Difficult to tell with everything being waterlogged.

Inside I searched for signs of intruders. There was no evidence anyone had broken in. My home was clear. Had Soul Patch and his crew greeted me inside my house to deliver their message, some of them might not have made it out alive. I have no patience with thugs invading my sanctuary. I would have immediately gone to all-out assault mode and not stopped until every one of them was subdued. In short, I would have shot first and asked questions later.

Incidents like the one I just experienced with Soul Patch and his crew reminded me that I was not in this alone. One of my greatest fears in dealing with hardcore criminals is that they would take revenge or their frustrations out on the people I love. That concern extended to my pets. They were adopted members of my family. None of them had anything to do with the life I had chosen. They should not be caught up in my turmoil. Still, it could happen, repercussions by association.

I spent extra time playing with Andrew and Booker. I gave more uninterrupted attention to my colorful and chipper Zebra finches, Toussaint, Coretta, Claude, and Truth, truly appreciating their boisterous songs. Gazing at my tropical fish contently inhabiting their aquarium world gave me a Zen-like calm, making me momentarily oblivious to the dangers from the outside world. My pets were in my will. If anything happened to me, Andrew and Booker were to go to Renita. The twins were a gift from Renita, after all. It was only fitting she should receive custody upon my death. My tropical fish and singing Zebra finches were willed to Destini's care. Being aware my pets would have good homes in my passing offered me solace. I made certain they had everything they needed before I left.

CHAPTER THIRTY-FOUR

I needed inside information. I went to The Lair to see Monty Holbrook. I was compartmentalizing my concerns so I could focus on the task ahead. The Lair was teeming with people and energy. I lucked up on a recently abandoned seat at the bar and ordered a cranberry juice. Monty stopped by before I could ask to see him. He must have spotted me when I walked in.

"How's it going, C. J.?" The dapper man with the winning smile and shining bald head asked.

"I've had better days," I said.

"Girl trouble?" Monty asked as if he knew of my troubles.

"More like jealous boyfriend trouble," I said.

Monty took the hint. "Let's talk in my office," he said, leading the way. Lair regulars acknowledged Monty and me with a nod or brief greeting as we made our way through the crowd. The din from The Lair went silent with Monty's office door closed and locked. I wondered if Monty had the room soundproofed. It was so quiet. Monty took a seat behind his desk, offering me one across from him.

"Tell Uncle Monty all about it," he said in a fatherly tone. "Quentin Drayton turning up the heat?"

Monty and I were around the same age. He often felt he needed to school me when it came to The Game. Most times, it wasn't necessary. I let his presumption slide. It never hurts to listen. Never know what you can learn.

"Yes," I said, "but that's not what I'm here to see you about."

"What can be more pressing than being on Quentin Drayton's shit list?"

"Ronnie Levers," I said.

"Who?" Monty asked, dropping his fatherly tone.

"He's a confidence man," I said.

"Doesn't ring a bell. Is he new to the neighborhood?"

"That's one of the things I'm trying to find out."

"What types of scams are we talking about?" Monty asked.

"He's got a friend's friend on the hook for seven figures."

Monty let out a low whistle. "Anyone that big time I would normally have info."

"He's been small time up 'til now," I said.

"Check with Ham," Monty said. "He keeps his finger on the pulse of hustlers and scam artists."

I've said it before, and it bears repeating. Tyrone Hamson—better known as Ham—is the kind of man who will smile in your face while taking your wallet, sleeping with your wife, and selling crack to your children. He has an insincere laugh and large dark soulless eyes absent of genuine emotion. I needed a hot tip. Ham was as good as the FBI when it came to Portland criminal info.

"Will do," I said.

"Need me to calm the waters?" Monty asked, knowing the contempt Ham harbored toward me.

"I'm good," I said.

"You think Ham would be over it by now," Monty said. "Don't get me wrong. Ham's a mean son-of-a-bitch with a long memory."

"Sadistic, some might say," I said.

"Nice guys, don't wear the crown, C. J. Not in his business. Or any other, I imagine."

The long memory Monty was referring to was an incident back when Tyrone Hamson and I first met. I was working on a missing person's case. I suppose I asked Ham one too many tough questions about his involvement. With a jerk of his head, he sicced one of his bodyguards on me. I broke the man's collarbone. Alan Biggs was his name. Alan retired shortly after that. Ham blames me. I suspect there were more reasons for Alan's retirement than a broken collarbone. It turned out Ham had nothing to do with the kidnapping. The combination of undue harassment by me and the loss of one of his most trusted senior employees put me on Ham's enemy list. A notation that could get me killed one day if I wasn't careful.

"What you did to Alan wasn't personal," Monty said as if reading my mind.

"It must have seemed that way to Ham," I said. "Being a new kid on the block. Like I was challenging his authority. Damaging his street cred."

"Not like Ham to take an incident like that out of context," Monty said.

"Maybe it's because I don't treat him like he walks on water," I said.

"Neither do I. Hell, most of the clientele in here treats him like one of the boys."

"I'm not like most of the clientele in here in case you haven't noticed, Monty."

"You have your bad boy moments," Monty said with a grin.

We both laughed. "You have a lot more good boy days than I do bad."

"True," Monty said.

"Ham probably sees me as a threat," I said. "Someone who could bring him down if I had a mind to."

"The law," Monty said.

"Pretty much."

"He ain't wrong, C. J."

"Can't say he is," I said. "Have you seen Ham tonight?"

"He's cuddled up with a little caramel cutie at one of the tables," Monty said. "One of Madam Karyn's girls."

"Is his date on or off the clock?" I asked.

"With Ham, who knows? If you need any help with this Drayton situation," Monty said, circling back to his earlier concern, "give me a holler. I'll come running."

I thought about telling Monty about my incident with Quentin Drayton's thugs but decided against it. Monty's involvement would only fan the flames.

"Thanks, bro'," I said. "I've got it handled."

"Famous last words," Monty said. I smiled. Monty didn't. "Don't go getting physical with Ham," Monty added. He had his no-bullshit face on. "The same rules apply to you as everybody else in here, C. J. You cause a problem. You're out on your ass."

"Gotcha," I said. I respected The Lair club rules. Although I didn't know who Monty had in mind to put me out on my ass with Ernest on vacation.

We returned to the din. An OG—original gangster—was wearing an outdated rust-colored pinstripe suit that hung on him like a zoot suit called for Monty to hang with him and his younger crowd. Monty excused himself to join them. My seat at the bar was gone. So was my drink. I looked around. I spotted a beige skin man dressed in a violet suit, matching silk tie, and mauve-colored shirt. His pencil thin mustache and wavy ponytail were tight. He wore a gold rope chain, diamond earrings, and rings on every finger. All of his jewelry looked expensive but not garish. Standing out was something Tyrone Hamson enjoyed. To his credit, he did it well. The sordid means he obtained his wealth was not to his credit.

Ham was snuggled up with said cutie at a table for two tucked away in a corner across the room. I waded through the crowd to get to them. She was pretty in a nubile way. Young enough to be his daughter with large natural breasts and purple-streaked hair, doing things young couples do when their entire world revolves around each other. They were drinking Cristal champagne. One of the first things I noticed when I arrived at Ham's table was there were no bodyguards with him. *He must consider this one of his nights off*, I thought. The second thing I noticed was no cigar. I couldn't remember seeing Ham without a cigar. Was he not smoking because of his lady friend? Did Ham actually care for this young woman? Ham whispered something into the young woman's ear that made her laugh before I spoke.

"Ham."

Tyrone Hamson looked up at me. His expression went from playful to mean. He had lost weight. I had considered him fat before. He had slimmed down to chubby. "I need to talk to you."

"Can't you see I'm busy?" He snarled.

"It'll only take a minute," I said in my most amiable voice. Normally I would introduce myself to his date and bully my way into gaining Ham's full attention. Not tonight. Tact was the operative word. I needed this man's help. If feigning servility would work, then I was all in.

"My time is money," Ham said with a sneer. Certain he sensed my manufactured vulnerability. A characteristic Ham was accustomed to exploiting. Ham was a believer in the law of the jungle. Not only did the strong survive, but they also preyed upon the weak. For Ham that translated to economic spoils. Profit almost always being his end game. "Even a minute cost you," Ham said, testing his advantage.

"How much?" I asked.

Ham glared at me. The young woman I had never seen before remained still and quiet. She wasn't new to the game. Sensing she was in the midst of an exchange that needed to play out. I also had the feeling she was ready to bail if something popped off. No weapons were allowed in Fullman's. That was especially true of The Lair. I had left my hardware locked in the trunk of my car. Ham regarded himself as a lover, not a fighter. Although his fighting rep was solid. Foremost, Ham was a businessman. Violence was a racketeering tool in his book. I remembered Monty's warning. The young woman had nothing to fear. Neither of us wanted a physical confrontation.

"Depends on what you want to talk about," Ham said.

"Ronnie Levers," I said.

Ham stared at me for a long moment. "Honey, could you give us a minute?" Ham sweetly asked his companion.

The young woman pouted. "I thought this was our time together, dumpling."

"This won't take long, sugar," Ham said. "I promise."

"Alright," she said, continuing to pout. "I'm holding you to that baby."

The young woman kissed Ham with puckered lips, leaving a perfect branding of red lipstick on his chubby cheek. She looked around as she got up, adjusting her short tight dress that hugged her curves and barely covered her lean upper thighs. Seeing someone she knew, the young woman waved and smiled before making her way through the crowd. I pulled the vacated seat around to my side of the table.

"You want a favor from me?" Ham said.

"I do."

"And I should do this for you. Why?"

"No good reason," I said. "You're a businessman, Ham. I'm looking to trade cash for information."

"Ronnie Levers. Now there's a name I haven't heard for a while. What you need to know about Ronnie Levers?" Ham asked.

"Everything you can tell me," I said.

"How much?"

"How much what?" I asked.

"How much are you offering for this intel?"

"What's the going rate?"

Garrett appeared. Pen and order pad at the ready. The Lair's newest waitperson gave us both a polite smile.

"Is there anything I can get for you gentleman?" Garret asked.

Ham yanked out the bottle of Cristal submerged in the silver champagne ice bucket and checked its level.

"Another bottle of Cristal," Ham said. "And some butterfly shrimp for me and the lady."

Garret turned to me. "And you, sir?"

"I'm good thanks," I said.

Garret let Ham know his order was coming right up and slipped away.

"I don't want your money, Cavanaugh," Ham said, picking up where we left off.

"What do you want?"

"Your services," Ham said. I had never dealt with Ham on his level. Bartering was unexpected. I needed to be careful. He was damn good at what he did, no matter what I thought of Ham. What he did best was ensnaring people into doing what he wanted.

"You want to hire me as a PI?" I asked.

"Not at this minute," Ham said. "When the time comes. I want you to do some work for me. No questions asked."

"As long as our deal has one stipulation," I said.

"Which is?"

"Nothing illegal. Not even remotely."

"I can go along with that stipulation," Ham said. We shook on it. Ham's hand was sweaty. I could not remember ever shaking Ham's hand when it wasn't.

"Tell me what you know," I said.

"Ronnie Levers. So he's back in Portland. I call him The Gypsy. He comes, and he goes. Rarely stays in one place long. Master of the small cons and scams. Nickel and dime stuff. The Gypsy never seemed worth my time, to be honest. Tell you one thing, though. He's never been busted. What's this dude done that's got you on his ass?"

"Graduated to the big time," I said.

"How big?"

"Big enough."

"Must be some serious coin for you to be involved."

"It's not always about the Benjamins."

Ham nodded with a sly smile. "If you say so, C. J. Sounds like Ronnie's got himself a real gem going."

"It's all a matter of perspective," I said.

"Hate to mess that up for the brother," Ham said.

I didn't want to get into a debate over how scams and cons could ruin people's lives. I needed to remain on Ham's good side for the moment.

"I hear you," I said. "Where can I find The Gypsy?"

"Not here. The Lair's not his scene. He prefers bars, pool halls, strip clubs, and casinos, from what I remember. He used to frequent a place over on Sandy. Diamondback."

"Like the rattler?"

"Yeah. It's a pool hall. Fancies himself a shark."

"Is he?" I asked.

"He's not bad from what I've heard. Wins more than he loses."

"Any weaknesses?"

"He has a fondness for the ladies. What hetero man doesn't?"

Ham's rumors and hearsays are typically reliable facts. "Thanks," I said, handing Ham one of my business cards.

"Don't forget our deal, C. J.," Ham said with a devilish smile.

"I won't. Give me a call when you're ready to collect."

"Believe me. I will," Ham said, " waving for his girl to rejoin him as I stood. The young woman had maneuvered her way to within earshot, believing neither of us noticed. I did. I'm confident Ham did as well. What she would do with her eavesdropped information was anybody's guess. My only concern was if she had any connection to The Gypsy.

I returned my chair to its original location, helping the young woman with her seat. She thanked me with a smile that belonged in a senior high school yearbook. Ham's date snuggled into the crook of his arm. Garrett was serving Cristal and butterfly shrimp as I walked away. I knew I had to work fast. Not only because of the trial ruling time crunch against Matteo Akraka. There was no guarantee Ham wouldn't double cross me by getting the word out to Ronnie Levers that I was looking for him. Especially if Ham discovered how much money was involved.

CHAPTER THIRTY-FIVE

Ronnie Levers was in the middle of fleecing a mark when she walked into the Diamondback. He had never seen her before. His eyes followed her like a hungry leopard stalking its prey.

Average height, early to mid-thirties, slender, wearing tight jeans, a hooded rain jacket, and leather rain boots. She dropped the hood, revealing blonde hair twisted up into a neat ponytail. She headed straight for the bar, not looking around. As if the only interest she had was shelved upon the tiered wall of multi-colored liquor bottles behind the bar. She took a seat at the bar. Distancing herself from the few people bellied up along its length. She removed her slightly water beaded jacket and draped it over the barstool next to her. Beneath, she wore an oversized rose-colored sweater. Alpaca, if he wasn't mistaken. Somehow that made her more attractive to Ronnie than if she were wearing a designer top. More accessible. The bartender had noticed her. He greeted her with a broad smile as she sat on the wooden bar stool. She placed her order. The bartender returned promptly with a glass of red wine.

"Hey, are we shooting or what?" the forty-year-old businessman asked. Sounding irritated, breaking Ronnie's trance.

"Yeah," Ronnie said, turning his attention back to their game of eight ball. Ronnie didn't want the man to discover he was being hustled. At least not right away. Not before he or the mark left the premises. He wasn't concerned about the businessman exacting revenge. Some of them would come after him when the law did not provide his marks with satisfaction. Ronnie ruthlessly discouraged their efforts. Sometimes he used a weapon, other times his fighting skills. If need be, he would employ the necessary muscle to bring his message home.

Ronnie had sized up his opponent for a couple of grand before the night was through. He was losing enough to keep the businessman on the hook. Giving him false hope, he had a legitimate chance of winning his money back and then some. The presence of that alluring woman changed his plans. Ronnie expedited his victory over the businessman running the table with ease. Ronnie collected his three hundred dollars, bringing his total winnings to eight hundred dollars, turning down the businessman's plea for double or nothing.

"Mind if I join you?" Ronnie asked the woman pointing to the bar stool opposite her coat. Her expression said she minded. Ronnie did not let that discourage him. "Tell you what," he said. "I'll sit here, minding my own business, leaving you to mind yours. If you want to talk, say the word or words, whichever you prefer. My ears are all yours. Of course, I can't promise I won't sit here talking to myself about you."

She shrugged. "If you want," she said. Sounding resigned rather than inviting. Ronnie scooted onto the barstool.

Ronnie Levers was handsome, and he knew it. He had been told so numerous times since middle school. Since puberty, he had been a chick magnet with wavy sandy hair, a disarming smile, twinkling blue eyes, and a charismatic personality. He was tall and fit and often mistaken for a male model. Ronnie looked the part. He sometimes dressed the part as well, depending upon his scam. Tonight, he was business casual with neat khakis, a solid buttoned shirt, a leather belt, and polished shoes. Wearing fake eyeglasses made him look professorial. Costumed to attract the type of pool player he was trying to fleece. His face had been smooth and blemish-free before the altercation with Matteo Akraka.

His cut lip, bloody nose, and minor facial bruises had healed. He still had a couple of facial scars from the beating he took from Matteo Akraka. Thin, pale scars made him appear ruggedly handsome. Akraka hadn't landed as many blows as he believed. Ronnie deflected or minimized the potential damage from most of his flailing punches. He had allowed Akraka to land a few to make his case. Levers had taken a variety of self-defense classes over the years. Aikido, Jujutsu, Tae Kwon Do. Martial arts training he harvested from street fighting tactics during his criminal life. He was able to defend himself in most situations. Had he wanted, he could have knocked Matteo Akraka out.

"Can I get you anything?" the bartender asked Ronnie.

"I'll have a whiskey sour," Ronnie said.

"Coming right up." The bartender darted away.

Her eyes were a gentle blue. Ronnie was glad he was sitting close enough to discover that fact. There was a warmth emanating from her clear skin that made her glow despite her despair. The bartender delivered Ronnie's drink as Ronnie was about to launch into a round of small talk. Her name was Barbara. At least he had gotten that far.

"Would you like another glass of wine?" Ronnie asked Barbara. "Or something else to drink, perhaps?"

"Not at the moment," Barbara said. Her pall of depression was solidly in place. Ronnie slapped down a ten and told the bartender to keep the change. The bartender thanked him, giving Ronnie a furtive look suggesting good luck with this one before he darted away to help another customer.

Ronnie toasted, "Here's to chance meetings blossoming into enduring friendships." Barbara clinked glasses with Ronnie. She took a sip of her wine without uttering a word or acknowledging his sentiment.

Ronnie's persistence ultimately paid off. Small talk ensued. General information was exchanged, most of his being fabricated. Barbara was currently unattached. She had never married. No children. She moved to Portland from a small town in Idaho that Ronnie had never heard of. Barbara lived in a one-bedroom condo in downtown Portland. Ronnie noticed the businessman he had fleeced storm out after losing to another player during a momentary lull in their conversation.

"I lost my job five months ago," Barbara suddenly said, gulping down the remainder of her wine. "Haven't been able to find another since. I'm three months behind in my rent. My landlord will evict me if I don't come up with my back rent in the next couple of days. Where am I going to come up with six-thousand, seven hundred and fifty dollars in the next three days?"

Ronnie got the bartender's attention. He ordered Barbara another glass of wine. "What about your family? Can't they help you out?"

The bartender replaced the empty with a full glass of red wine without sticking around.

"My parents died when I was little," Barbara said. "I was raised by my grandparents. My grandmother passed away last year. My grandfather a couple of years before her. They were all the family I had."

"What about friends?"

"Nobody with that kind of money. A couple I know might let me stay with them for a few weeks. No guarantees that will happen. I could be looking at becoming homeless."

Barbara's eyes became wet with tears. Barbara reached over and snatched a Diamondback cocktail napkin from the other side of the bar. She patted at her moist eyes, attempting to dry them before the tears spilled onto her cheeks without success. Ronnie offered her his clean handkerchief. Barbara accepted.

"Now, now," Ronnie said. "That's not even necessary." Ronnie had made his move hoping to have sex with Barbara tonight. He was genuinely feeling sorry for this woman.

"I feel so lonesome. I feel like a failure. Now I'm going to be," Barbara took in a deep gasping breath, "*homeless.*"

"Don't you worry about that," Ronnie said. "We'll figure something out."

"We?" Barbara said through her sobbing.

"I'm going to help you."

"Why would you do that? We just met."

"Let's just say I have a soft spot for a damsel in distress," Ronnie said.

Barbara's sobbing subsided.

"I know of a way you can make the money you need in a snap." Ronnie emphasized with a snap of his fingers.

Barbara eyed Ronnie, sniffling. Her face flushed. Her eyes wet with tears.

"Thank you for the drink. And the shoulder to cry on. But I'm not that kind of woman."

"No, no, nothing like that. That's not what I'm suggesting."

"What exactly are you suggesting?"

"Well," Ronnie eased his stool closer. Whispering into Barbara's ear. "It may involve a bit of trickery, if you know what I mean."

"What sort of trickery?"

"We're going to run a scam."

"What sort of scam?"

"Keep your voice down." Ronnie looked around to see if anyone heard Barbara. No one did or seemed to care. "The type of scam that will get you your rent money and a little more."

Barbara took a sip of her wine. Her emotions appeared to fluctuate between distress and hope.

"I don't know," Barbara said.

"Do you want to be homeless?" Ronnie asked.

"Of course not."

"Then I'm offering you a temporary solution. No one will get hurt. The only thing that will happen is that the pockets of someone who can afford it will be lighter."

"How? What are we going to do? You aren't making any sense."

"We are going to run a Badger Game," Ronnie said.

"A Badger what?"

"A Badger Game. All it involves is you getting a well-to-do married man in a compromising position that we photograph or even videotape. We then threaten to go public with our evidence unless he pays us."

"Sounds like blackmail."

"I prefer to call it compensation for marital longevity."

"Still sounds like blackmail," Barbara said. "Or is it extortion?"

"What it is, is an opportunity for you to get enough money in your pocket to keep you off the streets until you can get back on your feet."

"I don't know," Barbara said, hedging.

"That's up to you," Ronnie said matter-of-factly. "I'm trying to help you out."

Barbara thought about it. After a healthy drink of wine, she said, "Okay, I'll do it. As long as no one gets hurt."

"Excellent," Ronnie said, sounding genuinely pleased. "Meet me here tomorrow at six. I'll have everything lined up. Wear something sexy but not slutty."

"I don't own anything slutty."

"That's too bad," Ronnie said with a wry smile.

Barbara smiled back. Ronnie was falling for this woman. An honest attraction. He had not had a steady relationship for a few years. Not since Helena threw him over for the straight life and a billionaire named Gustav. Being with Barbara reminded him of how delicious romance could be.

"In the meantime," Ronnie reached into his pocket and pulled out a thick roll of bills. He peeled off four thousand dollars. Ronnie could have given Barbara the whole amount. What guarantee did he have she would return if he did? "Consider this a down payment on our agreement."

"My landlord wants it all," Barbara said.

"Tell him you'll have the rest in a week. He'll go for it. No landlord wants to go through the eviction process."

Barbara pocketed the money. "I can't thank you enough."

"Don't thank me yet. We still have work to do. I'll meet you back here at six tomorrow. Don't be late."

"I won't," Barbara said, nodding vigorously. "Mind walking me to my car? I'm feeling a little shaky and could use a strong arm to lean on."

"What kind of gentleman would I be if I didn't?" Ronnie paid the bartender what was owed, leaving the doubting man a generous tip. He helped Barbara with her coat. Retrieved his hooded rain jacket from the coat rack nearest them and put it on. Ronnie politely offered Barbara his arm. She took it. Her depression erased by a grateful smile.

*　*　*

For once, it wasn't raining. A damp cold hung in the night air like moss from a tree. I was standing by my car. Ronnie Levers and Barbara came toward me linked arm-in-arm. They were behaving with the giddiness of star-crossed lovers. I pressed play on the digital recorder I held in my hand. A crystal clear recording could be heard.

"What the hell?" Ronnie said as he rushed toward me, breaking the link with Barbara keeping pace. Ronnie heard his and Barbara's voices. I let the recording play a bit longer before turning it off. Long enough to make it clear to Ronnie the recording was of their bar conversation.

"What in the hell is going on here?" Ronnie said to me.

"Ronnie Levers meet Detective Abigail Miller," I said.

There was no time for staking out Ronnie Levers, hoping he slipped up. Carl needed results, and he needed them yesterday. This required immediate and drastic measures, a more direct approach. I had met Portland Police Detective Abigail Miller at Smoky's surprise party. A new transfer from Albuquerque, New Mexico, who happened to be a Smoky and Winston jazz fan. I contacted Abigail shortly after I met with Ham. Told her of my plan. Abigail was all in.

Detective Miller flashed her shield. "Bunco Division," Abigail added. "That recording is proof positive of a willful act of criminal conspiracy on your part to commit blackmail."

"You set me up!" Ronnie said to the woman he knew as Barbara. Shock rippled through his eyes, immediately replaced by rage.

"I came in for a drink," Abigail said. "The rest was your own doing."

"After you fed me that sob story about being on the verge of becoming homeless. I was trying to help. I felt sorry for you. I should have known better. Pity is a sucker's emotion."

"How'd you come by that wad of cash you pulled out of your pocket?" Abigail asked. "Good Samaritan work?"

"This won't fly," Ronnie said. "This was entrapment!"

"Not at all," Abigail said. "You see, Ronnie, you approached me. Now had I been the one to initiate contact, then you might have a case."

"You've got to be kidding," Ronnie said.

"The proof's right here," I said, holding up the digital recorder.

"This is bullshit!" Ronnie said, looking at me as if I had appeared out of nowhere. "Are you a cop too?" he asked.

"No," I said.

"Then what do you have to do with this?" Ronnie asked.

"A concerned citizen doing my civic duty," I said.

"What do you want?" Ronnie asked. In an instant, the rage had vanished, replaced by a steely calm.

"To arrest you," Detective Miller said.

"You didn't go through all of this trouble to run a sting on me for something that may get me locked up for a few months."

"You're right," I said.

"What is it?" Ronnie asked.

"Does the name Matteo Akraka ring a bell?" I asked.

"That's what this is all about?" Ronnie said. "Matteo fucking Akraka put you up to this. How do I even know you're a real cop?" Ronnie asked Detective Miller.

Abigail showed Levers her handcuffs. "Why don't I haul your ass downtown? Then we'll see how real this is."

"Here's the deal," I said. "You let Matteo Akraka off the hook, and this incriminating information goes away."

"You want me to relinquish my big score?" Ronnie said.

"You got it," I said.

"Not going to happen."

"You're looking at jail time," I said.

"Maybe. Maybe not."

"There's no maybe about it," Abigail said.

"We turn this over to the DA tonight," I said.

"Charges will be filed," Abigail said.

"That alone will put the brakes on your lawsuit," I said.

"How do you figure?" Ronnie asked.

"Being charged with a crime of this nature," Abigail said.

"Will call into question your credibility," I said.

"Guess what will happen next?" Abigail said.

"My lawsuit will be put on hold pending the outcome of my criminal case," Ronnie said.

"There you go," I said. "You've got a good attorney. Even he is not going to be able to get you out of this mess."

Ronnie thought for a moment. "I'll take my chances," he said with conviction. I believed him. One look at Abigail told me she believed him too. Levers was willing to gamble even though the odds were not in his favor, on to Plan B.

"Tell you what, Ronnie," I said. "We'll make you a deal."

"What kind of deal?"

"The kind you still walk away with a fist full of cash," I said.

"I'm listening."

"Whatever settlement you are awarded, you agree to accept the insurance payout—"

"Letting Matteo Akraka off the hook for the rest. I get it."

"What do you say?" I asked. A few people from the Diamondback had come and gone. None giving us more than a curious glance. The cold kept them moving. Ronnie's answer felt like it was taking forever.

"I shouldn't after the beat down that bastard gave me," Ronnie said. "That wasn't necessary."

"Do we have a deal?" I asked.

"What the hell," Ronnie said. "I would have settled for the insurance money in the first place if that asshole hadn't gone bonkers. It's only money."

Levers' last statement revealed more about him than our prior exchange. He wasn't a confidence man and hustler for the money. He was in it for the thrill. The adrenaline rush like daredevils get from testing their limits.

"And you'll drop the assault charges against Matteo Akraka," I added.

Ronnie thought for a moment. "If Akraka agrees to take anger management classes. Then I'll drop the assault charges." One final dig. Levers' figurative way of punching Akraka in the mouth.

"I'll pass that on," I said.

"Good." Ronnie put out his hand for the recording.

"No, you don't," Detective Miller said. I handed the recording over to the detective. "I'll be holding onto this until you make good on our deal. Then—and only then—will it be conveniently misplaced."

"How do I know I can trust you two?"

"You have our word," I said.

"I've heard that a time or two," Ronnie said. "Most times, they were barefaced lies."

"Our words are rock solid," I said.

"Do you have a choice?" Detective Miller added.

"Guess not," Ronnie said. "Can I have my money back?"

"Evidence," Abigail said. "In case you renege on our deal."

"May I have my handkerchief back? Or is that evidence too?"

Abigail yanked the handkerchief from her coat pocket and slapped it into Ronnie's open palm. The same palm that had been cut. A faint scar remained. Levers stared at Abigail as if committing her face to memory. "Detective Abigail Miller," he said. "Portland PD. Bunco Division." Turning to me, he said, "I didn't catch your name."

"I didn't throw it," I said.

"Right," Levers said. "You win some. You lose some."

Ronnie Levers left us whistling "The Gambler" by Kenny Rogers as we returned to the Diamondback, leaving me wondering who got the better of our deal. Tyrone Hamson came to mind. All it would have taken was a phone call from Ham to alert Levers I was coming. The ace up my sleeve was Levers would be on the lookout for me. Not an attractive undercover female detective. As long as The Gypsy held up his end of the bargain, Matteo Akraka was off the hook.

CHAPTER THIRTY-SIX

Destini and I had not seen much of each other since dinner with the Sabas. Destini and Liederman were pulling double shifts to keep up with the rise in Portland homicides. Debilitating department illnesses were still affecting available personnel. It seemed that combinations of ground level territorial beefs and plain crazy had reached a confluence of murder madness in the City of Roses. So much so that Homicide Captain Williamsen asked Destini and Liederman to work solo temporarily. Destini was taking work home and working weekends to keep up. I tried convincing my love to set up shop at my place, allowing me to pamper her during this stressful period. Destini declined. Said I would be too much of a distraction. I scheduled a morning delivery of flowers and chocolates to her office. The card was to read "Dreaming of you, C. J." The up side of Destini not accepting my invitation was that it afforded me more time to pour over the FBI surveillance data on Quentin Drayton.

I read through the last three months of written surveillance transcripts on Quentin Drayton. Nothing incriminating. He was careful. He was smart and elusive. There was no audio. I leafed through the photos. Pictures of him, his bodyguards, his sister, friends, acquaintances, and business associates linked to the drug trade but not doing anything marginally illegal. I saved the most engaging method of surveillance for last, the video. Much the same as the still photos were all I saw. There was nothing incriminating until this specific footage grabbed my attention.

Quentin Drayton's midnight blue DRAYDOG SUV was parked in the hotel parking lot. It was a clear day. According to the timestamp, Quentin got out of the front passenger side of his SUV at nine-forty-eight a.m., wearing top-of-the-line hip-hop gear. His sister, Carol Drayton, the driver, and another man seated next to Carol in the back seat remained inside.

Quentin said something to them before closing the car door. Quentin headed toward the hotel entrance. Four large men wearing black suits and open dark green overcoats jumped out of silver and pearl sedans parked across from DRAYDOG's SUV and escorted Quentin Drayton inside.

The cameraperson turned the camera back toward the SUV once Quentin and his bodyguards were out of view for whatever reason. At nine-fifty-six, the backseat bodyguard exited the vehicle, closing the door behind him; another large man dressed the same as his counterparts. He carefully surveyed the area. He opened the door and lent a hand to his charge once satisfied. Carol Drayton was about five-six, slender, wearing a fashionable sunset-colored business suit and heels. Her skin was the same rust-brown color as her brother. Her dark wavy hair weave draped over her shoulders. Her eyes were glued to her phone, looking the part of a successful, professional woman.

The bodyguard removed a piece of luggage from the trunk and set it down next to Carol Drayton, extending its telescopic handle. A slate blue business case covered in travel stickers. I paused the video to zoom in on the case. Australia, New York, Japan, Holland, Canada, Brazil, and London were the ones I could make out. Stickers were placed precisely on the case as one I had seen before. I could not believe my eyes. That was the same business case I saw Shelly retrieve from Epitome Self Storage Locker No. 137. What was Carol Drayton doing with it? I continued the video to find out.

Carol walked toward the hotel like a VIP. The vigilant bodyguard followed her, wheeling the case like any business traveler. Carol and her bodyguard disappeared inside the hotel. At ten-seventeen, Carol and her bodyguard emerged. Her bodyguard wheeling behind him an identical slate blue business case minus the decals. Why would Carol make an exchange like that if she knew they were being recorded? Maybe she expected all of the attention would be on Quentin, and nobody would notice her. It was also a detail even trained agents could miss. I was only aware of the discrepancy from having inside knowledge. The bodyguard loaded the new case into the trunk. Carol and her bodyguard returned to the backseat of the SUV as if nothing had happened. At ten-forty-four, Quentin and his bodyguards came out of the hotel. Quentin was escorted to his SUV. His bodyguards got into their sedans. They all left together.

If the contents of the business case Carol Quentin took inside the hotel contained what Shelly originally picked up from Epitome Self Storage—a safe presumption of illegal narcotics—then was Carol Quentin part of her big brother's organization after all? Quentin acted as a decoy in this transaction while his little sister sealed the deal?

The camera kept rolling, pointing into the parking lot. I presumed the agent forgot to shut it off. The official surveillance assignment was over. The agent probably wanted to jot down his observations and impressions while recent events were still fresh in his mind. At ten-fifty-eight, I saw the same decal slate blue business case Carol Quentin had taken into the hotel being loaded into the trunk of a burgundy sedan. The person doing the loading looked very familiar. I paused the footage to zoom in on his face. I could not believe my luck when I saw who it was. The burgundy vehicle exited the parking lot at eleven a.m. The agent had not seen the coincidence. I had read the agent's notes in the transcripts, and there was no mention of a burgundy vehicle, the business case, or the driver. I doubted anyone had viewed this footage since it had been shot. I had all the evidence I needed to formulate Shelly Morton, Adrian Morton, and Lerone Winbush's exit strategy from Thompson's grip. I made a copy of the entire video, capturing the most incriminating portions onto color stills.

CHAPTER THIRTY-SEVEN

The following day I called Detective Chris Thompson to set up a private meeting in my office. I stressed that it was urgent and for him to come alone. When Thompson arrived, I greeted him and dispensed with the amenities at the front door.

"I have something to show you," I said.

"Make it quick," Thompson snapped. "I don't have all day."

I locked the door. "In my office," I said, marching into my office and picking up a clasped manila envelope on my desk. I handed it to Thompson.

"What's this?" he asked.

"Open it."

Thompson unclasped the envelope and pulled out a stack of color prints. Stills I had captured from what I was now calling the Carol Drayton video.

"Pictures of Carol Drayton with one of her bodyguards standing in front of her brother's SUV," Thompson said. "So what?"

"Leaf through," I said. I had placed the stills in the same sequence as they had occurred in the video.

"Looks like she's checking into the hotel. Why are you wasting my time with this, C. J.?"

"Keep going," I said. Thompson got to the stills where Carol Drayton was returning to the SUV.

"Looks like she changed her mind about checking in," Thompson said.

"Go back to the earlier photos."

"Enough with the suspense," Thompson said irritably. "I have real police work to do. If you've got a point, make it."

"Take a good look starting from the beginning," I said.

After a heavy sigh, Thompson did as I asked. "What am I supposed to see?"

"Focus on the business case."

"Okay," Thompson said as he focused on the business case in each still.

"Notice anything special about the traveler?" I asked.

Thompson looked hard at a capture with a good view of the case. His detective curiosity was taking over his grumpy attitude. "Blue, metal, covered with stickers," he said.

"Go to the photos where Carol Drayton is returning to the car," I said.

Thompson leafed through until he got to a still with a clear picture of the business case the bodyguard was wheeling on their return to the SUV. Thompson's face lit with recognition.

"Notice anything different?" I asked.

"No stickers," he said. "What happened to the other case?"

"Looks like clear evidence of a switch to me," I said.

"What was in the case she took inside?" Thompson asked.

"Amway," I said. "What do you think?"

"Are you telling me Carol Drayton is a part of her brother's operation?"

"Could be something else," I said.

"Are you suggesting that Carol Drayton is dealing behind her brother's back?"

"From what I saw," I said. "It's a possibility."

Thompson let out a low whistle.

"Overall, Chris, I'm not telling you anything. I'm showing you photos in which Carol Drayton appears to be involved in something shady. I'm guessing her payment was in the case she brought back to the car."

Thompson said, "Damn. She sure had me fooled. How'd you come by these?"

"Never mind that," I said. I was not only not going to reveal my source. I also wanted Thompson to believe they were photos. I did not want Thompson to know I had video footage of the event. In case the detective didn't pan out. I needed the video available for another hand I could play.

"Now, hold on. Let's not jump the gun," Thompson said. "I'll admit what you have here is…compelling. "There's no hard evidence Carol Drayton was involved in doing anything wrong. We don't know the contents of either case. It's circumstantial evidence at best. Despite Carol Drayton's familial affiliation with Oregon's biggest drug dealer. We need more."

"Quentin Drayton is technically a narcotics supplier," I said. "There's a difference. He doesn't deal directly with the consumer."

"Semantics," Thompson snorted. "The bottom line is Carol Drayton went in with one case. She came out with another. It could be a drug payoff. Could be something altogether different. For all we know, she could have unloaded some old jewelry. It will take more than this to convince my superiors to move against heavy hitters like the Draytons."

I liked the fact Thompson used the inclusive "We." It suggested to me for the moment at least. He was willing to work in partnership. "That's the teaser," I said.

"You have evidence to nail this down?" Thompson asked.

"I most certainly do, Chris."

"Then let's see it."

"Here's where we negotiate, Detective," I said.

"You're kidding, right?" Thompson eyeballed me. My stone-cold expression answered his question. "Here we go," Thompson said, sounding exasperated. "Everything's a negotiation with you, Cavanaugh. Let me guess. Your terms involve your friend Shelly."

"I want you to cut Shelly loose," I said.

Thompson thought for a moment before answering. "I can do that."

"I also want the records of Lerone Winbush and Adrian Morton expunged."

"Tear up the paperwork on a couple of juvenile delinquents. Make like it never happened?"

"They were set up, Chris."

"So you say, C. J. Anything else? Maybe season's tickets to the Blazers while I'm at it," Thompson finished sarcastically.

"That about sums it up," I said, dismissing his sarcasm. "If you can work in the season's tickets. I'll take them."

"How do I know what you have is worth it? I've seen the advertisement but I haven't handled the product."

"Do we have a deal or don't we, Chris? I could turn what I have over to some other authorities. Say the DEA or FBI. Believe me. They would have no trouble making a conviction stick."

"What you have is that sweet?" Thompson asked. I nodded. The detective thought for a moment.

"Why not," he said. "I'll clear the decks for your pal Shelly and his teenage miscreants. If what you have holds up. Now let's see what I'll be trading in my leverage for."

I opened my middle right hand desk drawer. Pulled out another clasped manila envelope and handed it to Thompson. Thompson opened the envelope, staring at me as if he had his doubts.

"Is that who I think it is?" Thompson blurted when he saw the first still. Thompson was staring at the close up of a suave, clean-shaven man with tapered brown hair, chiseled features, and cool brown eyes.

I smiled. "Who do you think it is?"

"Kellen 'Missile' Westmore."

"If he's not Kellen Westmore, then he's certainly his doppelganger," I said.

"Now Missile *is* a drug dealer."

"Agreed," I said. I had done my homework on Missile since our first meeting years ago. Westmore started as a street corner dealer who worked for Portland drug kingpin Cecil Vogan. Westmore climbed the ranks over the years, becoming a trusted lieutenant in Vogan's organization. Westmore set out on his own when Vogan died in prison while serving a life sentence for drug trafficking/distribution and multiple homicides. Kellen Westmore's reputation was that he was cunning and ruthless. Missile became the man in Multnomah County and much of Oregon. That was until Quentin Drayton came along.

"Westmore's another dirtbag I'd like to put away," Thompson said. "There he is, holding that same sticker case in living color. Little sister is obviously not as attentive to the details as her big brother. She missed the decals if she knew she was being photographed."

"Or maybe she thought all of the attention would be on Quentin," I said, "and nobody would notice her."

"Could be," Thompson agreed with a nod. "We still don't know the contents of those cases."

"Certainly enough suspicion there to merit search warrants and to bring Carol Drayton and Kellen Westmore in for questioning," I said.

"That it is," Thompson said. "What's her game?"

"Meaning?"

"Do you think Carol Drayton is in with her brother, or does she have something going on the side?"

I had some ideas. Sharing them with Thompson might only muddy his investigative process. "As I said before, it's a possibility."

"Right," Thompson said, eyeballing me again. "You did say that."

"I'll leave unearthing the details to you, Chris," I said.

"And I will, C. J.," Thompson said with conviction. "You'd better believe I sure as hell will. How'd you come by this godsend material again?"

My immediate response was a smile. We both knew what Thompson was doing. Circling back to see if I would let slip my source. I didn't know how Thompson would exploit the information I gave him. I knew how I would play it. I expected that Thompson would do the same. One thing I would not do under any circumstances was reveal my source. If placed between a legal rock and a hard place, I would turn over to Aloisio Reis the same evidence I had given Thompson, only adding the FBI's video footage to the package. The FBI would take over, leaving Thompson and Portland Narcotics out in the cold. I would become an FBI protected witness. Portland PD would not be able to touch me. The same guilty people would be punished. The only difference being the FBI would receive most of the credit.

"I'm a damn good investigator," I said to Thompson's question.

"With friends in high places," he said.

"Sure doesn't hurt," I said.

Thompson could not stop grinning. The detective was on his way out with the evidence shoved into his trench coat pockets when I said, "Make sure you cite your source as anonymous."

"No problem," Thompson said, not bothering to look back or say goodbye.

I believed Thompson was as good as his word on cutting loose Shelly, Adrian, and Lerone. I was covering all of my bases just in case. Sometimes it's a dirty business on both sides of the track. I had borrowed one of Renita's video/audio recording devices. I placed the innocent looking baby Panda in my office. It had recorded our entire meeting. Our negotiation became part of the Cavanaugh Investigative Agency's digital archives. If Chris decided to renege on our deal, career advancement in Portland Narcotics would no longer be a realistic part of Officer Christopher Thompson's future by the time I was finished with him.

CHAPTER THIRTY-EIGHT

"You're early," Donna Haschak said matter-of-factly. Her gray eyes glanced up from her dual monitors for an instant while she continued to type. She had changed her dark auburn hairstyle from a medium length with bangs to a short, layered look. Donna appeared fit and right at home behind her modern adjustable height desk, wearing a two-piece business suit.

We had gotten to know one another over the years through our mutual connection to her boss. Patrick O'Malley preferred personal assistants who could handle themselves in a skirmish. Patrick was lucky to find Donna when his former P.A., who fit that bill, transferred up.

Donna had been a field operative and a very good one. Big things were in her DEA future until she was wounded during a firefight against an American drug cartel. Took a slug in the leg. The injury left her with a noticeable limp. She was reassigned to desk duty. Her focus was all about the DEA before the injury. She reprioritized her life. Working desk duty allowed her to maintain a regular work schedule. Donna met and married Trenton Haschak and settled down.

Patrick's private office was located in the Federal Building. Security was tight. Donna's reaction was minimal when I entered the office. I had no doubt Donna had seen me coming long before I walked in. All DEA offices in the building were tapped into the building security cameras. Donna and Patrick had a dedicated continual real-time monitor displaying the comings and goings of everyone who entered the building and appeared on their floor. If I posed any threat, then intruder protocols would have been enacted. Donna would have locked down the office with a press of a button at her desk. Alerted Patrick to the situation and immediately armed herself with the Beretta M9 in her upper right desk drawer.

"Gives me time to say hello," I said in response to Donna's greeting.

"Hello, C. J."

"How are things, Donna?"

"Living the dream."

"Missed you at Smoky's surprise party."

"The triplets came down with the flu. At the same time, if you can believe it."

"Sorry to hear that. The girls okay?"

"They're fine. Nine-year-olds bounce back fast. Maggie's been asking about you."

Maggie was the oldest of Donna's maternal triplets by three minutes twenty-three seconds, as she used to tell everyone when she was four. "Wants to know when you're coming by to play video games with her again."

I'm not a fan of violent video games. I don't find them entertaining. What I am is a quick study. I find it easy to memorize the handset controls and what controls to utilize in each situation. I only play them because so many people in my life do, including Destini and Renita. Maggie and I got into a fierce competition that ended in a draw the last time I was over Donna's house. Maggie was a good trash talker. Something she enjoyed as much as the game. She also wasn't above dirty tricks like slapping the controls out of your hands or blocking the screen during the heat of battle. I liked that kid.

"She wants to break the tie," I said.

"Yep. I warn you. Maggie's been practicing. No one in the house can touch her."

"I was a lot more lucky than good last time."

"Someone needs to bring my daughter down a peg or two. I'm going to lose it if I have to endure one more of her obnoxious victory celebrations. How about dinner next Saturday?"

"Sounds good."

"Bring your wife." Donna was referring to Destini. She believed us a perfect couple. Reminding me of that fact every time I see her.

"If Destini's free. She has a lot on her homicide plate right now."

Donna looked up at me for a long moment, still typing. "I'll ask her myself."

"Send him in." Patrick's voice came through the intercom.

I entered the inner office of Portland DEA Deputy Director Patrick O'Malley. The only significant change to his office over the past few years was his desk and chair. Donna had worn Patrick down with her contemporary office ideas. His old school wooden office desk and high back leather chair had been replaced with an ergonomic wire mesh chair and an adjustable height desk. Patrick was happy with the changes. Renita was on board for us to do the same. I was still thinking about it.

What hadn't changed was Patrick. He was still the tough, hardheaded, freckled Harvard Law graduate with a blue-collar background. His short carrot red hair was brushed back in waves with a touch more of encroaching steel gray. His quarter note muttonchops were groomed to perfection. He remained muscular due to a strict workout regimen, continuing erroneously, in my opinion, to blame his slight middle-aged paunch on a genetic curse rather than his deep affection for dark Scottish Ale.

Patrick did not mention why he wanted me to stop by his office. I had my suspicions. We exchanged good-natured greetings and a couple of pleasantries after we shook hands. Patrick offered me a seat across from his desk. I made myself comfortable.

"Thanks again for helping out on the Epitome surveillance," Patrick said in his even, measured tone.

"Any time. It looks like you've netted quite a few fish, judging by recent news reports."

"We have. A couple of them slipped the net, but we'll reel them in."

"That's not why I'm here, is it?" I said.

"No, it isn't." Patrick paused. His deep-set dark green eyes bore into me like an interrogator sizing up his victim. "Your journal entries and reports were excellent."

"Thanks, Patrick."

"Clear and concise…except for one gray area, C. J."

"Oh."

"Yeah. Maybe you can help me clear it up."

"No problem."

"Remember the time you were flying solo?" Patrick asked.

"Of course. Luca's wife was having their baby."

"Right. There was a person who appeared on the security cam footage. This person was obviously in disguise. Do you know who I'm talking about?"

"The dude wearing a cheap suit, phony beard, and a wig."

"That's the one."

"What about him?" I asked.

"We can't seem to ID him."

"Guess that's why he was wearing a disguise." My attempt at humor drew a blank stare from Patrick.

"The thing is, whoever he was didn't know about our surveillance op," Patrick said.

"Maybe the disguise was for the storage facility cameras."

"Makes sense. Nonetheless, we can't seem to track him down. He didn't leave any DNA evidence behind in the locker. We traced the rental car—"

"Excuse me. Rental car?" I was playing dumb. Patrick made no indication he was on to me.

"The perp in disguise arrived in a rental car."

"I hadn't noticed. I kept an eye on what was going on inside the facility. I didn't pay much attention to the parking lot. I must be getting rusty."

"I doubt that."

Patrick *was* on to me. Everything about him, from his eyes, expression, and body language, alerted me to that fact. He had no evidence to the contrary as far as I knew. I certainly wasn't going to volunteer any.

"As I was saying," Patrick continued, "we tracked down the rental. And you won't believe whose name it was under."

Patrick paused. He wanted me to fill in the blank. I didn't bite. "Who?"

"Quentin Drayton."

Patrick was right. I didn't believe it. His news made my shock reaction far more believable. Drayton would not be so sloppy to create an obvious drug deal connection to himself.

"You're kidding?" I blurted out. "The biggest narcotics distributor in Oregon, Quentin Drayton?"

"One and the same, C. J. When I asked Drayton why he rented a car in his name, he said, 'Why not?'"

"I never witnessed Drayton make any pickups from Epitome," I said.

"Neither did we. Drayton claims he was the person wearing the disguise."

"*What?*"

Patrick continued as if I hadn't spoken. "The funny thing is, Locker No. 137 is in his name. We have clear visual evidence of the disguised Quentin Drayton removing the carryon from his locker that we were able to trace to their delivery point tying Drayton to the entire chain of events."

"Why the Halloween costume?" I asked.

"My thoughts exactly!"

"You're losing me, Patrick. Quentin Drayton rented a car and wore a disguise. In order to make a pickup from his locker?"

"Baffles the mind, doesn't it? He had some cock-and-bull story about trying out something new. In case he needed to—and I quote—'go incognito in the future.'"

"That's…peculiar," I said. Truly at a loss for words.

Patrick nodded. "Any ideas?"

"None."

"Oh, I'm sure you might have one or two ideas, C. J. If you apply yourself."

"Are you serious?"

"Yes. Are you?"

Patrick was ready to drop the cat and mouse play. I wasn't going to let that happen. Shelly's future was at stake.

"Excuse me?" I said in response to his question.

"Who are you protecting, C. J.?"

"I don't know what you're talking about, Patrick."

"You recognized the person wearing that disguise."

"If Drayton's already copped to disguising himself, why do you doubt him?"

"Good question. I've been over every frame of that surveillance tape. I had an analysis done of that particular footage to verify what my eyes were telling me. The person in disguise was a different height and built as Mr. Drayton. He had a different gait than Drayton as well. And enough of his face was visible that you could make out his skin complexion didn't match Drayton's."

"Did you ask Drayton if he was wearing makeup?" I asked.

"No, I didn't. The thought never crossed my mind. Thank you, C. J., for sharing your great insight. I'll make certain to pose that question to Mr. Drayton when next we speak."

"You know me, Patrick. Always willing to help when and where I can."

Patrick gave me a sarcastic smile.

"Why would Drayton lie?" I asked.

"I asked myself that same question. I know he's not afraid of prison. He's been in and out of penal institutions for much of his life. He feels right at home. He's not afraid of dying, and he doesn't respond to threats. He's a tough, narcissistic, alpha male. Above all else, he's smart. Why would a person like Quentin Drayton not roll over on someone who could shave a few years off his sentence?"

"He's no snitch," I said.

"Granted, but as I said, he's smart."

"Maybe he's trying to protect someone."

"Like you're doing right now."

"Patrick, I have no idea what you are talking about."

"No idea, huh."

"Not one."

"I have a thought, C. J. Somehow, someone got to Drayton. Whatever they have is making him submit to this dumbass story that wouldn't fool a grade schooler."

"If he's sticking to his guns. You have no choice but to go along with it."

"Exactly! You see my point."

"Not really, Patrick. Why do you care? I certainly don't."

"I insist on the truth, C. J. I might bend or dismiss it to protect certain individuals, but I insist on knowing the facts."

"Sounds to me like you have them."

"That's your final answer."

"I didn't know I was being cross-examined."

"You're not. I'm asking as a friend."

"I've told you all I can on the matter, Patrick."

"But not all you know."

"All that's worth relaying."

"Is that how you're going to answer on the witness stand, C. J.? When they question you about the person in disguise?"

"My answer will be brief and precise. I will, of course, see no reason to refute Quentin Drayton's testimony that he was the man in disguise."

"Cedric Joseph Cavanaugh. A master of nuance."

"I've learned from the best."

"That is an area in which you have taught me a thing or two."

We stared at each other. Patrick gave me a light chuckle.

"Alright, C. J., I know you're lying, but I can see you're dug in. We'll just have to accept Mr. Drayton's word. He was wearing the disguise on that given day. The federal prosecutor will be satisfied with his explanation. They're focused on convicting Drayton. They will be more than happy to let some minnow get away in the process."

"What about the video analysis?" I asked.

"What analysis? It was never an official request, which means there is no official record of an analysis ever having been performed. I haven't shared my suspicions with anyone besides you. Drayton's already instructed his legal team not to pursue any line of query surrounding the individual in disguise so they won't request one."

How Patrick knew what Drayton's defense team was up to, I didn't ask. I nodded. I took no pleasure in deceiving my comrade. I believed I was doing so for the greater good. I hoped he had enough trust in me to believe the same.

"Thanks for coming in, C. J. I have a ton of paperwork." Patrick stood and extended his hand to me across his desk. We shook. He held on to my hand like a predator to its prey.

"Are you going to the FCC tonight?" Patrick asked.

"I might make an appearance."

"Tell Shelly I said hello. Today was his lucky day." Patrick grinned, then let go of my hand. "You know your way out."

Before I reached the door, Patrick said, "One last thing, C. J. What did you say to Agent Parker?"

"Lamar? Nothing special I can think of."

"Parker had been bugging me to put him in for a deep cover assignment. You've met him. I don't have to tell you the list of reasons why that wasn't going to happen. I've been stringing Lamar along because I don't want to lose him in his current capacity. He's damn good at surveillance work. I was eventually going to have to come out and tell him no if he persisted in his request. Working with you on a stakeout and Parker withdraws his deep cover request. He lets me know he's happy where he's at. What did you say to him to flip that switch?"

"Only the facts."

"Scared straight, huh?" Patrick said.

"More like a hard core shot of reality with no chaser."

Patrick gave me a knowing smile. The kind two people comprehend the meaning behind without a word from a shared and gritty history.

"See you around, C. J."

"You can count on it, Patrick."

CHAPTER THIRTY-NINE

My morning meeting with Patrick left me invigorated. Shelly was off the hook for the time being. If Drayton stuck to his story, Shelly would remain a free man. Cold rain turned to sleet as I made the short slippery walk back to my office.

I didn't know how Patrick knew about Shelly. His information could have come from a number of sources. Patrick's network ran wide and deep. Our meeting was a test, in my opinion. Patrick wanted to see if I would roll over on Shelly. Not out of fear or sanctimony but from DEA loyalty. I may have retired from the thicket, but Patrick knew law enforcement still ran deep in my veins. In his way, Patrick was assuring me that Shelly had nothing to fear from him. He was on board with what I was doing. Actions he could not officially sanction as Deputy Director of the Portland DEA. I always knew there were certain people for whom I was willing to bend the rules. I discovered Shelly Morton was amongst those few.

Detective Christopher Thompson was waiting for me in the hall when I arrived at my office.

"I was about to give up on you," Thompson said. "Thought you might be taking a sick day or something," he concluded with a smirk.

"I had a morning meeting."

"Oh yeah, with who?"

"A private matter. You want to come in?"

"I'm not standing here for my health."

We stepped inside. We were both wearing lined double-breasted belted trench coats and gable safari hats. No umbrellas; it's a northwest thing. We hung up our rain gear on the wooden coat rack in the reception area. Mine was still dripping wet. Thompson's was not. That told me Thompson had been waiting for a while.

I offered the detective some refreshment. He chose a Java Roast Breakfast Blend. I placed a pod into the single-serve coffee maker. We stood silent as the sound of hot water forced through the pod filled the gap. The aroma of light roast coffee filled the kitchen area. I was certain we were both using the quiet moment to go over our mental game plans. An occupational hazard those in law enforcement, particularly those accustomed to undercover work, find nearly impossible to turn off. Thompson took his fresh brewed coffee black, passing his nose over the steaming black Colombian brew, nodding his approval before taking his first sip.

"Delicious," Thompson said.

I was having black tea using the same method. The mild aroma of my choice did nothing to dispel the power of its predecessor. Small talk emerged as we waited. Civil discourse between acquaintances about local weather. Empty dialogue that distracted none of us from what lay ahead.

"What brings you here on this fine morning, Chris?" I asked as we settled into my office. We both grinned at my statement. For a northwest native, this weather was all good. I must have adapted more than I realized because I felt the same.

"I want to thank you for that Carol Drayton info, C. J. It helped put a lot of the pieces together."

"Glad I could help."

"Quentin Drayton's been trying to keep Carol out of the business. Give little sis a chance at a clean life. Although I don't know how that works. If you can launder money. I suppose you can do the same with lives. Anyway, little sis knew Shelly was giving Quentin headaches, so she decided to help him out. It turns out little sister is equally protective of her big brother when somebody messes with him."

"Carol Drayton set up those teenagers?" I asked.

Chris nodded. "Shelly thought it was Quentin Drayton."

"Natural assumption, how'd you figure it out, Chris?"

"The setup didn't add up. If Drayton felt burned by Shelly, he would have taken a more aggressive course of action, if you know what I mean. That's his nature. That's who he is. I looked into it. Found evidence that Carol Drayton was the one who set things in motion. Got names on the perps who carried out the setup as well."

"And you were keeping this in your back pocket. Why?"

"Never know when information like that could come in handy, C. J."

"You were going to let a couple of kids do time on a bogus bust."

"Sometimes I get so caught up in the chase I forget to take stock in the consequences."

I believed him.

"No hard feelings?" he asked.

"None," I said. "But I'm not the one who was almost railroaded."

"Understood."

Chris was holding back something. I could feel it. I needed to prod him into revealing what it was without giving up my inside info.

"This was all about Carol Drayton?" I asked.

"Kinda," he said.

"Besides the teens being set up, I still don't see how Shelly fits into Carol's scheme?"

"I had my partner keep an eye on Shelly after we made the deal. To make sure he was on the up and up."

"Trust no one," I said. "Believe only what you can prove."

"Exactly," Chris said. "He sees Shelly get into a rental car wearing a disguise. He follows him to Epitome Self Storage, where he sees Shelly come out of the place with a carry-on. My partner follows Shelly to a parking lot, where Shelly leaves the car with the carry-on in it. My partner has good instincts. Rather than follow Shelly, he sits on the car. Low and behold, one of Quentin Drayton's men gets in the rental car and drives away. Drayton's man drops off the rental, takes the carryon with him, and gets into a car driven by another of Drayton's men that is waiting for him across the street. My partner follows them back to Drayton's place. We assumed the carry-on was filled with product being delivered to Quentin Drayton. We were wrong about who."

"Who was the carryon delivered to?" I asked.

"Carol Drayton."

I nodded. Surprised but, for some reason, not shocked. "How are you acquiring all of these juicy details, Chris?"

"Like you, C. J., I hear things."

I looked sideways at Chris. He had a smug expression as he drank his coffee.

"This coffee is delicious," he said. "I'm going to get this at home."

I would pass along Detective Thompson's compliment to Renita. She made all of the coffee choices in our office.

"Take some with you," I said.

"Don't mind if I do," Chris said, enjoying another sip.

Then suddenly, it dawned on me. "You have someone on the inside!"

"Let's just say one of Quentin Drayton's lieutenants keeps me informed."

"Did you acquire him the same way you roped Shelly?"

"Of course not," Chris said, not masking his sarcasm. "He walked into my office one day and said he felt really, really bad about the criminal activities he had been involved in over the years and was hoping there was some way he could atone for his sins."

"Touché," I said.

"This informant overheard Carol tell her brother what she did, expecting praise for her ingenuity. Quentin immediately shut her down. Scolded her. He made Carol promise she would never do anything like that again, which she agreed to. I might have mentioned to Quentin on a recent impromptu visit while he was in lockup what might happen to Carol if he didn't cop to wearing the disguise on that fateful night."

Now it all made sense. Thompson's threat of exposing his sister was why Quentin Drayton was willing to take the fall. Did Patrick know about this? Maybe Patrick thought I was behind Drayton's coercion. Knowing me as well as Patrick did would make for a logical hypothesis. I had to smile.

"There may be hope for you yet, Chris," I said.

"I wouldn't count on it, C. J. The bizarre thing is Quentin Drayton has a hands-off policy on Shelly, his family, and everyone and anything to do with the Fremont Community Center. Anyone who violates that policy could wind up dead."

A decree like that suggested Quentin Drayton may have been trying to give others an opportunity he never had.

"How did Carol find out about the lockers if Quentin wanted to shield his sister from what he was involved in?"

"Quentin trusts Carol one-hundred percent, according to my informant. His best guess was Carol had been sneaking around, squirreling away information on Quentin's operations for some time."

"Was Carol looking to make a move on her brother?"

"Quite the opposite. Carol was looking to prove herself. She wants Quentin to make her part of his team."

"That's an interesting twist on family loyalty."

"Tell me about it," Chris said.

"You used the information I gave you to set up Carol Drayton. That in the end brought down her brother."

"That sums it up in a nutshell."

"How'd Kellen Westmore fit into this?" I asked.

"Westmore was on board because he assumed Carol was operating with Quentin's blessings, according to my source. I, unfortunately, have to let Missile's day of reckoning slide to make my deal work with Quentin."

"I'm guessing the incriminating Carol Drayton evidence will also disappear as part of Quentin Drayton's confession deal," I said.

"What Carol Drayton evidence?" Thompson said with a wry smile. Thompson knew with this collar in his jacket that he was virtually assured the Captain's seat when Richardson retired. Thompson had lived up to his rep. He was a bastard. Suppose that made me one too.

"I never told Quentin how I acquired my information about his sister," Chris said.

"To protect your source?"

"Yes, and you."

"Think it'll work?"

"I honestly don't know."

While Thompson's source was not devoid of my compassion, they fell into the neck deep in the game category. Whatever happened to him was collateral damage as far as I was concerned. I doubted Shelly would agree.

"Carol rented the car by phone and used one of her brother's credit cards to do it," Chris said. "Anyway, that's my story. I'm still not clear on how you knew about Shelly."

My involvement with the DEA surveillance operation on Epitome Self Storage might become public knowledge if I was needed to testify. My name would be listed in court documents that would eventually be made public. I saw no reason to jump the gun by telling Chris anything about it.

"As I said, I hear things, Chris."

"Yeah, I bet you do, C. J."

"What if Carol decides to talk?" I asked.

"Let's just say, Carol's been informed if word of Shelly's involvement gets out in any way, shape, or form, she will be presumed to be the source. In which case, both she and Quentin would be looking at a long stretch."

"Thanks, Chris, for helping me out on this one," I said.

"Did I have a choice?"

I answered with a slight shoulder shrug. Thompson laughed.

"We SOBs have to stick together," he said.

I laughed. Chris had done his due diligence. I didn't know who he talked to or what they had said about me. If he was referring to what he discovered about my DEA history. His description was close to the truth. In some ways, we were cut from the same cloth.

Chris finished his coffee. "Man, that's good. It's been fun, C. J. but I have to get back to work."

"Let's get you some of that coffee to go."

I went to the kitchen and tossed a handful of breakfast blend, along with a few other single-serve coffees, into a white T-shirt plastic grocery bag with the red words "Thank You" cascading down both sides. By the time I entered the reception area, Chris was bundled up and ready to leave. I handed him the bag.

"I presume you won't be pulling any strings now, C. J."

"That's a safe bet."

We shook hands. The detective's grip was firm and warm.

"This doesn't make us even. You owe me, C. J. I had to burn some hard-earned capital to clean up your friend's mess."

"Justice isn't enough for you."

"Justice comes at a price."

"Consider the coffee a down payment."

Chris smirked. "See you around, Cavanaugh." My gut told me he was right.

"You can count on it," I said.

We exchanged business cards and went our separate ways.

This day had turned out to be a winner despite the weather. I fired up my PC. After a few moments, I opened the front door of my office and checked the halls. No one was about. I locked the door. I returned to my inner office and closed the door. I was being paranoid, I know. I wanted to make certain no one could overhear me. I picked up my landline to give Shelly Morton the great news.

CHAPTER FORTY

Life at the Cavanaugh Investigation Agency had been interesting while Renita was on vacation. Weeks of professional intrigue my partner would have savored. Of course, I will downplay the events when I tell Renita about them. Lessen her disappointment at not having been part of the show.

For First Class Homicide Detective Destini Pendleton—aka my sweetheart—police life was returning to normal, doing the same for our relationship. Homicide had straightened out its personnel shortage issues. Destini had more time to herself. Free time she was happy to share some of with me.

I was in the middle of summarizing a background report on a candidate for a corporate President of Overseas Operations when my office landline rang.

"Cavanaugh Investigation Agency," I said.

"We got 'em!" Aloisio could not contain himself. I could see him in my mind's eye. His face lit up like a child on Christmas gifted their favorite toy.

"Congratulations," I said, pulling myself away from my report.

"Turns out they did have a base of operation. A front company called Burnish Works. They owned and operated out of a building in Boise City, Oklahoma. The Oklahoma FBI bust went down so fast. Burnish Works didn't know what hit them!"

"Were they mobile as you suspected?"

"Yes. Nationwide. Your guy Contact was one of their mobile operators. We got him, by the way. His real name is Stewart Blunt, in case you're interested. We'll be able to round up most, if not all, of their mobile units. I'm not holding my breath on capturing many of their operatives. They've probably scattered like dried leaves in chaotic winds."

"Nice poetic metaphor, my friend."

"I have my moments."

"What about the arsonists?" I asked.

"We'll have better luck with them. We know who they are. We should capture them before they take flight or go underground. Sarah has already arrested her target."

"We're you in on the Oklahoma bust?" I asked.

"Front and center."

"What about Sarah?"

"She wanted to be there, but I vetoed her request."

"Why?"

"She's a good undercover operative, C. J. I didn't want to expose her. It makes it easier for her on her next assignment."

Aloisio Reis hadn't been made Oregon FBI Special Agent in Charge for nothing. Like any good chess player, he was thinking ahead in this relentless battle against perpetual crime.

"Thanks for your help on this one, C. J."

"You, agent Nelson and your team did most of the heavy lifting. I came along at the right time to add my finger to the bow."

"You got our foot in the door. Why did you ever give up undercover work? You have a knack for it."

I thought about his question for a somber moment before answering. "It was time."

There was quiet. "That agent Nelson," I said. "She's pretty sharp."

"Don't I know it. Sarah's destined for greater things than working for me. I wouldn't be surprised if she turned out to be my boss one day."

Neither would I, I thought.

"Don't forget to pay me for my time," I said. "This wasn't a freebie."

"I won't," Aloisio said. "We'll do lunch soon, C. J."

"You're buying."

"Don't I always."

"Unless I need a favor. What's going to happen to Aidan Madigan?"

"He's going to be indicted along with the rest of them."

"Don't you think he and his family have already suffered enough, Aloisio?"

"Madigan's condition got to you, huh?"

"That and his wife. His wife and children had no part in this mess. They shouldn't be made to suffer for his sins."

"In my opinion, C. J., Madigan should have thought about his family before he became wrapped up in this mess."

In his way, he may have been doing just that, I thought. I remained silent. People faced with far worse circumstances than losing their business did not turn to crime to resolve their dilemma. I had no defense for Madigan on those grounds. Aloisio sighed.

"Maybe we'll be able to work out a plea bargain with the Federal Prosecutor once the smoke clears."

"Thanks, Aloisio."

"You're getting soft on me, C. J."

If only he knew the events of recent history, I thought. "You're just now noticing," I said.

"To be honest, yes."

"Any leads on your internal breach?" I asked.

"Agent Reis," I heard a voice in the background say.

"Hold on, C. J.," Aloisio said. I couldn't hear anything being said. I assumed Aloisio had muted his phone.

Aloisio said in a hurried voice when he returned, "I've got to go, C. J. Talk to you later."

He hung up. I savored the victory for a moment before getting back to the background report.

CHAPTER FORTY-ONE

It was Friday. The last couple of days had been laid back by comparison to the previous few weeks. I didn't feel exhausted from my most recent professional challenges. I felt quite the opposite, a peculiar soothing mix of invigorated calm. My investigative work had returned to normal, background checks and insurance claim verifications. Renita and Ernest were due to fly into Portland International Airport on Saturday. I didn't expect Renita back in the office until Monday.

I was whistling John Coltrane's "Wise One" in the kitchen and filling my eco-friendly stainless steel water bottle with filtered tap water when I heard the office door open. I stopped mid-fill to see who it was.

Two women of nearly equal height and age stood shoulder to shoulder in the reception area. The lithe woman on my right with luminous green eyes and full red lips had tumbling long, thick gray hair. The plump woman on my left had dense short dark gray hair, a full round face, sparkling brown eyes, and a rosy complexion. They were both dressed in stylish form-fitting blue jeans and hooded single-breasted raincoats. The woman on my right wore fire engine red UGG rain boots that matched her raincoat. The woman on my left wore taupe winter duck boots that coordinated well with her tan raincoat. A sunny winter's day with blue skies, we knew that could change in an instant.

"Are you," the woman on my right paused to look at my business card held aloft in her hand, "Mr. Cedric J. Cavanaugh?"

"Yes, I am."

"Good," the other woman said with satisfaction as if they had solved a mystery.

"My name is Cleo Berge," the woman on my right said.

"And I'm Doris Berge," said the woman to my left.

They unbuttoned their coats.

"A pleasure to meet you both," I said, helping them off with their coats.

"Likewise," Doris said.

"We would like to hire you, Mr. Cavanaugh."

"To do what exactly?" I asked, hanging up their raincoats on the coat rack.

"To find our husbands' killer," Cleo said.

"That's a job for the police, ma'am."

"Please don't call us, ma'am," Doris said. "It makes us feel ancient."

"We have plenty of good years left," Cleo said.

"Just because we're grandparents," Doris added, "doesn't mean we want to be constantly reminded of it."

"Except by our grandchildren," Cleo said.

"Of course, they are so adorable."

"Ryan and Jessica."

"Ryan's mine," Cleo said. "Jessica's hers."

"Six and three."

"Cute as buttons."

They spoke in concert as if of one mind.

"What should I call you?" I was finally able to squeeze in between their interchange.

"Doris and Cleo will do," Cleo said. Doris agreed with a smile. I nodded.

"Doris, Cleo, homicide is a job for the police."

"According to the police, our husbands were *not* murdered," Doris said. Her smile replaced with an expression of irritancy.

"We believe otherwise," Cleo said, mimicking Doris' mood.

"What makes you think your husbands were murdered?"

"They drowned," Cleo said. "At least they were found that way."

"What do you mean 'found that way?'"

"According to the coroner's report," Doris said, "our husbands drowned in the Pacific Ocean."

"Since the coroner found no evidence of foul play," Cleo said.

"They ruled our husbands' deaths as accidental drownings."

"You're not convinced."

"Our husbands' bodies were discovered lying side-by-side on our fishing yacht," Cleo added. "The yacht was spotted adrift near Yaquina Head off the Oregon coast by a fishing trawler heading out to open water."

"If they accidentally drowned in the ocean, then who placed their bodies on the deck of our yacht?" Doris asked as if stating the obvious.

"And why didn't the person—or persons, we're not certain how many people were involved at this point—report their finding to the authorities?"

"Unless whoever did it was responsible in some way," Cleo stated conspiratorially. Doris agreed with a couple of quick nods.

"Good questions," I said before either could speak again. "I'm sure the authorities found those circumstances suspicious. Didn't they investigate?"

"They did," Doris said. "And still they concluded their deaths were due to drowning."

"Accidental drowning," Cleo said as if the words left a bitter taste. "The *authorities* theorized a fishing trawler found them and placed our husbands back on their boat, expecting someone would find them."

"Probably didn't want to get involved, according to the police," Doris said.

"Especially if they had undocumented workers on board," Cleo added. Doris and Cleo nodded to each other in agreement. I noticed the widows were wearing simple gold wedding bands. Had they remarried, or were they mementos from their dead husbands? Questions for another time. "Where did you get my card?"

"Shelly Morton gave it to us," Cleo said.

"A dear, sweet man.," Doris said.

"We met Shelly some years ago at a Friends of Multnomah County Library dinner event."

"Shelly told us about the Fremont Community Center that he was running."

"We were curious."

"So we paid Mr. Morton an impromptu visit."

"We like doing that sort of thing," Cleo said.

"Showing up unannounced. Surprising people, like now."

"You see some of the most interesting reactions when you catch people off guard."

"It can be quite entertaining," Doris said.

"Or startling."

They burst out in tandem laughter. I imagined they recalled some of their more amusing surprise reactions. I was also hoping I hadn't been added to their list.

"Once we saw the good Shelly was doing for the young people in that struggling community," Cleo said after their amusement had faded.

"We knew we had to get involved," Doris said with heartfelt sincerity. Cleo gave her friend an approving nod.

"We were recently voted onto the Fremont Community Center Board of Directors," Cleo said with pride.

"Was it three or four months ago?" Cleo asked Doris.

"I believe it was three, dear," Doris answered Cleo. "We attended our first board meeting as official board members the other day," Doris said, returning their attention to me.

"To discuss the budget, future projects, youth activities, those sorts of things," Cleo said, almost dismissively.

"We happened to mention to Shelly about the tragic passing of our husbands."

"And how dissatisfied we were with the sloppy police investigation—"

"More like no investigation," Doris interjected.

"Precisely, lack of investigation into their murders."

"Murders?" I said. Still waiting to hear any evidence substantiating their claims like motive, means, or opportunity.

"That's the way we see it," Doris said. "Haven't you been paying attention, Mr. Cavanaugh?"

I opened my mouth to speak. Before I could, Cleo said, "The long and the short of it is Shelly recommended you."

"More like highly recommended you."

"He gave us your business card."

"You want me to do what exactly?" I asked.

"Help us find justice," Doris said.

"I see," I said, taking a moment to let what I had heard sink in. To my astonishment, Cleo and Doris looked on in silence. "Step into my office, ladies, and let's discuss this matter further."

I know the term "lady" has become a volatile word amongst some women these days, a Victorian description that should be banished from consideration of all women. I associate the term to women of gentle manners and refinement. Most women I know do not fit into those categories, although they can project those qualities at their choosing. Doris and Cleo were women who I believed lived the part in every fiber of their beings.

"Can I get you anything to drink?" I asked.

"Tea if you have it," Cleo answered.

"The same for me," Doris said. "We're not coffee drinkers."

"We know that's almost sacrilegious, especially in this part of the country, but it's what we enjoy," Cleo said.

I liked these women more and more. "Tea it is. I'll show you our choices."

"Oh, very nice," Cleo said. They both smiled. An endearing and gracious smile. The kind of smile that would subdue the meanest soul.

"There's one other thing you should know, Mr. Cavanaugh, about our case," Cleo said as I led them into the kitchen.

"What's that?"

"It's what I believe is referred to as a cold case," Doris said.

"How cold?"

"Over five years," Cleo said.

Law enforcement doesn't have a particular timestamp for cold cases, I thought. *Cases become cold when they are no longer actively investigated. I regard cold cases as being ten years or older.*

"You wouldn't by chance have anything to do with the Berge Building?" I asked them both.

"We used to own it," Cleo said.

"The same Berge Building that burned down not long ago?" I asked. The Berge fire was listed as accidental because they couldn't prove it was arson.

"Yes," Doris said.

"What a relief it was to be rid of that dreadful place," Cleo said. "We sold it to The Sickle Development Group."

"Not dreadful in the building itself," Doris said. "The building itself was gorgeous in its day."

"I didn't mean 'dreadful' in that way at all," Cleo said.

"Dreadful in a sense," Doris said, acknowledging her friend's apology with a light pat on her shoulder. "We believe it led to the deaths of our husbands."

"Most certainly," Cleo said.

I showed the ladies our tea selections. Cleo chose jasmine. Doris selected ginseng. I stuck with filtered tap water.

Rather than using mugs that Renita and I typically offered our guests and drank from ourselves, I felt these ladies deserved a bit more civility. We didn't stock good china. We are an investigation agency, after all not a five-star restaurant. Our department store purchases were still a cut above our mugs. I served the ladies their teas in teacups on saucers with metal teaspoons balanced on the rim of their tea saucers.

They noticed a few unopened packages of tea biscuits on the counter. Renita had bought them for me. They were delicious. I seldom ate any. I was watching my diet. Renita ate more of them than I did. With her coffee, interestingly enough.

"Kedem tea biscuits are our favorites!" Doris said.

"Might we have one or two?" Cleo said.

I held up a package of biscuits in each hand.

"I'll have chocolate," Cleo said.

"Make mine vanilla."

I removed two saucers as dessert plates from a kitchen cabinet to place their cookies.

"Oh, we'll only need one," Doris said.

"We don't mind sharing," Cleo agreed.

I smiled at them and returned one of the saucers. I opened the packages and set them on the counter. Cleo helped herself to four chocolate cookies. Doris picked out four vanilla cookies. They arranged the cookies in a tidy circle about the saucer alternating between chocolate and vanilla. Once done, they appeared pleased with themselves. We didn't have cloth napkins. Paper napkins would have to do.

I escorted the ladies into my office with their steaming hot tea carrying their dessert plate for them at my insistence. They drank their tea straight like me. I sat down behind my desk once I had seated them. I was intrigued by their story. I flipped open a Steno notepad I had sitting on my desk and grabbed a pen from my world map pen and pencil holder, the holder a birthday gift from my favorite nephew.

Cleo said, "This tea is delicious." Doris agreed with an "um-hmm" sound.

"Thank you," I said. "Ladies, I'm not making any promises. I'll do a thorough investigation if I decide to accept your case. Report to you the facts of my discovery. If those facts do not align with your suspicions, I will not alter them to fit your theories. Do you understand?"

I had expected looks of trepidation or second thoughts, if only for a moment. Instead, Cleo and Doris looked at each other, smiled broadly, and with exuberant unison, said, "Completely!"

I smiled inwardly at their response, not wanting to break my detached professional decorum.

"Alright then," I poised my pen over the first sheet of the notepad, "let's start at the beginning."

Michael R. Lane is the founder of **Bare Bones Press**. He is a published poet and writer who turned to indie publishing. His novels include the *C. J. Cavanaugh* mysteries, *Exchange Student* and *The Family Stone*. His short story collections are *Long Journey Home*, *UFOs and GOD* and *Emancipation*. He has also penned five books of poetry, *A Leap Year of Haiku*, *Love & Sensuality*, *Mortal Thoughts*, *Sandbox*, and *A Drop of Midnight*.

www.ingramcontent.com/pod-product-compliance
Lightning Source LLC
Chambersburg PA
CBHW021150310726
48971CB00002B/570